The Dress Shop *of* Dreams

BALLANTINE BOOKS TRADE PAPERBACKS

NEW YORK

The Dress Shop *of* Dreams

A Novel

Menna van Praag

The Dress Shop of Dreams is a work of fiction. Names, characters, places, and incidents are the products of the author's imagination or are used fictitiously. Any resemblance to actual events, locales, or persons, living or dead, is entirely coincidental.

A Ballantine Books Trade Paperback Original

Published in the United States by Ballantine Books, an imprint of Random House, a division of Random House LLC, a Penguin Random House Company, New York.

BALLANTINE and the HOUSE colophon are registered trademarks of Random House LLC.
RANDOM HOUSE READER'S CIRCLE & Design is a registered trademark of Random House LLC.

This book contains an excerpt from the forthcoming book *The Witches of Cambridge* by Menna van Praag. This excerpt has been set for this edition only and may not reflect the final content of the forthcoming edition.

ISBN 978-0-8041-7898-3
eBook ISBN 978-0-8041-7899-0

Printed in the United States of America on acid-free paper

www.ballantinebooks.com

9 8 7 6 5 4 3 2 1

Book design by Dana Leigh Blanchette
Title-page images: © iStockphoto.com

For Mum
with infinite love

& for Al, as ever,
with infinite thanks

Acknowledgments

Big, big thanks as ever to my magical agents, Andrea Cirillo and Christina Hogrebe, for always believing and being there. Gigantic thanks to Linda Marrow, for everything. You're a beautiful soul and a brilliant editor. Enormous thanks to all at Random House—especially Jennifer Hershey, Anne Speyer, Kim Hovey, Lindsey Kennedy, Maggie Oberrender, and Kathleen Fridella—who helped shepherd this book from my hands and into the big, bright world. Colossal thanks, of course, to all my gorgeous readers—this book is for you, I hope you'll take it into your hearts.

Huge thanks, as ever, to Alice Jago, who tirelessly read endless drafts of this book and still had something fantastic to say each and every time she did so. Massive amounts of gratitude to Laurence Gouldbourne, who—twice—gave me the great gift of plot and story inspiration when I'd hit a wall. Enormous thanks also to Penny Macleod, who contributed so very much.

Thank you, Mum, for first inspiring this story and for always inspiring me. Thanks to Andy and Leah, I look forward to seeing you play Cora and Walt. Thanks to Caitlin for the inspiration of her beautiful creations. Thanks to Lenore (aka Etta) for letting me into her miraculous den—and for the magic star. Thanks to Artur—for all the love and cake—and for making everything possible.

The Dress Shop *of* Dreams

Chapter One

When ordinary shoppers stumble into the little dress shop, they usually leave without buying anything. Nothing seems to fit or suit them very well. The music clouds their chatter and the shimmering silk walls hurt their eyes. After a few minutes they stumble out onto the street again, muttering to their friends about fashion and wondering why they ever bothered to step inside in the first place. But when a different kind of shopper discovers the shop, they find that opening its little blue door is the very best decision they've ever made. These are the women who aren't really looking for the perfect cocktail dress, the jeans that'll lengthen their legs or the skirt that will slim their silhouette. No, these women are looking for much more than that; they are looking for a lost piece of themselves. Which is exactly what Etta Sparks can give them.

When such a woman absently ruffles through the racks of

expectant dresses, casting furtive glances toward the counter, Etta sits pretending not to notice, until the time is right. Although she isn't actually psychic (being able to see only what the dresses show her) Etta has many gifts, and one of them is knowing when someone is ripe. She can see when a shy woman is on the edge of feeling brave. And then she steps forward.

"That would look beautiful on you," she'll suggest gently. "Why don't you try it on?"

They always shake their heads at first, of course. But Etta can see the desire in their fingertips, the tiny flicker of hope in their eyes. So she chats about anything: the weather, the music, the sweetness of strawberries, the latest film, a particular book, the sensuality of silk . . . Then, when the woman is ready, Etta picks out a dress—in their favorite color, one that will make their eyes sparkle, their hair shine and their skin glow. And, now that she knows their greatest wish, Etta makes them a promise. A promise she knows to be true.

"Wear this dress and you'll find what you're missing: confidence, courage, power, love, beauty, magnificence . . ." Etta says, while they regard her rather skeptically. "You will. I promise. Wear this dress and it will transform your life."

Etta doesn't mention that it might be a bit of a bumpy ride, at least at first. When a woman needs courage, for example, life might throw a few things at her to draw it out. When a woman needs to love herself, she might be lonely while life leaves her without external hearts to hide in. Other things are simpler, like beauty and magnificence, since as soon as a woman slips the dress over her head and stares into the mirror, she instantly feels more beautiful and magnificent than she's ever felt in her life.

Fortunately there is nothing that, with a little nip, tuck and the stitching of a special little star, Etta's dresses can't provide. For these are dresses that unlock the wisdom and wishes of women's hearts, dresses that help them to heal themselves and, eventually, attain their deepest desires.

Etta loves to watch when these women step out of the changing room, their faces lit with delight and disbelief.

"My goodness," they say. "But it's so . . . I look so, so . . ."

"Beautiful." Etta nods. "Yes, you do." And she watches them, swallowing a happy sigh and everything else she wants to say but really shouldn't.

"You just need a nip here," she says, taking a threaded needle from her pocket and making six quick stitches in the shape of a star, "a tiny tuck here. And voilà!" Etta steps back, a knowing smile on her lips and a sparkle in her eye. "You are perfect."

It happens the same way every time. The woman usually stands in front of the mirror for a while, turning this way and that, checking to be certain it isn't an illusion. And, when she is at last sure it's real, a blissful smile spreads into her cheeks and flushes through her whole body. In the mirror she sees herself as she truly is: beautiful, powerful, able to do anything. And she sees that the thing she wants most of all, the thing that seemed so impossible when she first stepped into the little dress shop, is really so possible, so close, that she could reach out and touch it.

"Yes," Etta says then, "as easy as pie. Speaking of which, the bookshop on the corner does the most delicious cherry pie. You really should try some."

The woman nods then, still slightly stunned, and agrees, saying that pie sounds like a perfect idea. So she stumbles out of the shop in a daze, new dress tucked tightly in her arms, and wanders down All Saints' Passage to the bookshop. There, she has the best piece of cherry pie she's ever eaten and leaves with a stack of books that will make the transformation complete.

Cora blinks. She yawns and stretches, then rubs her eyes and gazes up at the ceiling. 564 fleurs-de-lis gaze back down at her. As her body wakes, she could swear faint echoes of jazz drift away and fireworks still sound in the distance. It's that dream again. The one so vivid it feels more real to her than reality. The one she's been having nearly every night of her life. The only one she remembers every morning when she wakes up.

In her dream Cora is standing at her bedroom window, tiny hands splayed on either side of her freckled nose against the glass, watching fireworks explode, scattering light like fistfuls of stars. Down in the garden a hundred lanterns hang above a hundred heads, luminous rainbows of silk bobbing along to the jazz. Champagne corks pop and trumpets blow into the air amid claps and cheers. A beautiful black woman sings on stage, her voice as bright as the feathers in her hair.

Cora sees her parents standing close to the singer, sharing a glass of bubbling, sparkling water. They sway together, her father's arm around her mother's waist, her beautiful head tucked against his chest. Cora wants to join them. She wants to sing, dance, clap and cheer. She wants to freeze-frame the fireworks and count each burst of light. She wants to open her mouth and swallow the sparks and stars as they fall from the sky. But Cora is too young for the party. She was sent to bed hours ago and really should be asleep. Instead she watches the celebrations, listening to the laughter and the jazz tapping on her window, until the last firework explodes and the moon fades away in the milky dawn.

Cora would swear it was a memory, but she understands it can't be. Her parents died twenty years ago today, on her fifth birthday, and she only knows their matching black hair and green eyes, their tall gangly figures and faraway stares, from photographs. There was never a party, and certainly not such an extravagant affair, of this Cora is certain. Her parents were prominent academics at New College, Oxford, who never frequented frivolous events. Maggie and Robert Carraway spent most of their days, and many of their nights, in the biochemistry department. When they weren't cross-pollinating plants, discovering new species or generally trying to save the planet, Cora's parents were teaching her the basics of complex tissues, encouraging her to experiment on sunflowers or taking her on tours of English woodlands, European mountains and African deserts. They usually forgot birthdays, anniversaries and the like. They would have forgotten Christmas, too, if the luminous trees and light displays throughout the city hadn't reminded them. Not that they were neglectful, far from it. They simply lived in their own world—a world of cells and organisms, of ecosystems and genetics, of research and theories, but a world in which their daughter was at the very center. The Carraways took Cora everywhere. They kept a cot in the biochemistry lab for when they worked late. She took trips to European conferences. She ate all her meals in the university canteen. She played with papers, pencils and chemical equations. A year before they died they published a letter in *The Times* calling for the government to fund research into sustainable foods capable of growing in barren climates to feed and sustain starving communities. The letter hinted that they were focused on creating such foods, but since all their papers burned in the fire that killed them, Cora never knew for certain.

All of this early history has been recounted to Cora by her grandmother, since Cora doesn't remember a day of it, having suppressed the memory of her life with her parents along with their deaths. As a child Cora asked questions about them all the time and Etta gave her carefully selected stories in return. Nowadays Cora tries not to ask too often, not to focus on impossible fantasy and lost hope, though of course she can't stop the dreams. But the one thing she holds true to is that letter (Etta's copy, framed on Cora's bedroom wall) for it reminds her of why she does what she does, spending every day in the lab trying to fulfill her parents' legacy, to do a great thing that would make them proud.

Cora slides out of bed and crosses her room, counting the floorboards as she steps across her tiny flat on Silver Street, provided virtually rent-free by the university in return for her devotion to their biology department. And so, for forty hours in the lab and twenty hours teaching each week, Cora has fifty-three square meters in the center of Cambridge in which to sleep and eat. Not that she does much of either there. The flat is simple and sparse. The floors are wooden, the walls white. She owns no TV, no stereo, no ornaments. She never buys flowers or bowls of fruit. If Cora ever had visitors, they'd think she had only just moved in. If there was a fire the first, and only, thing she'd bother saving is her laptop. No paintings or photographs adorn the walls, no books are on the shelves. Everything she needs for work she has at her rooms in Trinity College. She survives on sandwiches and snacks from coffee shops at lunchtime and vending machines late into the night while she's scouring over plant plasma and peptides.

The only bright and beautiful thing in Cora's flat are her pajamas: Indian shot silk, the color of a sunset, sprinkled with 34 pink peonies and 69 blue morpho butterflies. She trundles into the kitchen now, opens the fridge and pulls out a bag of coffee beans. She weighs the bag in her hand—1,233 beans, approximately. These, along with a week-old loaf of bread, are the only edibles in her flat.

Cora switches on the kettle, marking the seconds until it boils. Whenever Cora is worried—about life, science, loneliness—counting soothes her. She's always had an extraordinary ability to count, to just *know* facts and figures at a glance. Of course, to her it's perfectly ordinary, since she's always been able to do it. But she understands that other people can't and that those same people might find her strange, so she tries to do it only in private. While sixty-seven seconds tick by, Cora imagines her day. In an hour she'll be at the lab. Three hours and fifty-five minutes after that she'll eat lunch. Or, more likely, forget to eat lunch. Six hours and twenty minutes after that she'll nod at her colleagues when they leave for the day. Three hours and forty-seven minutes later she'll leave. Then she'll come home and go to bed. Three days a week she adjusts the schedule for an evening visit to a bookshop. Within that she fits in her teaching commitments and visits to Etta. Otherwise, her days all follow the same pattern, yesterday, today and tomorrow.

Then, as she pours the hot water into the French press, Cora remembers the date. March 14. Which means that today is a bit different; today she's having dinner with her grandmother. Today is her birthday.

Chapter Two

Even though Cora must have stepped into her grandmother's shop twenty thousand times, she usually walks past the little blue door and the window draped in dresses. If she's lost in thought, counting the cobbles on the street or the bricks on the walls, then it only takes a second before she's back onto the main street and has to turn around again.

Apart from A Stitch in Time, there's one other shop on All Saints' Passage that Cora frequents—a bookshop, with a little red door and a little window crammed full of fiction—a rotating stock of 983 volumes. Inside, both places are much bigger than it seems possible they could be. Bigger than Cora's flat; not big enough to get lost in but big enough to hide in (which she does three times a week), if no one was particularly intent on finding you. She has known the owner, Walt, since she was a girl. Apart from her grandmother, he's her closest friend, and if Cora was interested in romance she'd be interested in him. However, since she isn't, she hardly gives him a second thought.

No matter how many times she's done it, every time Cora walks into the dress shop she gets a jolt of surprise. Stepping through the door is like stepping back in time. 1,349 (at her last count) dresses in every style hang on racks, clustered together as if holding hands and gossiping among themselves. Sequins flash from sleeves, sparkling beads swish from hems, and every color that one could possibly imagine (and a good number that one couldn't) shimmer and twinkle like galaxies of stars bottled in jars. Rows of shoes sit on shelves above the clothes, dyed every hue and tone, each pair a perfect match to one of the dresses beneath. The walls are wrapped in silk, the floor carpeted in velvet, the colors changing according to the shifting seasons.

Music is the breath of the shop, though Cora has never seen a record player. Music—from Stravinsky to Sinatra—plays every moment of the day and night, gentle and low when the shop is empty but quickening whenever the bell above the door chimes and someone new steps inside. Then the tinkling piano riffs speed into double time joined by wild saxophones, trumpets and beating drums. Perry Como, Dizzy Gillespie and Fats Waller sing and shout, their voices leaping and jumping, bouncing off walls and sweeping through the air so each new customer glides like Ginger Rogers off the street and into the shop. Cora has seen dowdy women with gray faces and buttoned-up shirts skip across the floor, their faces suddenly lit with shock and delight. Even Cora, who's never danced a step in her life, sometimes catches her disobedient hips swaying to the beat of "Ain't Misbehavin'" or "It Don't Mean a Thing."

Tonight Cora dawdles along the tiny, tight passage, counting as she goes: 86 leaves on the ivy inching up the wall, its vines concealing 28 bricks. She doubles back after missing the little blue door. The shop greets Cora with "One O'Clock Jump" as she rushes past curtains of clothes to arrive in the sewing room, tucked away behind the counter, where her grandmother sits with a skirt of crimson silk on her lap. It's the same shade the walls turn on December 7 until the twelfth day of Christmas when they sparkle bright white, the color of fresh fallen snow. Now the walls are green-blue silk, for early spring.

"Happy birthday," Etta says, giving her granddaughter a kiss. "And you're still late, as usual. I suppose the life cycles of amoebas are far more fascinating than your boring old grandmother."

"Of course not." Cora smiles. This is how it goes every time, this is the routine between them. Etta has no idea what her granddaughter spends her days doing, no matter how many times Cora has tried to explain. "You aren't old or boring. Life would probably be a lot easier if you were."

"Pish-posh." Etta gives a dismissive wave as she stands, dropping the silk skirt onto her sewing table. The room where Etta works her magic, mending and altering the clothes she sells, is even more chaotic than the shop itself. Hundreds of ribbons and threads hang from hooks on the walls, swathes of fabrics are piled up on shelves, open drawers overflow with buttons and beads of thousands of different shapes and sizes: 3,987, to be exact. It is an Aladdin's cave of couture.

"How do you find anything in here?" Cora asks, yet again. "I'd go crazy." Her lab, home and office are all obsessively well ordered, everything in its never-changing place.

"I don't need to know where anything is." Etta shrugs. "Whatever I need finds me. It's as simple as that."

Cora frowns at her grandmother. She has never been able to

make sense of her. Not since she was a girl. They are polar opposites. Where Etta loves flamboyance and frippery, color and chaos, Cora likes everything in life to be structured and simple, plain and predictable. She prefers even numbers over odd. She likes to know what's going to happen next, or at least be able to estimate the probabilities. Etta had long ago tried to sprinkle some frivolity into her granddaughter's life, telling her that little girls were meant to have fun. She bought Cora silly toys, organized treasure hunts and *Alice in Wonderland*–themed tea parties. She turned a corner of the shop into a playroom where they could dress up together and dance to the Charleston with feathers in their hair. But it was no use. Cora went along with it all, dutifully smiling whenever her grandmother asked if she was having a good time. But her heart was never in it. After her parents died her heart was never really in anything again.

"I know this is the only time you ever eat properly." Etta clears space on the table and produces two plates of roast-chicken salad. "I'm going to wait until you eat every bite. We're having cherry pie for pudding. Walt's bringing it over later. I would have baked a cake, but I know how much you love his cherry pie." As she says this, Etta gives her granddaughter a sideways smile.

Cora frowns. "What?"

"Nothing," Etta says. "Then we're having cheese and biscuits after that; I've a rather delicious-looking Barkham Blue I've been saving for the occasion."

Cora resists the urge to raise her eyebrows. "It's only a birthday," she says. "It's not a reason to celebrate."

Why not? Etta is about to say, but she holds back because, of course, they both know the answer to that. As they sit down the bell in the shop tinkles and Etta jumps up from the table.

"That'll be our pie."

Cora eyes her grandmother suspiciously as she hurries out of the sewing room and onto the shop floor. A moment later she is back, bustling through the doorway, one hand wrapped around the elbow of a tall, thin man dressed in blue jeans and a white shirt, whose messy black hair falls over his eyes but doesn't conceal his large but handsome nose.

"Hi, Walt," Cora says.

He nods in return and, with a sizeable nudge from Etta, stumbles forward into the room. He hands a plate of cherry pie to Cora and steps back.

"Happy birthday," he says, his eyes fixed on the plate. "I made it twice as sweet, and with ground almonds instead of flour."

"Thank you," Cora says. "It smells delicious."

"I only took it out of the oven twenty minutes ago." Walt lingers a moment then steps back toward the doorway. Etta grabs his arm as he passes her.

"Stay for some," she says. "It'd be wrong to eat it without you."

Walt glances at the food on the table. "No," he says, "you're still eating, I—"

"Nonsense, it doesn't matter, we're nearly done."

Walt hesitates then shakes his head. "No, I'd better go. I, um . . . like to do a stock check on Thursdays and it's getting late."

As Walt disappears, Etta throws a look of frustration in her granddaughter's direction, but Cora just returns it blankly. Etta turns and hurries after him. She stops Walt as he reaches the door. The dresses displayed in the window rustle as if a breeze had just blown through them.

"Wait," Etta says and he turns, fixing his gaze just above her head. "You know, some people don't see the things right under their noses. They mistake the everyday for what's ordinary and unimportant."

Walt glances down at the tiny woman and meets her gaze, seeing the acknowledgment and affection in her watery blue eyes.

"Especially those people searching for something," Etta continues. "They don't know exactly what they're looking for, but they always imagine it'll be far away and hard to find. They think it'll come with whistles and bells. Those people need shaking up to see something as simple as"—Etta dropped her voice to a whisper—"true love with someone they've known forever."

Wide-eyed, Walt shakes his head. The thought of him shaking Cora up makes him slightly sick with nerves. "I don't really know what you . . ." he begins. "Anyway, I've got to go. Enjoy the pie."

Walt turns the wooden doorknob but Etta is too quick. She grabs the back of his shirt and holds on.

"You've got a loose thread, just let me fix it for you."

"Don't worry." He pulls away. "It doesn't matter."

"It'll only take a moment," Etta says as she plucks her special needle from her pocket. "Wait."

Since he has little choice in the matter, Walt waits. Less than a minute later he leaves with a tiny red star stitched into the lining of his shirt.

When her daughter and son-in-law died, Etta was the first and only family member on the scene. She rushed to the hospital, scooped her sobbing (but otherwise unscathed) granddaughter up in her arms and promised the little girl that she'd protect her forever, that she'd never suffer again. And so, when it became clear that—as some sort of subconscious coping mechanism—Cora had suppressed all memories of her parents, happy and sad, Etta let it be. She allowed her granddaughter's heart to remain shut down even as she grew older. But now she realizes it must stop, or the cost will come at too high a price.

Etta's always been aware that the numbing of Cora's heart has suppressed her urge for laughter and desire for love as well as protecting her from pain. Most of all it's left Cora oblivious to *him.* Of course, it didn't matter while Cora was younger. Etta knew Walt would wait then, but he won't be able to wait forever. Eventually, he'll give up. And Etta can't let that happen. If Cora doesn't have the chance to love the man who loves her more than anything else, it would be a tragedy, a loss on a par with Etta's own: the man she thinks about late at night with a bottle of bourbon and a box of chocolates. Fifty years ago, when Etta lost him, she still hoped life might be full of other lovers. And it was—just none who held her heart the way he did. Now Etta knows that great love only comes once in a lifetime, if you're lucky.

Etta stands at the bathroom sink, looking into the mirror. Cora is downstairs, doing the washing up. Etta turned sixty-nine two months ago, but she doesn't look a day over sixty-one. Which is some comfort, she supposes, but not much. Every day she sees a new wrinkle in the mirror, another line etched on her once beautiful face. She pulls the sagging skin back from her eyes, stretching it almost taut again, consoling herself that the one advantage of her fading sight is she can't see her fading face so sharply. Her granddaughter insists that she's still beautiful, but Etta knows she's not. Cora only thinks that because she loves her; she's blinded to the depressing truth by sentimental feelings. But Etta doesn't suffer under such illusions.

She hasn't been with a man since her husband passed away twenty years ago, the same year her daughter died. If she hadn't had Cora, Etta would have given up on life herself. While she was in her fifties, even in her early sixties, Etta still harbored hopes that she'd experience intimacy again, that one day she'd be held tight in a masculine embrace. But she knows it probably won't happen again, not now.

Cora and Etta sit on the sofa in the living room halfway through watching *Gone With the Wind.* Etta gazes at the screen while Cora fidgets.

"You know we've watched this film 28 times before, don't you?"

"Hush," Etta hisses, "we have not."

"We have. And it's two hundred thirty-eight minutes long. That's one hundred eleven hours. That's four and a half days of our lives in the Deep South."

Etta smiles. "And every minute very well spent."

"You're obsessed with Clark Gable."

"Well, there's nothing wrong with that. A girl could do a lot worse than Gable."

Cora smiles. "You know he's dead, right?"

"I'm old," Etta says, "not senile. And, at my age, one has to take what one can get. Unlike you, who could be with a real flesh-and-blood man instead of her grandmother on her birthday night."

"I'm perfectly happy as I am."

"Are you?"

"Yes, I am."

"Very well." Etta shrugs. "If you insist."

"I do."

"Then there's not much I can do about that," Etta says. It's a lie, of course. Etta has rather powerful means at her disposal, methods she uses every day to transform the women who venture into her little shop, but she's been putting off using them on her granddaughter, hoping that it might happen naturally instead. As the years pass, however, Etta's hopes have dwindled, which is why, tonight, she's pinning them on Walt instead.

She hopes that her pep talk with Walt may have had some effect. Perhaps, for the first time, he'll stop waiting in vain for Cora to notice him and do something to seize her attention instead. Etta doesn't hold out much hope, since she must have given him a hundred similar nudges over the years and he's never found the courage to act on them. Of course, this time is different, for this time he has a little red star stitched into the lining of his shirt to help him along. If *that* doesn't work, nothing will, and then it'll be time for Etta to take matters into her own hands.

Chapter Three

Walt has loved her forever, for nearly as long as he's been alive. He was four years old the first time he saw her. It's his earliest memory. A simple, ordinary day, made special and extraordinary by first love and first words.

Walt's father had been shopping with his son on a Sunday afternoon when he'd wandered into All Saints' Passage and found the bookshop. A silent boy, Walt still hadn't spoken, so there was no reason to think he'd be interested in reading yet. But when Walt snuck through the door, under his father's arm, he let out a gasp of delight.

He had stepped into a kingdom: an oak labyrinth of bookshelves, corridors and canyons of literature beckoning him, whispering enchanting words Walt had never heard before. The air was smoky with the scent of leather, ink and paper, caramel-rich and citrus-sharp. Walt stuck out his small tongue to taste this new flavor and grinned, sticky with excitement. And he knew, all of a sudden and deep in his soul, that this was a place he belonged more than any other.

Hours later, staggering along the passage with armfuls of books, Walt had glanced up at another shop window to see two bright green eyes and a mop of blond curls peeking out under a beaded hem. The eyes blinked as he stared and the sad little mouth opened slightly. Walt stopped.

"Come on, Wally," his father had called, "we're late for dinner."

He'd said this as though there was someone at home cooking it for them, a wife and mother who anxiously expected them. He always spoke this way, as though denying his wife's death could bring her back, if only momentarily.

"But Daddy," Walt protested, "I want see the girl."

His father had dropped the books then, pages fluttering to his feet. Tears filled his eyes and fell down his cheeks. Four years of silence, of doctors, specialists and speech therapy. Four years of nothing and now a whole sentence, in an instant. It was a miracle.

"What girl, son?" The question was a whisper on his lips.

Walt turned back to the window, ready to point, but the girl had gone.

There are people who like to connect, to make eye contact and smile. Walt is not one of them. At school he learned to make himself invisible, to watch people without being seen. And so he watched Cora growing up: staring out of the shop window while raindrops slid down the glass, wandering along counting paving stones, flower petals, leaves of ivy and anything else that inhabited All Saints' Passage, sneaking into the bookshop to read biographies of Marie Curie and Caroline Herschel while entire afternoons slipped out of sight. He watched, biding his time before he finally found the courage to speak with her. And, even then, when they formed a tentative friendship in the years that followed, he was never able to look Cora in the eye and tell her how he felt.

When Walt turned sixteen, with enormous relief, he abandoned school to fulfill his second greatest wish (his first being the wish for Cora) and work in the bookshop full time. When Walt turned twenty his father died, finally succumbing to the broken heart he'd been nursing for two decades. With the inheritance Walt bought his beloved bookshop along with the flat above it, and as soon as he moved in he stayed. He's there for twelve hours a day, every day, even though the shop is only open for eight. But he loves the empty hours best of all, when he can walk along the aisles and bask in the warmth of the books, their glittering gold letters, their stories softly pulsing between pages just waiting to be opened and read and loved.

Mondays, Wednesdays and Fridays are Walt's favorite days, for these are the ones when Cora—at exactly 6:26 P.M.—opens the door and steps inside his kingdom. She stays for an hour while Walt gazes on, his eyes peeking out above Shakespeare or Milton or García Márquez. He watches her weave along the aisles until she reaches the science section, slides a book off the shelf and sneaks into a hidden corner to read it. When Cora slips into the book she forgets herself entirely, allowing Walt to watch without worry, to gaze unabashedly at the wispy curls that fall over her face, delicate fingers cradling the book, lips absently mouthing the words, breath that occasionally quickens with excitement and shivers through her body in the most alluring way.

The very second the hour is up Cora, without looking at her watch, shuts the book then stands. On her way out she stops at the counter for a slice of cherry pie and a double espresso. She declines cream with the pie but takes four sugars with the coffee. Sometimes, if the book has been particularly brilliant and she's forgotten to eat lunch again, she'll have a second slice.

Sometimes Cora chats absently about scientific subjects Walt can't understand, though he listens avidly anyway, nodding along and making agreeable sounds in what he hopes are the right places. Sometimes Cora only nods hello and says nothing, just eating, lost in thought. Since Walt rates the odds of his lips ever touching hers as less than his chances of winning the lottery, instead he bakes cherry pies so he can watch her eat. And, despite the sadness of knowing that this is the closest he'll ever get to Cora, it's still the most sensual moment of his day.

Apart from his love for Cora, Walt has another secret. A secret he'd love to share with her but knows he never will. He has always loved to read aloud, to hear words float about a room, to swim in stories and breathe in poetry. And he has a powerful voice, a beautiful voice, as deep, thick and rich as melted chocolate. Characters seem to come alive when he speaks, sliding off the page to stalk the bookshop aisles and relive their fictional lives in 3-D and Technicolor. At night, after Walt flips over the "closed" sign on the front door, he sits back behind the counter and opens doors to other worlds: bookshelves transmute into swamp trees, floors into muddy marshes, the ceiling into a purple sky cracked with lightning as he floats down the Mississippi with Huck Finn. When he meets Robinson Crusoe, the trees become heavy with coconuts, the floorboards a barren desert of sand dunes whipped by screeching winds. When he fights pirates off the coasts of Treasure Island, the floors dip and heave, the salty splash of ocean waves stings his eyes and clouds of gunpowder stain the air. As a rule Walt sticks with adventures and leaves romances untouched, preferring to escape his own aching heart rather than being reminded of it.

Occasionally, picking up a book during a quiet afternoon, Walt forgets himself and reads aloud to an unsuspecting and delighted customer. And, two years ago, on one fortuitous Friday, that particular customer happened to be the producer of BBC Radio Cambridgeshire. Walt didn't need to be told that his was a face made for radio (not that the producer even thought this, let alone said so) but he needed some persuading that his voice was, too. He'd be perfect for the *Book at Bedtime* slot, the producer urged. Every night at ten o'clock he could pour words into perfect silence and assist drowsy listeners to slip off to sleep. It was the thought of *Cyrano de Bergerac* that convinced him. Cyrano had been Walt's personal hero for the last fifteen years, and he'd always wished that they'd shared an eloquent tongue as well as an enormous nose and an unfortunate penchant for unrequited love. But now, since he didn't have any great words of his own, Walt was being offered those of great writers—now he could have a voice without a face. He said yes.

Tonight, Walt is sharing the wretched tale of Madame Bovary with his listeners. The story has sharpened its fingers on Walt's fragile heart, snatching up little slices of flesh. This is exactly what he's always striven to avoid, but for some reason his producer (a sorry sucker for romances) insisted on this particular book and now it's wrapped the tragic twists of its plot around Walt's chest, constricting his breath so the woeful words are barely audible anymore:

"Her real beauty was in her eyes. Although brown, they seemed black because of the lashes, and her look came at you frankly, with a candid boldness . . ."

The sentence scratches his throat. Walt thinks of Cora. He thinks of what Etta said: *Some people don't see the things under their noses. They mistake the everyday for what's ordinary and unimportant. These people need shaking up*. He isn't a fool, he isn't deluded by desire, he knows perfectly well what is possible and what is not. Cora is just a friend. She's never shown the slightest physical interest in him so he knows absolutely that he'll never experience anything with her, let alone *passion* and *rapture*. But he's always accepted his hopeless situation fairly happily: the sight of her smile, the smell of her double espresso, the sound of her footsteps on the floorboards, this has been enough. Seeing Cora three times a week is enough. Almost.

It isn't as though Walt has no other options, at least in theory. He has fans: women who phone the radio station asking for his address, phone number and marital status. They call him the Night Reader. They send him lustful letters and, occasionally, their underwear. They declare their undying desire, their dreams of making love to him while he sprinkles them with words and kisses until they explode. Of course, he never replies. And not because he believes they'll change their minds as soon as they see him, but because he simply isn't interested in anyone but Cora. And it's been that way since the first time they spoke.

He was five and she was eight. He was sitting on the steps outside the bookshop, half-reading *The Three Musketeers* and half-watching her standing in front of a willow tree that grew over the alleyway wall, counting the leaves that dripped down to the pavement. Walt knew that was what she was doing, not only because he knew her quite well by now, but because she mouthed the numbers staring into the branches. Why he was suddenly seized by the courage to finally address her, he never knew. Perhaps the devious Milady de Winter, who'd just swept onto the pages of the tale, dared him to do it.

"What's your name?" he asked.

She'd turned to him with a deep frown, instantly terrifying him. About to turn to escape back into the bookshop, Walt was stopped by her shrug.

"Cora."

"That's a funny name."

"It isn't, actually." Cora's frown deepened. She pulled herself up to her full height of four foot three inches. "Officially my name is Cori, but Grandma calls me Cora. I'm named in honor of Gerty Cori, the first woman winner of the Nobel Prize in medicine. I bet you didn't know that."

"No," Walt admitted, embarrassed. "I didn't."

"What's your name?"

"Walt," he offered quietly, expecting her to retort that his was an even sillier name, but she didn't.

"After the scientist?"

Walt frowned, thrown. "What scientist?"

Cora shrugged. "Maybe Luis Walter Alvarez or Walter Reed, but . . . actually Walter Sutton is the most famous. He invented a theory about chromosomes and the Mendelian laws of inheritance." Cora let slip a little smile of satisfaction at the blank look on the boy's face. "Or maybe Walter Lewis—"

"No," Walt interrupted, "I've never heard of any of them."

"Oh." Cora folded her arms and tilted her nose upward. "Then who are you named after?" she asked, as if this was a given.

"Walt Whitman," he retorted. "The poet."

Cora considered this for a moment then shrugged again, a careful gesture this time, as if she were unburdening a heavy coat from her shoulders. "That's okay, I guess. But poems, stories and that stuff are a waste of time anyway. They don't answer any questions. They don't help anyone."

Walt swallowed the protest that rose up inside him and slid his book out of sight. "Don't you like reading at all?"

"What a silly question," she said, and then seemed to regret it and was kinder. "I have to read, to find things out. I'm studying to be a scientist," she added. "When I grow up I'm going to save the world."

If he'd been curious, enchanted and infatuated with her before, that was the moment he actually fell in love.

"How?" Walt asked, though the answer didn't even matter. Just the fact that she *wanted* to do such an incredible, enormous, ambitious thing was enough for him.

Cora shrugged for a third time. "Maybe I'll discover a cure for cancer, or invent a special food that can grow anywhere and feed everyone, or a way to kill every mosquito or . . . something special like that, anyway."

Walt just stared at her. Most of his time was spent lost in stories or playacting out their plotlines—pretending he was twenty thousand leagues under the sea or journeying to the center of the earth—and most of his thoughts were wasted on similarly pointless subjects. He'd never considered even attempting to do something so noble and amazing. That this girl had not only considered it but was, he was certain, actually going to do it, left him without words.

Cora narrowed her eyes at Walt, seeming to suspect him of mocking her with his stare, then her face relaxed. "What are you going to do when you grow up?"

"Work here, in this bookshop."

Walt replied without thinking, then instantly regretted it. Someone who was going to save the world would never be interested in someone who was going to work in a bookshop. But it was the truth, this was his one and only ambition in life, and Walt was quite incapable of lying.

"Oh," Cora considered. "Why?"

"I don't know." Now it was Walt's turn to shrug. The die was cast, there was no point in trying to snatch it back now. "Because . . . because I belong here."

"Oh," Cora said and Walt knew, with a sinking heart, that he'd given the wrong answer. "I've got to go home for tea," she said. "Bye." And with that she turned away, leaving him to gaze after her.

It's a memory Walt has recalled so often that every second of it sparkles, like a ruby polished a hundred thousand times. It's a great shock to Walt then, what happens next as he's sitting in the studio, speaking softly into the microphone, following Emma's tragic fate. The air in the studio booth is so still that the words bounce off the walls and echo through the room:

". . . her gown still hanging at the foot of the alcove; then, leaning against the writing table, he remained there until evening, wrapped in a sorrowful reverie. She had loved him, after all!"

It is this last sentence that does it. Those six little words tip the delicate balance of his fragile life, smashing it like crystal onto stone. And suddenly it's clear to Walt what he must do. He has to act. He has to do something different. Something special. He has to shake Cora up.

Chapter Four

When his shift at the radio station is over, when he's finally slammed *Madame Bovary* shut, Walt runs all the way back to the bookshop. Fumbling with the lock, he yanks at the door, scurries through the maze of bookshelves to the counter, then opens a drawer under the till and plucks out a book. He hurtles upstairs, through the hallway of his tiny flat, and falls onto the sofa in the living room. Sweating and panting, he sits up and waits to catch his breath. The book he holds is bound in rough red leather, worn at the edges and along the spine. Inside the words are handwritten, dotted with diagrams, faded with age and in a language Walt can't understand. It had been his mother's book, tucked, along with a pack of tarot cards, another book and a gold pen, into the side of his cot on the night she died.

Eva O'Connor had lived just long enough to see her son into

the world and hold him once. Walt's father hadn't known about the rare condition that killed her and at first simply thought his wife was sleeping, a well-earned rest after twenty-six hours of labor. Walt was born at home and it wasn't until nearly a week later that David O'Connor found his wife's notebook alongside *Leaves of Grass,* which was how Walt got his name. The bereaved husband and new father saved both books and gave them to his son on his tenth birthday. Walt has been trying to make sense of his mother's legacy ever since.

Walt's parents had met in an unorthodox way, a story that Walt had heard a thousand times and always cherished. Eva had been a fortune-teller before she married; David, a slightly drunken visitor to the fair on Midsummer Common who went into her tent on a dare. In the ten minutes that followed she read his cards, then kissed him, and their lives changed forever. When the fair left Cambridge three days later, Eva didn't go with it. Two years later Walt was born. As a boy he'd begged his father to tell him what his mother had read in the cards, but David had always claimed he couldn't remember, saying that the delightful shock of the kiss had knocked the memory right out of him.

Walt must have gazed at the pages of his mother's book a million times, desperately trying to make sense of the confusing and complex mess of curling letters, dots and lines. In an attempt to decode it he's studied more than a thousand languages—past and present—but Eva's words don't match any of them. Sometimes he thinks it might be her own secret code indecipherable to anyone else but her. But why, then, would she have left it for him?

The year before David died, while they were carving out a pumpkin to celebrate Walt's birthday on Halloween, he jokingly suggested it might be a spell book, which is why Walt consults it now. He'd laughed off the idea at the time but, since an air of mystery and magic always surrounded the memory of his mother, Walt secretly enjoyed entertaining the notion.

As he opens the book, tentatively holding the pages like the wings of live butterflies between his fingertips, Walt hopes that *this* time it will all suddenly make sense. He needs a spell or, failing that, a miracle to shake Cora up.

Walt closes his eyes and mumbles a prayer, a request for help. In the silence that follows he waits. Nothing happens. He opens his eyes. Still nothing. And then, just as he's about to shut the book and stand, Walt hears the voice in his head. It isn't his voice; it's female for a start, and it doesn't rise up from his consciousness. Instead each sentence seems to drop, fully formed, from the sky. *Mum* is the first thing Walt thinks, though of course he can't remember the sound of her voice. Then he stops thinking and listens.

Seize your courage and show her your heart.

Walt sits up straight and still, holding his breath. The words fire through his blood, igniting every artery and vein in his body so his head pounds until he can't think straight. But Walt doesn't care about momentary intellectual impairment; he doesn't care about thoughts, rationality and judgment. It's all unimportant. His mind doesn't matter because he has his heart. And something else of which Walt isn't even aware: a little red star sewn secretly into the lining of his shirt.

Walt needs to act now. Right now. This second. Even if it is past midnight, it doesn't matter. What he is actually going to do, along with the appropriateness of this undecided action, is irrelevant and immaterial. Walt has been waiting a lifetime for anything approaching a chance with Cora and he won't wait another minute for his sudden courage to disappear.

Unsure of exactly what he's going to do or say, Walt snatches up his mother's notebook then dashes out of the flat and through the shop before he can change his mind or doubt himself. When he's standing on the pavement he stops. Then takes a breath. What on earth is he doing? It doesn't matter, it only matters that he's doing it. He's taking action. He's doing something. He's not a coward, he's not scared anymore.

Walt wonders if Cora will still be at her grandmother's. He suspects so. Etta will probably have persuaded her granddaughter to stay and watch old films. He hopes so, since he doesn't know where Cora lives, and is rather embarrassed to ask Etta but he will if it comes to that. For now though, he'll try his luck. As he walks Walt wonders how Etta will take to a late-night visitor. Not too badly, he hopes, since it was Etta who put him up to it in the first place. Or at least put the idea of doing something crazy and courageous into his head.

When he reaches the front door of the shop he hesitates. Pulling himself up to his full height of six foot three inches, he knocks. He listens to the silence. All Saints' Passage is dark, lit only by moonlight, without the assistance of streetlamps. As the owners of the only two businesses on the street, Walt and Etta joined together to petition the city council for lighting but have so far been fobbed off with postponed promises. Walt taps his forefinger on the spine of his mother's notebook and ponders his next move.

Cora is in the bathroom, splashing water on her face so she'll stay awake until the four-hour film finally ends, when she hears tiny taps rattling the glass of her grandmother's windowpane.

She twists off the tap and walks into the next room. Another tap hits the glass. Cora hurries across the carpet, past the quilted bed. She fiddles with the catch and pulls the window open.

"Walt?"

He smiles sheepishly. "Happy birthday, again."

Cora frowns. "What are you doing here?"

"I, um, I wanted to show you something."

"In the middle of the night?"

"It's pretty special," he says.

"But it's late," she says. "Why don't you show me when I come to the bookshop tomorrow? That might be easier. Oh, and thanks for the pie. It was even more delicious than usual."

Walt watches as she reaches up to pull the window closed again. The little red star stitched into his shirt tightens its threads.

"No, wait!"

Cora frowns, her arms paused for a moment, her fingers tight on the wood of the window frame.

"It's a book," Walt blurts out, "my mother's notebook. It's in a special code and I thought . . . I thought you might help me decipher it."

"Oh?" Cora releases her fingers. She still can't understand why on earth Walt is coming to her with encoded diaries at—she glances at her watch—12:06 A.M., but now her interest is piqued. She reaches out her hands above his head. "Why don't you throw it up and I'll take a look."

"No." Walt shakes his head, holding the book tight to his chest. This isn't going at all the way he might have hoped. It's no use. He'll have to stop hiding behind other things and come right out and say it. And quickly, before she disappears again.

"Okay, it's not exactly that, not right now anyway," Walt

stumbles, unable to believe he's on the brink of finally confessing, declaring, announcing, trumpeting his love. "I've come to tell you . . ."

"Tell me what?" Cora folds her arms.

Walt takes a breath so long and deep he starts to feel dizzy. "How I feel."

"How you feel about what?" Cora's frown deepens.

"About you."

"Me?" Cora gazes down at the man standing on the pavement underneath her window and wonders what she's missing.

In the silence blood pounds through Walt's head and he starts to hyperventilate. The little red star tightens its threads again.

"Yes." Walt's voice is soft but strong now, unwavering. "I want to tell you, I have to tell you, that I love you."

The anxious discomfort that has been rising up inside Cora bursts forth in an entirely unexpected bout of laughter. The laughter cracks through the air, a whip that snaps across Walt's chest and flays his fragile skin. The laughter surrounds Cora in a brittle, oblivious fog. Walt begins to feel his legs give way under him, caught between collapsing on the pavement and making a mad dash in any direction. He has to save himself, he must claw his way out of this hideous situation or he'll never be able to face Cora again. He'll have to sell his beloved shop and move to Mongolia.

Suddenly it occurs to Walt what to do. He starts to laugh, sounding shrill and forced at first but, driven by sheer desperation, he manages to smooth out the sound and inject a little levity. Then, in a stroke of divine inspiration for which he's infinitely grateful, Walt starts to hiccup.

Cora stops laughing. "Are you drunk?"

Walt nods, adding a delirious giggle for effect. "Too much tequila," he slurs, "sorry. I suddenly had an unstoppable urge to perform an impromptu Romeo and Juliet. I thought you might fancy a birthday show."

Cora frowns. "I thought you were doing a stock check."

Walt looks momentarily horrified. "Well, yes, um, I finished early, so I decided to get a drink—to celebrate."

Cora's frown deepens. "It's not my birthday anymore, anyway, and you're crazy."

Walt took a bow. "Guilty as charged."

Cora stares at him, brows furrowed, and for one long torturous moment Walt isn't sure whether she's going to believe him. Then she gives a slight smile and shrugs.

"Go to bed, you crazy fool, and we'll forget about it."

Thank heaven for that, Walt thinks. *Thank heaven for that.*

"Free cherry pie next time you come in," he calls up to her, "all you can eat."

"And espressos," she says as she starts to pull down the window. "For the rest of the month."

"Done."

When the window closes, a dull thud of wood against wood, Walt stands awhile longer looking up at the dark glass. When a gust of wind ruffles the pages of Eva's diary and blows down his neck, Walt slowly turns and walks away.

Etta stands in the corridor, her hand against the wall, her heart sunk to the floor. Having heard the commotion she'd sneaked upstairs and, having arrived just in time to catch Walt's declaration, quickly followed by its rebuttal, Etta is more sorry than she can say. She doubts very much that, given the twenty years' worth of love and longing that had been channeled into this one act, Walt will ever attempt it again. Which means that she'll have to take Cora's closed heart into her own hands and get ready for the inevitable mess of confusion and pain to come.

Cora nearly runs into her grandmother in the corridor.

"What are you doing?"

Etta sidesteps the question. "Why don't you stay tonight?"

"I . . . I don't have anything with me, my pajamas . . ." she says feebly.

"Oh, come on. It's late and you don't have a date," Etta prods her granddaughter.

"I suppose it'll already be morning by the time we finish this epic melodrama," Cora concedes. Every now and then her grandmother invites her to stay the night and she can never say no. Although she prefers the solitude of her own flat, and a night uninterrupted by snuffles and snorts, in a bed uncluttered by a sexagenarian who kicks in her sleep, Cora will never leave her grandmother alone when she doesn't want to be. When her parents died it was Etta's bosom she buried her head in, it was in Etta's arms she cried. It is Etta who gave Cora everything she needed to survive.

"Okay then," Etta says as they walk back toward the living room together. She stops at the airing cupboard and makes a show of rooting around for a nightgown while, as Cora waits, Etta quickly stitches a little red star into the corner of the first one she finds. After a moment she hands it to Cora. "This'll fit you fine."

"I'm not sharing your bed again," Cora says as she takes it. "You snore dreadfully."

"What rot," Etta huffs. "I most certainly do not."

While they watch the last hour of *Gone With the Wind* for the twenty-ninth time, Cora thinks about Walt and what just happened. Had he really been drunk? Or had he actually meant something by what he said? If so, Cora doesn't understand it. He can't care for her, certainly can't love her; that much is impossible. She isn't a lovable person. She's cold and calculating and doesn't really want anything in life except to make a great scientific breakthrough. Excepting Walt himself, she has no real friends to speak of. The only person who really cares for her is Etta and, Cora suspects, this is only because blood and biology compel it.

When the credits finally roll on *Gone With the Wind* Cora eases herself off the sofa and tucks a patchwork quilt (88 hexagons in every hue of blue) around a snoring Etta, then walks across the living room and into her grandmother's bedroom. She hasn't got the energy to brush her teeth, she just wants to fall into bed. Now that Etta won't be sharing it with her, Cora actually stands the chance of a good night's sleep.

Cora slips off her underwear and reaches for the nightgown her grandmother has given her, made of cotton and lace, all in cream with blue ribbon trim. There's something about it she almost recognizes; the memory of something tugs at her fingers but does not rise up. When she pulls it over her shoulders it slides over her skin like silk, falling to her toes where the fabric floats just above the floor.

"It's like being hugged by a cloud," Cora whispers, rather surprising herself.

And when she slips between the sheets she's asleep before she closes her eyes. In the living room Etta opens hers.

Tonight, for the first time since the tragedy, Cora won't dream of a party, she won't wake to whispers of laughter and jazz. She won't feel a blush of wistfulness that can be washed off in a moment or two. In a few hours she'll know true sorrow for the first time in twenty-five years, every feeling that she's suppressed all her life will surge up and engulf Cora again. In a few hours she'll wake up weeping, her heart cracked wide open. This, Etta knows, is the cost of love. It's a great shame, she thinks, that the heart cannot feel joy without also feeling pain, that it cannot know love without also knowing loss.

Chapter Five

An hour after she's fallen asleep, Cora wakes screaming. She sits bolt upright in bed, her own terrified voice mixing with the screams in her dreams and the smell of smoke now so powerful it almost chokes her.

Etta is already waiting at her bedside. And when her granddaughter stares at her with horrified eyes, Etta strokes her fingers through Cora's curls and places a glass of brandy in her open hands. Despite the fact that Cora never drinks anything stronger than coffee or tea, she swallows it in a single gulp, then coughs and splutters until tears are running down her cheeks.

"It's okay, dear girl," Etta says softly. "It's over now. It's all over."

Cora stares at her grandmother as if she's speaking a foreign language. She shakes her head and opens her mouth but no words come out.

"Do you want another drink?"

Cora shakes her head again. She reaches for Etta's hand and clutches it until Etta can't feel her fingers anymore.

"It's all right," Etta whispers. "It will be all right, I promise."

At last Cora finds her voice. "What happened? I can't, I don't . . ."

"You had a nightmare," Etta says. "You had a—"

"No, it wasn't a dream. The dream I've been having every night of my life, *that* was a dream. That never happened, I know, it's only what I wished—but this was real, a memory, I just don't understand how it could be."

"What did you see?"

Cora still can't quite believe what she did see. "My parents. Our house was on fire. I was trapped, screaming, and . . . I don't know, it all went black, but I think they saved me."

Cora stares at Etta's bedspread, adorned with 168 embroidered butterflies. She stares at them, then begins to multiply and divide them, trying to slow the frantic pump of her pulse. Etta shuffles out of the room and returns with another brandy. "Drink up, dear girl, it'll help."

"It *was* real?" Cora splutters. "But how . . . Why am I finally remembering this? All my life I couldn't remember what happened. Why now? And how?"

Etta glances at the ceiling. Cora eyes her suspiciously.

"You did something, didn't you?"

"It was time," Etta says, not yet offering her granddaughter the whole truth, knowing that now is not the right time to talk about Walt. Cora must mourn her parents first. "I couldn't let you spend the rest of your life in a cocoon. It was time to unlock your heart."

"What did you do?"

"I have my ways," Etta admits. "I know you've wondered about my dresses, you just won't let yourself believe in magic and the power of clothes to give a person confidence, hope, courage . . . Mine just happen to be a bit more—"

"What did you do?" Cora interrupts.

"I sewed something special into your nightgown," Etta admits, "a little red star . . ."

Cora has, on some level, always been aware that there is something *different* about Etta's dress shop, though her scientific reasoning has never allowed her to ask or investigate into exactly what. Of course she doesn't believe in anything not firmly underpinned by a fixed foundation of provable facts. But she's unable to deny that something slightly strange, something perhaps beyond the realms of her understanding, is happening now. Still, Cora doesn't want to know what, so instead of asking how she asks why.

"But why are you doing this? You know I don't want to remember the past. I don't want that reality. I prefer dreams. There's no point, nothing good comes from pain like that."

Etta collects herself. She knew this wasn't going to be easy. "You may be a brilliant scientist," she says, "you may have one of the biggest brains in the world. But, my dear girl, you know absolutely nothing about the heart."

"The heart?" Cora frowns.

"When you shut down your heart you protect it from pain but you prevent it from feeling anything at all," Etta explains. "Which is why you've never fallen in love."

"Love?" Cora's frown deepens, wondering what her grandmother is going on about. "What's that got to do with anything?"

"You might not miss it now," Etta says. "But trust me, you will one day. And I can't let that happen. I can't let you lose the love of your life. I can't let you wind up alone when you're my age, wishing . . ."

"Wishing what?" Cora asks. She's never seen such a look of sorrow on Etta's face before and, for a second, she forgets about her parents.

"Nothing," Etta says, the look suddenly gone. "It's simply a shame that one's own particular magic never seems to work on oneself, that's all. Anyway, the point and purpose here is that it is time to open your heart. I'm afraid that means unearthing all that pain you buried so long ago and . . ."

Cora wonders what her grandmother isn't saying. It seems as if sweet, innocent Etta might be keeping quite a lot of secrets. Cora narrows her eyes and frowns, formulating a carefully phrased question. But, before she can speak, the sound of her parents' screams ring in Cora's ears.

"You never told me I was there," she says, tears clouding her eyes, "and you always said it was an accident."

"I know, sweetheart, I'm sorry." Etta takes her granddaughter's hand, wishing there was a softer way to say what she's about to say, wishing she didn't have to say it at all but she knows that now that Cora is starting to remember, she deserves to know the truth. "But you were there. And I don't believe it was an accident. At least, it wasn't *their* accident—something, someone else was involved. I don't know what happened. But I do believe there's more to it than the cold, hard facts. I'd bet my life on it."

"What do you mean?" Cora still grips her grandmother's hand, looking up at her through red eyes. Time folds in on itself and all at once Etta sees Cora as a girl, sobbing after scalding herself on a Bunsen burner, failing to get 100 percent on a chemistry test, being rejected by Oxford University. That she'd got 98 percent, that she'd been accepted by Cambridge, didn't matter. Cora's standards were uncompromising and untouched by reason or rationality. All the same, Etta feels her heart contract when she sees her granddaughter in pain.

"So what are you saying? You think they were murdered?"

"I don't know," Etta admits. "I don't know anything for certain. The police ruled your parents' deaths as accidental. They didn't have enough evidence to the contrary and I didn't have the energy to push them. I brought you home. Keeping you safe seemed to be the only thing that mattered after Maggie died. So I let it go."

"But you might be wrong. It might just have been an accident. You don't have any evidence either, do you? You don't have any proof."

Etta shakes her head. "Yes, I might. And no, I don't. But, dear girl"—she reaches out and cups Cora's cheek in her hand—"not all of life's answers are found in your head, some you have to sense with your heart."

Cora frowns, used to her grandmother's sentimentality and suspicious of it. "Okay, well, just tell me everything you *do* know, everything you remember. And stick to the facts."

So Etta does, until patches of gray morning light slip slowly into the room and neither of them has words or breath left. Cora's parents' scientific papers all burned in the fire, Etta believes, and no further details are known. But the day before they died, Maggie had called her saying she wanted to talk about something very important, something for which she'd have to be sitting down. At the time Etta had been distracted by a rush of customers and, after quickly checking it wasn't the imminent arrival of another grandchild and thinking she'd have endless hours to discuss details later, promised to call her daughter back tomorrow. Of course, then it was too late. This is everything, the whole truth as she knows it, Etta promises. There are no more secrets, at least none that she is keeping.

Something happens to Cora while her grandmother speaks: an unfolding, an unspooling of her outer layers to reveal her core. At first she simply wants all the facts laid out before her so she can organize and assimilate them, reshuffling stories and memories, nightmares and dreams, into a revisionist history of her past. But, as Etta talks about her parents, about truths Cora never knew or had forgotten, Cora begins to do something she's never done before. Slowly, in effortless exhaustion, her mind switches off, shuts down, and emotions flood through her body.

Etta watches her granddaughter cry, head bent to her chest, shoulders shuddering slightly, fingers wrapped together, twisting around and around each other as if whittling down the bones. It is nearly noon before Cora slides under the covers, allowing her grandmother to tuck the duvet into a tight cocoon, and closes her eyes. Etta creeps out of the room with soft, slow steps.

She turns at the door to glance back at her beloved granddaughter now asleep in her bed. Cora's eyes are swollen and red, her skin burnt and blotchy with sorrow, but something else is happening, the very thing Etta intended; a lightness is beginning to wash over her, a shadow of joy. It's only a whisper of possibility now, a potential, but Etta can see flickers of it at the edges of Cora's body. A space is opening up in her tight chest, a gap that could let love slip in. The tears she's shed have started to erode the ice. Her heart is beginning to thaw.

Walt slides *Much Ado About Nothing* off the shelf and slips it alongside *The Merchant of Venice*. Five minutes later he returns it to its rightful place. The attempt to suppress his sorrow beneath unnecessary stock reorganization isn't working. That morning he'd rearranged the entire romance section into alphabetical order. In the afternoon he'd returned all the books to their original places.

Last night, like Cora, he hadn't slept. He'd run home, limbs pumping, adrenaline pushing away tears, and fallen into bed. He'd lain there all night, fully dressed, and stared up at the ceiling, replaying every hideous second of the awful event over and over and over again. As the morning light slowly crept across the room, Walt managed to drag himself out of bed and tug off his clothes. Finding a funny little red stitch in his shirt, he'd pulled out the thread with his teeth and dropped it onto the floor. Then Walt had taken a shower and, as the hot water spat onto his skin, he'd known that this was it. His life as it had always been was over. He could no longer pretend. He could no longer keep hoping and deluding himself. He had to let go, just as he should have years ago. That much was clear now.

"Oh, bloody hell."

Walt abandons Shakespeare and slouches back over to the counter to find solace in a slice of cherry pie. He glances at the clock and frowns. It's 6:48 P.M. She didn't come. It's Friday evening and Cora isn't sitting in the science section reading *The Life of Mary Somerville* or something similar. She is a creature of unwavering habits, of precise and exact routines. But now she's deserted him. The world has been knocked off its axis and is spinning in a different direction.

His half-finished copy of *Madame Bovary* sits next to the till, taunting him. Walt glares at it, then snatches it up, fingernails digging into the paper. After last night he suspects Cora will probably shun his bookshop for a while, perhaps forever. He wouldn't blame her. She probably thinks he's some sort of mad stalker and will avoid ever having to see him again. This, Walt considers, should be a good thing. At least it will save him from the abject humiliation of having to look Cora in the eye again.

What will he do now? Perhaps he'll be able to employ great reserves of willpower and, eventually, one day, he'll forget her. Or at least be able to go a whole hour without thinking of her. He will find other things to fill the gap, fun and wonderful things, until the gaps have gone and he's left with a life, a life he will love. This plan should leave Walt feeling free, released from chains and ready for anything. But it doesn't. He only feels disorientated, untethered, a forgotten sheet left to flap in the wind.

The second time Walt spoke to Cora he'd been six, she'd been nine and crying. The sight of her, fragile shoulders hunched over and trembling, so moved him that he forgot to be shy. He'd just wanted to hug her, cuddle her like his father did when he couldn't sleep and called out for his mother. Cora sat on the pavement in All Saints' Passage, almost hidden by the branches of the willow tree hanging over the wall and brushing the paving stones. Walt sidled up, scuffed shoes on tiptoes until he stood just inside the curtain of branches.

"Are you okay?" he'd asked, immediately regretting it because of course she wasn't.

When Cora looked up, eyes swollen and bloodshot, he expected her to tell him to push off, to leave her alone. But she didn't. Sorrow had temporarily rubbed off the rough edges, leaving her tender, exposed. She swallowed several times before speaking.

"My science teacher, Mr. Heatly," she said, wiping her eyes and sniffing. "He says no one can save the world. He says we're all insignificant and ultimately useless, that no matter what we do it'll never stop millions of people from suffering. He says I should give up and surrender to the inevitable."

"He sounds like an idiot," Walt said, thinking that if he ever met Mr. Heatly he'd kick him in the shins. "You shouldn't listen to him."

The look that Cora had given him then—a glorious mixture of gratitude, hope and expectation—had nearly stopped his heart. If someone had told Walt, in that moment, that he could give ten years of his life in exchange for Cora's happiness, he would have.

"Thanks," Cora said. "That's naïve but nice of you."

Walt smiled then and his near-stopped heart had soared.

Now Walt paces up and down behind the counter, hoping his frustration will evaporate as he moves. He rubs the end of his nose (something he used to do for endless hours as a child, in the hope that he could rub some of it away), lost in thought. His old way of life has collapsed. He needs to find a new way of being: new thoughts to fill the cavern left in his brain that now must be emptied of Cora, new actions to pass hours no longer marked by anticipation, a new life to replace the old.

Then Walt stops pacing. He has an idea. An idea so different, so startling and wild, it makes him sneeze with shock.

Chapter Six

An hour later Walt walks into his producer's office and stands in front of his desk.

"Hey, Dylan. I've come for the letters."

Dylan sits up in his chair, leaning forward. "But you said—"

"I know. I've changed my mind."

There are many things Dylan wants to say in response, but thirty-six years in the world have taught him such impulses are usually best suppressed, so he holds his tongue and shrugs. "I've been throwing most of them out, because you told me to . . ." He ducks under the desk and gropes around, pulling out a shoebox with letters spilling over the sides. "Here is the last two weeks' worth."

Walt leans over the desk and takes the box. "Thanks."

After his shift, during which he reluctantly shares another

three chapters of *Madame Bovary* with his late-night listeners, Walt takes the box of letters home and spreads them across his bed. The envelopes are multicolored: pastel pink, lavender purple, fire-hydrant red among the creams and whites. *In for a penny, in for a pound,* Walt thinks, and reaches for the red one.

Less than a minute later he drops it to the floor. "Bloody hell." He's not a prude, well, perhaps he is. In any case, he's too embarrassed to finish the letter. It emits waves of desire from where it lies on the floor. Walt quickly picks up another, safer letter, sealed in virginal white.

Dashwood Cottage, Cambridge
01223 290478
Monday, March 4

The Night Reader,
I'm sorry, I don't know your real name. And I'm sorry to write to you like this. I'm not a crazy person, a deluded fan who thinks she knows you just because she listens to you every night. I'm not in love with you, though you've got the loveliest voice I've ever heard, and my mother always said you can tell everything about a man from his voice. But she's on her fourth marriage, so perhaps I shouldn't listen to her. Anyway, that's not the point. I'm just writing to say that your voice is magical. I've already said that, haven't I? Okay, let me say it properly. Your voice is like birdsong. It woke me up.

Ten years ago my husband died. I stopped going outside. I stopped speaking to people. Six months ago I turned on the radio. You were reading The Great Gatsby. *After that you read* The Awakening, *then* A Passage to India. *Now, as I write this, you're reading a book about a woman hitchhiking across America.*

I'm turning 40 in December and I've only now started to see the world again, to see color and light. And everything is sharper, brighter, more alive than I ever remember it being before. You've opened my eyes and my heart. You've saved my life.

With love and thanks,
Milly Bradley

After Walt has read the letter three times he does something he's never done before in his life. He picks up his phone and, not thinking of the late hour or what on earth he's going to say if she answers, he dials the stranger's number.

On Wednesday Cora calls in sick and cancels all her tutorials. In the four years she's been working with Dr. Baxter it's the first time she's taken a single day off (for ill health or holiday) and, though he's surprised, he tells her not to worry, that she's welcome to a week off if she needs it. Cora is assisting the eminent Dr. Baxter in his research for the Emergency Nutrition Network to develop alternative food sources to combat acute malnutrition. Last year he'd been awarded the Nobel Prize in Biochemistry, for the world-changing creation he'd made decades before: genetically modified wheat that grew without water. So the work they do together is extremely important, and Cora is a little loath to miss a single day of it. She assures him she'll be back as soon as she feels better. Strictly speaking she isn't actually sick, though she has a strange ache in her chest she's never felt before, but Cora needs time to investigate another potentially life-changing subject.

At lunchtime Etta brings Cora a tray with a bowl of homemade garlic and truffle pasta and a plate of lamb, new potatoes and braised broccoli. After setting it down on the bedside table, Etta pulls open the curtains and the room lights up with a flood of midday sunshine.

"I didn't make dessert," Etta says. "I thought you could go to Blue Water Books and get some of that cherry pie you love so much. I made these for you." She sets a pair of new trousers on the wooden chair next to Cora's bedside. Etta pats down the duvet then, one by one, plumps up the cushions on each of the chairs in her bedroom.

Cora eyes the trousers suspiciously: dark blue cotton, 28.4 inches at the waist, 36.7 inches long: a perfect fit. "What'll happen if I put those on?"

Etta swallows a smile. "Nothing. I haven't touched them. If you don't want to go to the bookshop, I'm going to Fitzbillies for a coffee and Chelsea bun, maybe two. You're welcome to join me."

Cora sits up in bed. "You know, those things will kill you, the rate you eat them."

"That may be true." Etta smiles. "But I can't imagine a better way to go."

Cora raises her eyebrows and pulls the tray of food into her lap. It's too rich for her taste but, in the absence of a good old sandwich, she'll eat it anyway.

"I'm going to Oxford," Cora says, twirling her fork around in the pasta. "I've decided to see if there's any truth to your suspicions." She eyes her grandmother. "So you should tell me now if there's anything else you're keeping from me. Okay?"

"No," Etta says, glancing out of the window. "No, of course not."

"Hum." Cora gives a suspicious sniff. Then she swallows a mouthful of pasta. "Delicious."

Etta smiles. "Thank you."

As she watches her granddaughter gobble up the pasta as if she hasn't eaten in a month, Etta is already almost regretting what she's done. She might have known that Cora would want to investigate the facts for herself, though she didn't think she'd do it so quickly. Etta doesn't want Cora diving into the past, walking a painful path paved with sorrow, blood and broken glass, getting lost in the pain of events she can't change. She wants Cora to wake up to the opportunities of hope and love in the present. Unfortunately, having awoken Cora's heart, and given how strong-willed her granddaughter is, Etta has no hope of controlling events now, so she may as well not bother.

An hour later, having exacted a promise from Cora that she'd give herself a day to think about it before doing anything rash, Etta is ensconced in her usual corner in Fitzbillies, famous purveyor of what are supposed to be the stickiest, sweetest Chelsea buns in the world. She remembers going to the café as a girl, it having been a fixture on Trumpington Street since 1922, though she was never allowed an entire Chelsea bun to herself in those days. Now, although she can eat as many as she likes, Etta can never manage more than one. She teases her granddaughter by suggesting otherwise, but the stodgy, sticky concoction of raisin-studded dough drenched in syrup is a challenge to consume. However, delicious though they are, the Chelsea buns are not the reason Etta has been coming to this café three times a week for nearly fifty years.

The real reason Etta comes to this particular café is because of a man and a promise she made. Before that, when she was barely eighteen, Etta once had a brief affair with a hypnotist, who'd told her he could look into an audience and spot—at a hundred feet—those who would fall under his spell and those who wouldn't. He used this gift to pick his volunteers. There was a tightness in the ones who would successfully resist him: stiff shoulders, firm jaw, unyielding stare. The people he picked were eager, fluid, restless, those who wanted to step into the alternative reality he was offering them. But, very occasionally, he'd be wrong. There were some, he had explained, who seemed suggestible on the surface: bright eyes, easy smile, sitting forward in their seats, when really their minds were as inaccessible as their bank accounts. Etta, he'd said, was one of them. It's perhaps unsurprising, then, that she's always been immune to her own magic.

When Etta's heart had been broken, by the only man who ever held it, she'd tried everything in her box of tricks to help it heal. But nothing had worked. She'd closed the shop for a week, had tried on virtually all the dresses, made little nips and tucks with her needle, stitched stars into them with her special red thread, yet the following Sunday her heart still hung heavy in her chest: a broken pendulum of bruised flesh swinging slowly back and forth.

Now she sits at the window gazing out onto the street. Her coffee is cold now and her Chelsea bun half finished, though she can't actually remember eating it. As she picks a raisin out of the dough and squeezes it between her thumb and forefinger Etta is seized by a sudden longing so strong and sharp it makes her gasp. A moment later, when she can breathe again, Etta closes her eyes to think of the man she lost to God almost fifty years ago.

—

Milly is not a woman of moderation. She was once. She used to take baby steps through life, always tentative, always second-guessing herself. When her husband died—snatched from her suddenly by a drunk driver—she got even worse, going from baby steps to stopping walking altogether. Because she knew the terrifying truth: no matter how careful you were, how prudent and well-protected, you were never really safe. You could be hit by a car crossing the street, you could walk under a falling chimney, you could get cancer even if you never left your house. No matter what you did, death would get you sooner or later. Which made everything else meaningless. So Milly surrendered, waved her white flag and gave in. Until she heard Walt.

It was just before midnight. Milly was in bed, staring up at the ceiling, knowing she'd be conscious for hours yet. Half-heartedly she reached for her radio alarm clock and tuned it in. When she heard his voice she froze the dial and sat up. That was the moment she started to come alive again, piece by piece, word by word.

Walt's words fell around her like warm rain that settled on her skin, slowly and gently soaking in. Milly closed her eyes and listened. She felt her husband's hand in her hair, his kiss on her mouth. Her cheeks flushed with a heat that spread through her body, lapping in waves across her chest, flooding to her fingers and toes until she was lit from within by life again. At first she was an oil lamp—her light flickering and pale. But as weeks passed and *The Great Gatsby* progressed Milly's light grew stronger until, by the time Walt finished *A Passage to India,* it shone like a sunrise. That was when she wrote him a letter.

And now Milly is about to meet him. The Night Reader. In person. It's all she can do to stand up straight. Her heart thunders, her head throbs. Now she is no longer a woman of moderation. She is illuminated. She is fire and ice. She is passion, excitement and joy. After being in the desert for so long her appetite for life is unquenchable. Now, when Milly unwraps a box of chocolates she eats every one, when she uncorks a bottle of wine she drinks until the last glass and when she falls in love she gives her whole heart. When she opens the door to the bookshop Milly holds her breath. When she steps inside all she hears is blood rushing in her ears. And, when she sees him behind the counter, her mouth drops open.

Cora wanders along All Saints' Passage, absently counting the cracks in the paving stones beneath her feet: twenty-seven by the time she reaches the end of the street. She glances left and right, at the pretty boutiques, at the students and tourists wandering past. She's not in the mood to mix with people or even be near them. She needs to decide what to do next. *Books,* Cora thinks. That's what she needs now, the company of books and their characters: the company of famous female scientists who'll sweep away her thoughts with their brilliant, beautiful lives. She turns back into All Saints' Passage and steps into the bookshop. She hurries, head down, past Walt and a woman, about forty and rather frumpy, standing next to the coffee machine. Out of the corner of her eye Cora sees the woman tentatively tasting a slice of cherry pie while Walt watches. She hurries past, pushed forward by the memory of the last time she saw Walt and still embarrassed, though surprisingly not as much as she thought she would be.

"Oh my goodness, it's delicious!"

The words explode behind Cora as she reaches the science section. Cora frowns. The woman's voice sounds as her own might if she suddenly made a significant scientific discovery.

That's what it would take to elicit such excitement in her, not simply a slice of cherry pie.

Two hours later Cora's head is gloriously empty, her own reality washed away by someone else's. It's the first time she's read without checking her watch and she's surprised how quickly the time passed and how much better she feels. And it's not the usual lifting of spirits she feels after an immersion into the lives of inspirational women, it's something more. She can't quite put her finger on the emotion, but it's strong and deep. Cora glances down at her T-shirt and trousers, deeply suspecting that Etta's little red stitches are secreted somewhere in the lining of her clothes.

Reaching the counter Cora glances up again. Perhaps today, given how long she's been reading, she'll have two slices of cherry pie. She stops alongside the coffee machine.

"A double espresso please," she says, without looking up.

"Sure."

The machine whirs into action and Cora's caught by the sound of the word, the lightness of tone, the laughter beneath it. Happiness. He sounds happy, she realizes. Cora has never considered Walt a particularly happy person, not that she's really given it much conscious thought until now, and she wonders if it's the effect of this new woman.

Walt, his back to her, slips the tiny china cup under the stream of coffee. It's a minute before he turns around and when he does she's surprised. Not by the fact that he's smiling, but by the fact that she wants to keep looking at him. Cora never likes to look people in the eye, not if she can possibly help it. She likes to stay back, keep a safe distance. Or she did. But now even that is shifting.

There is something intriguing about Walt, something new

that captures her attention, piques her curiosity. Perhaps because, all of a sudden and without her noticing, he's transformed from a bookish boy into a handsome man. And not just any man, since she's seen so many men and never wanted to look twice at any of them. So Walt, statistically speaking, is an anomaly. Simply scientifically there must be something very special about him. She's just not sure exactly what.

Walt slides the espresso across the counter, along with a bowl of sugar cubes and a spoon. "Here you go."

"Thanks." Cora feels herself smile. Strange. She straightens her face. "And I'll have two slices of cherry pie, please."

"Oh." Now it is Walt's turn to smile. But his is tucked inward, a reflex, a smile indicating a secret feeling, not one he's consciously meaning to share. "I'm afraid we've got none left. I baked one this morning but . . ."

With an apologetic shrug he nods at the empty plate discarded on the counter. Its white expanse is smeared with red cherry juice and scattered with crumbs. Someone else has eaten her pie. With a pang of annoyance Cora thinks of the woman she saw feasting on it a couple of hours before. They have shared it. A pie for two. The woman must be Walt's girlfriend. A new girlfriend, the reason for all the smiles. So he *was* drunk the other night under her window. Of course he was, how could she have imagined otherwise. Cora feels a quick twist in her chest. But it's a different sensation from the first. Odd. New. Unrecognizable. Jealousy? Regret? Disappointment? Cora frowns. What has Etta done to her?

Chapter Seven

The next day, having kissed her grandmother good-bye, placating her worries and promising to be back before too long, Cora sits on a bus bound for Oxford, rumbling past endless fields of flat yellow dotted with trees, interrupted by an occasional village. An unopened biography of Dorothy Hodgkin lies in her lap. She gazes, glassy-eyed, at the dirty window but doesn't see the countryside beyond. Cora has taken this trip with her grandmother once a year for the last twenty years. Every year on the first of June, her parents' wedding anniversary, they board the bus at dawn and return at midnight: an eight-hour journey to a hidden graveyard. They leave a bunch of white roses on each of the two graves. Cora has never done it alone.

Etta had offered to shut the shop and accompany her granddaughter to the Oxfordshire Police Station. In fact, she'd almost insisted. But Cora had been firm. It was something she had to do by herself, she'd said, though she isn't entirely sure why. Perhaps so she can back out at the last minute if seized too sharply by the fear circling her now—silently waiting, like a shark in shallow waters. What will she say when she arrives? What does one say to the police in order to find out the particulars of a twenty-year-old case? What procedures will she have to go through? Will any evidence even have survived? Is Etta right in her suspicions, or not?

As the scenery slips past, Cora, wanting a distraction from more distressing thoughts, allows her mind to rest on Walt. She's surprised at just how many memories she has that contain him. Has she really seen him so often? How odd that he's never stood out before now. Or perhaps the fact that he's been such a fixture in her life, like oxygen in water and air, is exactly why she's always taken him for granted.

Her thirteenth birthday fell on a Wednesday. Etta had wanted to organize a party but Cora begged her not to do so. After sitting around the shop that morning, squirming about in the silk skirt—cream sprinkled with lavender lilies—her grandmother had sewn, Cora had left at lunchtime, claiming she had plans with a friend. A few hours after that Walt found her squeezed into a corner in the back of the bookshop, face buried in a biography of Jocelyn Bell Burnell.

"Happy birthday," Walt said softly.

Cora glanced up with a frown. "How do you know it's my birthday?"

Walt blushed and shrugged.

"When's your birthday?" Cora snapped.

"Thirty-first of October," Walt said, softer still.

"Halloween." Cora considered this. "Same day as Adolf von Baeyer and Sir Joseph Swan."

"Who are they?"

"Scientists," Cora said. "You must have heard of Sir Swan?"

"Sure." Walt lied. "I don't know who else is born on your birthday, but I bet—"

"Albert Einstein." Cora let slip a smile of pride and closed her book. "Sorry I snapped at you. I don't like birthdays very much."

"Why not?"

Cora glanced down at the book again, tracing her forefinger over a woman's face. While he waited, Walt sat down a few feet away, took off his backpack and set it down on the floor next to his knees.

"My parents died on my birthday." Cora spoke without looking up. Her finger stopped on the *B* of Burnell. "So birthdays always make me sad."

"Oh," Walt said. "I'm sorry."

Cora shrugged. "It's not your fault."

"I just, if my dad died, too . . . being an orphan, I can't imagine it. I'm sorry I brought it up." Then Walt brightened. "I've got something that might cheer you up."

"Yeah?"

"It's a bit of a secret. My dad gave it to me last year, on my tenth birthday. I'm not supposed to show it to anyone else."

"Really?" Cora leaned forward, fingers twitching.

Walt unzipped his backpack and very carefully pulled out a book. It was quite small, just bigger than a deck of cards, bound in dark red leather with an inscription embossed in gold on the front that Cora couldn't quite make out.

"My dad had my name engraved on the front." Walt held it tight between both hands. "It's—"

"Walt! Where are you?"

At his name, Walt sat up, eyes wide with shock, his mouth straightaway shut with a guilty grimace.

"Oops," he whispered. "That's Dad. I'd better go."

Cora nodded, glancing once more at the book as Walt slipped it back into his bag. As he started to scurry away, Cora stood up.

"Wait."

Walt turned back.

"Thank you," she said softly, and smiled.

He had never shown that book to Cora again. Not, she realizes, until the night he came to her window. It had been the same book, red leather and gold. How could she have forgotten that? The book must be something pretty special and she's honored that he'd wanted to share it with her. But what was it? Cora makes a mental note to investigate the matter on her return home.

The priest looks down at his fingers resting on the feet of the statue. St. Francis wears sandals, the nails of his ten marble toes smoothed away by thousands of hands over hundreds of years. Father Sebastian can't remember how long he's been standing there. What was he meant to be doing? What time is it? He's hungry. It must be nearly midday. Confession. That's what he's supposed to do now. Before he stopped by St. Francis, Sebastian had been on his way to the confessional.

He shuffles across the stone floor, his soft leather shoes sliding past the pulpit, shaking himself free of his memories so he'll be able to listen to his parishioners. He knows most of them think he nods off while they talk, sleeping through their minor transgressions, dozing during their petty sins. Probably they'd prefer it that way. But Sebastian never sleeps during confession, despite the soft velvet cushions and dim light. It wouldn't be right. And he tries to be as good as he possibly can, after the great wrong he once did, always vainly attempting to level his lopsided balance sheet, even though his heart isn't really in the religion of it anymore. In fact, if he's honest with himself, Sebastian's heart hasn't been with the church in a long time. He goes through the motions, the rituals, the pomp and circumstance, but at the end of each day he feels more detached, more alone than when he woke.

Sebastian settles into his seat and leans his head against the wood, letting a small sigh escape his lips. He feels the presence of someone else alongside him, another soul seeking redemption. And, before he even speaks, Sebastian knows who it is. He can't help a smile.

"I've met someone, Father. A woman." The words tumble out in a rush of excitement. "A real woman, one who actually looks me in the eye without laughing."

"Well, that's a wonderful thing," Sebastian says. "And I'm very happy for you. But, strictly speaking, you aren't really supposed to be here, are you?"

"I didn't steal someone else's place," Walt protests. "There was no one waiting, so I just thought—"

"But you're not a Catholic, dear boy," says Sebastian gently. "And you don't have anything to confess, do you?"

"No," Walt admits. "But I like talking to you. You're such a good listener."

The priest smiles again. He knows the real reason Walt comes to him. For, while he listens carefully to each of his parishioners, there is no need. He's always been able to see people's stories on their faces: their greatest regrets, fears, hopes and dreams, hanging in the air around their heads and hearts. He only has to look at a person to suddenly feel exactly what they feel. And so it was with Walt, ten years ago. But still Sebastian listens, because it's the right thing to do and because, while he does so, he is able to forget about himself.

"I think," Walt continues, buoyant as a balloon, "I think she might actually . . . like me. Not just my voice, but me."

"But this is not Cora?" Sebastian frowns. "The one you're in love with?"

"No." Walt sinks back to the floor. "Not her, I'm trying to forget about her."

"Oh. Okay." Father Sebastian feels the sudden stab of pain in Walt's chest as if it had just happened to him and decides not to pry. "And who is this new girl?" He's vaguely aware that, in these politically correct days, he shouldn't really call grown women "girls" but he can't help it. Any woman not of his generation seems like a girl to him.

"Milly." Walt smiles. "Her name is Milly. And she's nearly forty. Seventeen years older than me. But it doesn't matter. I don't even notice. She wrote to me. I called her. She's really quite lovely."

"Oh." Sebastian scratches his nose. "I see." But that is a lie. Another sin to add to his infinite list, though of course there was only one that really mattered, the one he tries every day to forget.

"I'm not being fickle," Walt protests, as if finally giving up on a twenty-year-long unrequited love could be interpreted as being capricious. "I'll always care for Cora, of course I will. But I've got to get over her. She's never going to love me back and I need . . . I need to be loved back."

Sebastian traps another sigh—of deep longing—in his chest and holds it there. He's always had very strong willpower, been good at fasting, at holding secrets, denying himself sustenance and rest. But not love. He's never been able to stop loving someone simply because he should. If only. Then the last fifty years of his life would've been considerably more bearable.

"Of course you're not fickle," Sebastian says, suddenly realizing the boy might interpret his silence as judgment. "No one could say that of you. And I'm happy. You've found someone. If you're lucky you'll fall in love. I'm happy for you, I truly am." The priest's nose twitches again and he scratches it. Another lie. He'll have to chant Hail Marys while polishing the vestry windows tonight.

"Thank you," Walt says. "I'm happy too." But, although this is certainly true, although Walt feels happier than he has in his whole life, something the priest said is starting to trouble him. Will he fall in love again? Is it possible? Because, since he decided to finally let go of Cora, he hasn't felt his heart at all. Not a quickening, not a skip, nothing. It just sits in his chest, beating out its dull monotone, ticking out the time for the next fifty years, until it reaches its last beat, never to be moved or touched or captured again. And Walt is starting to suspect that perhaps neither he nor his heart is actually capable of loving anyone else.

Cora stands on the steps of the Oxfordshire Police Station. Now that she's actually here, she's unsure whether she wants to go in. It has taken her all morning to get there. When the bus dropped her off in the city center, Cora had intended to hurry directly to her destination. But instead she found herself dragging her feet, forgetting directions, taking wrong turns. She lost hours counting leaves and bricks and cigarette stubs dropped on the streets, drifting around Oxford, avoiding personal places and stumbling across famous ones: Bodleian Library, Balliol College, Ashmolean Museum.

Cora can't remember the house she lived in as a girl, so she couldn't purposely avoid it, but she stayed clear of New College, where her parents worked. She has no memories of being there either yet isn't ready to confront any memories that might return to her, now that she knows things weren't as she'd always thought.

"Are you all right?"

Cora blinks and brings herself back. She's standing on the steps—on the 7th of 17—of a police station. A tall young man is standing beside her with a slight look of concern.

"Are you all right?" he asks again.

Cora nods.

"Can I help you with anything?"

She frowns at him. "Are you a police officer?"

He nods. "I'm a detective."

It seems to Cora that he wants to touch her arm, to reassure her of something though he doesn't know exactly what. Over the last few days she's been getting these senses of strangers, little snapshots into their hearts, and wonders if it's normal. She's spent so much of her life disconnected, wrapped up in her head, that she doesn't know what it's like to connect, to see and know other people.

"I want," Cora begins, "I'm here to talk to someone about . . . my parents."

The police detective nods and waits.

"They died twenty years ago," Cora says. "Here in Oxford, in a fire. It was ruled an accidental death but . . . I'm not entirely sure it was."

"Oh, I'm sorry," he says. "Please, then, follow me."

Twenty minutes later Cora is at the police officer's desk, holding a plastic cup of tepid tea between her palms, sitting forward in her chair. She watches Detective Henry Dixon's fingers as he types and stares at his computer screen. When it seems as if he's completely forgotten she's sitting there at all, he looks up.

"I'm sorry," he says, "it takes a while to access some cases and—"

"I should really be going through all sorts of procedures and paperwork before anyone does anything," Cora interjects. "So please don't apologize. I'm very grateful. Really."

She'd overheard Henry quietly arguing with another police officer while she sat in the waiting room, so she knows he shouldn't really be doing this.

Henry gives a quick smile. "I'll be as fast as I can."

Etta sits at her sewing machine, stitching the hem of a bright blue silk dress, her foot tapping restlessly against the leg of her chair. She's trying not to worry about Cora but can't help it, her thoughts keep pulling back to her granddaughter no matter how hard she tries to wrench them away. Etta wishes a customer would come into the shop and distract her but the bell above her door hasn't rung in hours. When Etta finishes the hem she threads shimmering beads onto a needle, two at a time. Then, as she pulls the needle through the silk, she suddenly hears the blessed bell. Etta jumps up from her table, nearly knocking over the sewing machine, and hurries into the shop.

A very beautiful redhead steps onto the carpet and "Let's Twist Again" starts to play. Etta smiles. It's one of her favorite songs and she knows this customer is going to be fun. The woman walks slowly around the shop, lingering over each dress as though she wants to buy them all and can't bear to choose just one.

"Which one would you like to try on?" Etta asks, not needing to be tentative.

The woman turns with a brilliant smile, still holding the hem of a bright yellow minidress, and fixes her bright green eyes on Etta.

"I want to wear them all," she exclaims. "I want to take them all home."

Etta laughs. "That's exactly why I live above the shop."

"Well, I'm not surprised. So would I. It's quite the loveliest dress shop I've ever stepped into, and I've stepped into a lot."

"Compulsive shopper?" Etta asks.

The woman shakes her head. "Costume designer."

"Oh." Etta brightens. She knew this was going to be fun. "For films?"

"Not yet, but I'd love to." The woman holds out her hand. "Greer Ashby. It's lovely to meet you."

"Etta Sparks. My pleasure." Etta gives Greer a quick glance, assessing her situation with an expert eye, but can't see anything in particular, no missing pieces, that her customer needs. "So tell me—since, embarrassingly enough, I can't seem to figure it out—what can I do for you?"

Greer smiles. "I'm up for an award, for a play."

"How exciting. What's it called?"

"Ninety-nine Nights," Greer says. "My sister-in-law wrote it and asked me to do the costumes. It's a gorgeous play. You should see it."

"Oh, I will," Etta says, "I will."

"Anyway, I need a very special dress. And I can see I've come to the right place."

"Indeed you have," Etta says, thinking that she might just stitch a little red star inside the lining of the dress Greer chooses, an extra shot of confidence to spur her in the direction of those films. "Indeed you have."

Milly stops walking outside A Stitch in Time. She's on her way to see Walt, but the window glittering with dresses brings her to a halt. It's filled with dozens of dresses draped over each other in every shade of blue. They sparkle and shimmer, every inch of fabric scattered with sequins, glitter and beads giving the effect of ocean meeting sky on a bright summer day.

Milly is not a fan of dresses. She can never find a flattering one and now just usually buys garments without first trying them on, because it's easier and less painful that way. But there is something about this shop. It almost seems to be an art gallery rather than a dress shop, a place that will make you feel serene just by stepping inside and breathing in all the beauty.

"Bye Bye Love" fills the shop as Milly opens the door. Etta looks up from behind the counter to see her new customer: wearing a baggy dress two sizes too big, a heavy woolen coat and clumpy shoes, her mousy brown hair cut in an unflattering bob around her round face. She wears no makeup but her skin is clear and her eyes are bright. These eyes widen as she glances about the shop, mesmerized and slightly scared. Slowly Milly approaches the closest rack of clothes and reaches out to touch a dress. Etta watches her. This customer is exactly the opposite of her last one; this one she'll have to treat with kid gloves.

When Milly's fingers touch the lapis blue silk she pulls back, as if having just received a slight electric shock. For a long moment she stares at the dresses until a slow smile creeps onto her lips. Milly reaches out again, this time letting the silk slip over her fingers like water. Then she turns to go. But Etta is beside her before she finds the door.

"You haven't tried anything on."

Milly stares at Etta as if she's seen a ghost.

"None of them would fit me," Milly mumbles. "I'm far too old and fat for pretty dresses." She hates clothes shopping. The hours of despair searching for something remotely suitable, the few seconds of hope, the bitter disappointment when the mirror reveals every dimple of cellulite, saggy skin and rolls of belly fat. In fact, she can't now imagine why on earth she stepped into the dress shop in the first place. What was she thinking?

"Don't be silly." Etta laughs. "You'll look beautiful. I promise."

"No." Milly shakes her head. "They're far too glamorous. They'd look ridiculous on me."

"These aren't ordinary dresses," Etta assures her. "No one looks ridiculous in them, only completely and utterly fabulous."

Milly laughs then, a full deep laugh, and Etta knows she's in.

Etta sticks a small hand into a rack of crimson ball gowns and plucks out one of her loveliest creations. The bodice is made of spiderweb lace, thousands of roses embroidered over herringbone, ending at the waist with waterfalls of dark red silk cascading to the floor.

"Oh my goodness," Milly gasps. She takes a tiny step backward. "Oh, no. No, I couldn't. I couldn't possibly—"

"Just try it. For me," Etta says with a smile, ushering her toward the changing room. "Make this old woman happy, then I'll let you go. Please."

Milly gives a sigh, relenting, as Etta knew she would. Her

current customer is a chronic people pleaser, absolutely incapable of refusing a direct request.

"Wonderful, thank you." Etta grins. She waits outside the changing room, standing guard to be sure Milly doesn't discard the dress too quickly after putting it on. She needs to coax her out into the open, to help her have a closer look; she needs to make a few adjustments and add a secret red star into the lining with her little needle and thread.

Chapter Eight

After half an hour, Henry sits back from his screen and rubs his eyes. "I've found your parents' file," he says. "They died in a fire, on March fourteenth, 1993, right?"

"Yes." Cora nods.

"Okay," Henry says. "So, the inquest gave a ruling of accidental death. The fire wasn't arson. It wasn't set on purpose. The police investigators didn't find any accelerant, anything of the sort to suggest that someone intentionally started it." He glances back at the screen, then gives Cora an almost apologetic look, his dark brow furrowed. She notices that his eyes are a bright, bright blue. "The police report concluded the fire was caused by an unattended candle falling onto a pile of papers and books."

"Oh," Cora says, not sure whether she's disappointed. "Okay."

"Was that not what you wanted to hear?"

Cora shakes her head. "No, it's not that. It's just, my grandmother . . . she thinks it wasn't simply an accident. She thinks that perhaps someone else was involved."

"She thinks they were murdered?"

Cora shifts in her plastic seat. "No, not exactly. Well, I'm not sure. She's not sure. I just wanted to see what I could find out."

"Does your grandmother have any evidence?"

Cora shakes her head. She grips the side of his desk, suddenly feeling like a three-year-old telling a grown-up that fairies are real. What evidence does she have, what proof? Cora wants to jump up from her chair and run away. What is she doing? What is she doing asking to see the details of a case about which she knows nothing? Now she looks like an idiot. Or a lunatic.

"Family members often can't bring themselves to believe that the death of their loved ones was a tragic accident," Henry says softly. He reaches across the desk, resting his heavy solid fingers on her light, jittery hands, grounding her, bringing her back to reality. "It's not unusual to want someone else to be responsible. So they have a person to blame, to hate. Cruel twists of fate can be harder to—"

"Yes, of course," Cora says, about to stand up and excuse herself, when all of a sudden, a memory rises up within her: she's sitting at one end of a small oak dinner table, kneeling on a chair to read a book. Her father sits at the other end of the table and, in the middle, her mother. Both smile, completely absorbed in their own books, stacks of papers piled up around them. The room is dark except for candlelight flickering from five candlesticks dotted about the table.

Cora pulls her hands away from the desk and the warmth of his fingers. She jumps up, knocking the plastic chair back so it hits the floor. She turns to pick it up.

"Sorry," Cora says, "sorry, I've wasted your time. I didn't

mean, I thought perhaps . . ." And, in a puff of embarrassment, she hurries out of the room, leaving Henry staring after her, before she can finish the sentence.

Milly's smile is radiant, gazing at herself, a beautiful figure resplendent in the crimson gown of lace and silk. Etta grins, compliments swallowed when she sees they're clearly not required.

Only silence is needed now, to let Milly's shock and delight sweep away sorrow and self-doubt. "I can't, I don't . . ."

"Believe it, my dear." Etta leans forward. "Sometimes a painting just needs the right frame to reveal its true beauty."

Milly takes another slow turn in front of the mirror, unable to pull her eyes away, unable to stop smiling. "I feel like I'm falling in love."

It's then that Milly's greatest wish shimmers onto the mirror. And, when Etta meets her sweet customer's eyes again, her smile is tainted with sadness so subtle and soft that Milly couldn't possibly see it. Etta doesn't want to say what she's about to say, but knows she must.

"Love is a glorious thing, my dear. And you have two loves in your life now, do you not?"

"Yes." Milly nods, shocked. "But how did you know?"

Etta smiles again. "I know something else too, from personal experience: don't give your heart to someone who can't return it with their own."

Milly's smile drops. "Why would you say that?"

"So you can have your greatest chance at happiness," Etta says. "Because it hurts less if you walk away now."

"You don't know," Milly protests, "you don't understand."

"Oh, my dear." Etta places a soft feathery hand lightly on

Milly's arm. "I know about love, especially the unrequited kind. And I really don't recommend it as a subject of study."

Milly glances down at the hem of her dress and squeezes her eyes tight shut. When she opens them again she won't look in the mirror or at Etta.

"This dress doesn't really suit me, and I'd never have a chance to wear it. I don't go to parties," she mumbles, hurrying back into the changing room, pulling the curtain closed behind her. A few minutes later she runs out of the dress shop, clutching her bag to her chest, leaving the crimson ball gown in a puffed-up heap of silk and lace on the dressing room floor.

Etta gazes after her as the door falls shut. This is the first time a customer has rejected her magic, has discarded a dress that was meant for her. It's a troubling turn of events. Could it be that she's losing her touch?

"Wait!"

Cora turns at the bottom step to see Henry running down toward her.

He stops on the step above her, not out of breath, but still confused by what he's doing and why. Cora can't look him in the eye.

"I've got something for you, just in case." Henry hands Cora a single sheet of white paper folded in half. She takes it and unfolds the page, expecting the telephone number of a good psychiatrist.

"A coroner?" Cora frowns. "Why are you giving me this?"

"I'm not sure," Henry admits. "But if you're suspicious about your parents' deaths then you need to see the coroner's report. It can give you more answers than I can. And, if you find something particularly revelatory, conflicting evidence or something that was overlooked before then you petition to reopen the case."

"I, I . . ." Cora is so touched by the police officer's generosity that she can't bear to tell him he was right in the first place, that her grandmother was wrong. "Thank you."

"You're welcome."

They stand together on the steps in silence. Cora is the first to tip into embarrassment. She shifts from the step onto the pavement, gives him a wave, then walks away without looking back.

Cora doesn't go to the bus stop. Instead she drifts aimlessly around Oxford, turning thc piece of folded paper over and over in her pocket. She isn't at all sure what to do next. Calling Etta should be the first step but, strangely, she doesn't feel like talking with her grandmother right now. She just wants to be alone. Contacting a coroner feels like a slightly scary prospect, too startlingly sharp and bleak to face.

Cora wanders along Woodstock Road, counting windows: 148 by the time she reaches Jack & Jim's, a twenty-four-hour café on the edge of Little Clarendon Street perpetually populated by students who stake out tables while writing essays and drinking endless cups of coffee and tea. Suddenly missing Walt's cherry pie, Cora stops to buy a chocolate-pistachio cookie before she turns right at the end of the street and heads toward the art house cinema.

With a vague idea of losing a few hours in fiction, Cora continues to count windows as she walks. Then, halfway down Walton Street, she stops. She's standing in front of a house: a house with six steps leading up to a bright yellow door, with seven windows including one in the attic and one in the basement, and walls of brick painted white. The color on the door is new—it used to be dark blue—and she doesn't remember an attic. But there is no mistaking the house now that she's seen it. She can feel it vibrating with a shiver into her bones. This is the house she lived in as a girl. This is the house where her parents died.

Chapter Nine

Cora stands on the steps of the house for a long time. So long, in fact, that she begins to feel strangers staring as they pass by. She doesn't know what to do. She wants to move, but she can't leave any more than she can knock on the door. Slowly, she studies the building, scrutinizing the thousands of bricks surrounding her, for once too overwhelmed by emotion to count them, imagining the flames rushing greedily across the bricks, the black smoke staining stone and cement. Cora is almost surprised that no marks remain, no scars, no testament to the trauma of her childhood. How can such an event simply have been painted over and forgotten?

A surge of anger rises up and catches in her throat. Tears blur her vision. The dead are so easily replaced. Some other family lives in the house now, utterly oblivious to those who preceded them. Cora glares at the bright yellow door: the color of sunflowers and bright summer days. It's not right. It ought to be dark blue, it ought to be black with soot and sorrow.

Suddenly all Cora's reticence and nervousness are swallowed up in another surge of anger, one that propels her up the steps to the frightful door, where she curls her fingers into a fist and raps her knuckles on the wood.

If the door hadn't opened so immediately, Cora probably would have fled as soon as the fury subsided. But a moment later she's staring into the face of a middle-aged woman who regards her with a surprised but polite smile.

"Oh, I'm sorry," she says, "I thought you were the postman. I'm expecting . . ."

She trails off as Cora glares up at her.

". . . Anyway, never mind. May I help you?"

Cora opens her mouth. Silence stretches between them until the woman starts to inch back behind the threshold.

"I used to live here," Cora blurts out. "When I was a girl."

"Did you?" the woman brightens. "How lovely. It must have been a long time ago, we've been here nearly twenty years, but you don't look—"

"We left when I was five years old," Cora says, thinking now that the woman seems sweet and slightly posh, and that such people probably don't take well to being told that strangers died in their homes. "I was walking . . . It's the first time I've been back."

"Oh." The woman's smile deepens. "Well then, would you like to come in? You must have some lovely memories, if you can remember that far back." She chuckles. "By lunchtime I can barely remember what I had for breakfast."

When Cora doesn't answer, the woman reaches out her hand. "I'm Judith Dowes."

Cora reaches out her hand in return. "Cora Carraway."

"A pleasure to meet you," Judith says. "Do come in."

She steps aside, holding the door open, and before Cora quite realizes what she's doing she's stepped into the house to join her.

Walt sits in the bookshop, half-reading *The Inimitable Jeeves*, his feet up on the counter. He glances at the phone next to the till. He wants to call Milly but isn't sure he should. He really likes her but, simply due to the fact that she isn't Cora, Walt worries that he just won't be able to love her. And Milly, he senses quite strongly, is a woman for whom liking won't be enough. She needs to be loved: deeply, utterly and completely. And this troubles him.

Walt snaps the book shut. Perhaps he should back off, let her go, spare her any possible pain. For the last thing Walt wants to do is cause Milly any suffering. He probably wouldn't be able to live with himself if he did. A vegetarian for the last fifteen years (after watching a particularly gruesome video at school about nonorganic farming), Walt can't even bring himself to kill wasps or flies. As a child he was once stung by a hornet and, though it hurt like hell, he'd let the perpetrator live.

Walt is staring at the phone again when it rings. His feet fall off the counter as he lunges forward to pick it up. He knows, with a deep certainty down in his bones, who it is. And it's not some silly customer enquiring whether or not the new John Grisham is out.

"Hello," he says, forgetting even to add *Blue Water Books*.

"Hi, Walt," Milly says. He can hear the smile in her voice. "It's me."

"Yes, I know." He's ridiculously pleased to hear from her. And realizing that makes Walt think that perhaps he's wrong, perhaps he really can get over Cora, perhaps he can love someone else after all, perhaps, perhaps, perhaps . . .

"How did you know?" Milly asks.

Walt shrugs before realizing she can't see him. "I suppose I just wanted it to be you," he says. Which certainly isn't a lie. "What are you up to?"

"Actually, I'm outside," Milly says. She takes a quick breath. "I wondered if you fancied lunch?"

Walt and Milly get a little lost on their way to lunch. They walk through town, taking a right turn toward the river when they probably should have taken a left, until they're wandering along The Backs, following a gravel path that runs behind Trinity College, King's College and Clare College. They watch students pushing punts along the river, zigzagging and crashing into the banks while tour guides with clutches of tourists glide effortlessly past.

They stroll under willow trees dipping their leaves into the water, sneaking glances at each other, listening to tourists being told about Lord Byron keeping a pet bear at Trinity College, followed 150 years later by Prince Charles, who only kept fish.

"Did you do your degree here?" Milly asks.

They stop to study the Bridge of Sighs: its intricate stone latticework and delicate spires reaching into the sky. It's Cora's favorite bridge. At least that's what she told Walt when she was fifteen. She liked to sit on the bench in Silver Street that overlooked it, admiring the architecture while pondering important thoughts. Words from a passing punt drift up, telling them this was one of Queen Victoria's most beloved places in the world.

"No," Walt says, shaking himself free of the memory. "I didn't go to university. Did you?"

"No," Milly says. "I was never very good at lessons. I couldn't get my head around spelling and sums. My teachers thought I was stupid. But I just wasn't really interested. I daydreamed too much."

"What did you dream about?"

"Silly things," Milly says. "Getting married, having kids."

"That's not silly."

"Makes me sound like a 1950s housewife."

"Well then, so was I." Walt smiles. "I never wanted a big life either. I just wanted to own Blue Water Books and be a husband and a father."

"You did?"

"Yes," Walt assures her, though he stops short of telling Milly exactly whose husband he'd wanted to be. "And I agree with Queen Victoria, Cambridge is one of the loveliest places in the world. I've never wanted to be anywhere else." He knows, of course, that he isn't really qualified to say, since he's never actually been any other place in the world than this, but he believes it anyway.

"I think so too. My husband was from New York, but we met in Cambridge. Whenever we visited his family, I was always so scared by how big and fast everything was. I couldn't wait to come home."

For a moment Walt is thrown, then he remembers her letter. Of course. She's a widow, her husband died a decade ago.

"Are you okay?" he asks. They're standing together beside a tiny stone wall, viewing the bridge, their fingers only a few inches apart. Walt wants to slide his thumb over to touch her skin.

"I wasn't," Milly says softly, "not for a long time." *Not before you.* The words sit on her tongue but she doesn't say them. "I am now."

"I'm glad," Walt says. "I mean, I'm glad you're okay now, not . . ."

Milly shifts her hand slightly so her little finger sits on his thumb.

"I know what you mean," she says softly. "Thank you."

They return to the bookshop, where Walt leaves a note on the door apologizing for early closure, then spend the rest of the day walking around the city, hand in hand. Walt manages to focus most of the time, to refrain from pointing out places that Cora likes and memories he has of them as kids together. And, most of the time at least, Walt manages not to think of Cora too often and to remember who he's with and why.

They say good-bye when the sun sets, promising to speak soon. And, as Walt ambles back in the direction of his flat, his only regret, the only piece missing from a rather perfect day, is that he hadn't kissed her.

Cora stands in her old bedroom. At some point in the last twenty years it has been transformed into Judith's office. A long wooden table, painted white and entirely covered with piles of paper, is pushed against the back wall; two other walls are lined with fitted bookshelves (containing 987 books); into the fourth wall is cut a large window overlooking the garden. Cora presses her nose against the glass, her eyes misted over as she remembers her dream. It's the same garden, though of course there are no fireworks, no champagne, no jazz and, most important of all, no parents. And she's not five years old anymore. She's twenty-five and all alone.

A surge of sadness pulls Cora away from the window and back to the door. As she steps into the corridor Cora turns to take one last look back, placing her hand on the wall. She sniffs the air. It's as if a bonfire has been lit in the next room and smoke is drifting down the hall. It's the sweet, woody scent of camping and marshmallows crisping under a night sky scattered with stars. Then it shifts, suddenly bitter and sharp, threatening to flood into Cora's lungs and choke her.

Cora swallows and blinks. She steps forward, stumbling along the corridor toward the stairs, but now it's dark and she can't see farther than a few feet. She gets down on her hands and knees and crawls to the stairs but when she peeks down the tunnel of steps her face burns as if she's stuck it into a bonfire. At the bottom of the stairs the air has turned the color of a sunset after a storm. And then she hears the screams.

The next thing Cora feels is a hand on her shoulder, fingers pinching into her skin, shaking her hard. She blinks again and looks up. The light in the hallway is bright and clear again. Judith is standing over her, eyes wide with fear. Cora is on her hands and knees, white-hot with embarrassment.

"Are you all right?" Judith asks, her voice high and sharp.

Cora stands quickly, pulling herself up against the wall.

"I'm sorry," she says, "I'm so sorry."

"You were screaming," Judith says. "You were screaming for your mother."

"I'm sorry," Cora says again, already halfway down the stairs. "I'm sorry."

She jumps the last few steps and as she hurries along the corridor, something on the wall catches her eye—a framed faded page of annotated equations—but mortification pushes her onward out of the house and onto the street. Cora knows without any doubt at all that, whatever the police report may claim, her parents' death was not a plain and simple accident. It's not just a fault of fate. It might not have been murder, exactly, but it's certainly more than a candle falling against some papers. Much more. She has no proof, no evidence. But, in a life dictated by scientific certainty, she has never been more certain of anything.

Etta sits at her sewing table, a skirt of moss green silk half-covered in sequins between her fingers. She rubs the fabric, squeezing comfort out of it like juice from an orange. Every few minutes she thinks of Cora and hopes she's okay. Etta should have gone with her granddaughter; she should have followed her even when Cora refused the company. It's too much to bear, investigating the death of her parents alone. There's no knowing what she might discover, how the shock of it will affect her.

Etta has spent a good deal of the last twenty years wondering exactly what happened to her daughter and son-in-law. What had Maggie been going to tell her before she died? She wanted to know but had never tried to have the case reopened once the police ruled it as accidental. Etta had just waited patiently, privately mourning, knowing that it wouldn't make any difference; that nothing could alter the past, nothing could change what happened.

Occasionally she wonders whether she'd undo the past if she could. Then she'd still be the light, bright woman she was born to be, a tranquil pond without a drop of sadness. But then she'd never have known her daughter; Maggie wouldn't have blessed her life and Etta isn't sure she could undo that. However, when it comes to Maggie's father, it's another story altogether.

Etta met the love of her life when she was nineteen. They

had sat together in church, back in the days when Etta attended every Sunday afternoon. Her mother sat between them but Etta felt his eyes flit to her during the service, the warmth of his gaze on her skin. The following week she found herself, almost accidentally, next to him in front of the rows of candles being watched over by a painted wooden statue of the Virgin Mary.

"You again." He smiled.

"Me again." Etta bent forward to light her candle, hiding her own smile. "Who are you praying for?" she whispered.

"Isn't it impolite to ask?" he said, but his tone was playful.

"I'm afraid politeness isn't one of my virtues," Etta said, thinking he had the most beautiful smile she'd ever seen, one that went right through his body from his head to his toes.

"No?" he asked. "Then what are?"

Etta laughed. An old woman sitting in the pew behind them shushed under her breath. "Oops. See, I told you so. I even offend people in church."

"Well, then," the lovely boy asked, "who are you lighting your candle for?"

Etta gave an enigmatic smile while she searched for a name. "My sister," she said, plucking out the first relative who came to mind, then affected a sad look. "She's got herself in trouble."

"Oh," he said, "I'm sorry."

Etta glanced over at him, caught by the sincerity of his words. Suddenly she felt bad. And, for a long time afterward, when she looked back at what happened, Etta wondered if it had all been some sort of karmic retribution for that lie.

Henry Dixon can't concentrate. He has an important case he should be working on, he's quite sure, only he can't remember what. As he focuses on his computer screen, he glances down at the keyboard and wills his fingers to type something. Anything. But instead he stares until the letters smudge into one another and Henry can't see his hands anymore. What was it about that woman that lodged her into his head like this? Ever since he chased her down the steps, a highly unprofessional move, she's taken residence in his mind, dislodging all his other thoughts to make room for questions: Who is she? Where did she come from? What really happened to her parents?

Henry is interested in Cora's case, but he's even more interested in her. Though exactly why, he can't tell. She's pretty, certainly, but not in a heart-stopping, head-spinning sort of way. She looks more like a librarian than a film star. And, while she seems nice enough, he didn't feel the flash of kismet, the spark of soul mates, when they met. So what's going on? He doesn't get out enough, that's it. Since his divorce, Henry hasn't been on anything approaching a real date. He tells himself it's because no one wants someone else's ex-husband, especially not one with shared custody of a five-year-old son. But he knows it's not that, not really. He's scared. A detective who's seen more gruesome things than he'd care to remember is scared of going out on a date. It's pathetic really. His little boy, Mateo, who believes his dad could win a fight against Superman, would laugh if he knew.

And then Henry feels it. That itch. The stirring in his soul. The twitch in his fingertips. The one he gets when something doesn't quite make sense and he needs to understand it. It's what happens whenever he finds a supposed suicide or accidental death and suspects suspicious circumstances. It's how he feels when everyone else tells him to drop it, to close a case he knows should remain open. Which must be why he can't stop thinking about that woman. Because she needs his help.

Chapter Ten

Walt shifts in his seat and snatches another glimpse of the clock. Three minutes have passed. He swallows a sigh and starts the sentence again:

"Her mind did become settled, but it was settled in a gloomy dejection. She felt the loss of Willoughby's character yet more heavily than she had felt the loss of his heart."

Walt takes another breath before reading on. He taps his foot against the desk leg and considers faking convulsions or a coughing fit. Instead, with yet another deep breath, and great reluctance, he reads on. Why the hell does Dylan insist he read this rubbish? All these characters are so silly. Marianne, especially, is too ridiculous. Why can't she just control herself; why can't she accept that Willoughby doesn't want her? Why does she explode with sobs at every opportunity and fling herself about like a lovesick teenager?

While Walt descends inexorably into the depths of *Sense and Sensibility* his mental rant against its characters continues, syllables of complaint tapping behind his aching eyeballs, upset tugging inconveniently at his heart. In truth Walt knows why Marianne makes him so angry: her sorrow, her broken soul, her inability to accept that she can't have the thing she wants most in the world, remind him of himself, of Cora. Which makes him feel guilty again because he knows he shouldn't be thinking of her. He doesn't need to, not when he has Milly. So why can't he stop?

It's not during the day so much anymore, he's okay during the day. But at night, while he reads, he can't seem to help it. At night he doesn't just think of Cora, he yearns for her. Walt blames it on these blasted books that his boss insists he read: romances full of unrequited and ill-fated love, stories that bring back his past too sharply, getting him to think about things he shouldn't. Now Walt wonders what Cora might be doing. Is she asleep? Is she reading in bed? Is she making love to some undeserving suitor? Is she, could she possibly be, listening to him?

Walt isn't sure which of the last two options he likes least. Certainly he hates to imagine another man touching Cora. But the idea that she might be listening to him fills Walt with conflicting emotions. Guilt: because he knows Milly listens to him every night without fail, and to hope Cora's doing the same seems somehow disloyal. Embarrassment: because he's reading ridiculous romances that Cora, being a sensible scientist only interested in nonfiction, would sniff at. Comfort: because this at least would be a connection between them. Joy: at the feeling of this connection. Which brings him back to guilt again.

—

Dylan sits in his office with his eyes closed. He should have been home hours ago, but he can't help it. Hiring the Night Reader was the best professional decision he ever made (the listening figures are off the charts, it's the highest-rated hit show among women aged twenty-five to forty-five), but it's been his personal undoing. Now every night of the week he stays late at work, writing e-mails, composing letters and filing papers until Walt starts to read. Then he switches on his radio, sits back in his chair, closes his eyes and smiles as the words drift into the air:

"Early in February, within a fortnight from the receipt of Willoughby's letter, Elinor had the painful office of informing her sister that he was married . . ."

Dylan has absolutely, completely and utterly fallen in love with Walt's voice. Not in the way that women all over Cambridge have. His feelings aren't remotely sexual; instead he feels like a child again: as if his father (before he got dementia and Dylan became the parent) has tucked him into bed, opened a book and taken him to Wonderland or Narnia or Middle-Earth. He feels small and safe again, wrapped up in a blanket of words, rocked with their rhythm until he falls asleep. As a child, Dylan would look forward to this moment all day. From the moment he woke, he anticipated returning to bed again, for that last hour of the day when he'd be at the center of something magical. Which is exactly how he feels now and has done every day for the past two years, ever since stepping into that shop and hearing Walt's voice for the first time.

Before that day Dylan had a perfectly fine life. He wasn't a recluse or a hermit, quite the opposite. He had plenty of friends and was never shy asking women out for lunch or dinner. Not that, since turning thirty, he's ever had a relationship that actually involved a woman staying the night, partly due to a fear of commitment but mainly because his septuagenarian father, Ralph, tends to sleepwalk naked. But, aside from bathing, feeding and generally ensuring his dad's safety, Dylan had always been a vigorous specimen of manhood: thirty-six years old with a full head of dark hair and a long, lean, muscular body with a fairly healthy social life. And now, thanks to Walt, he's acting like a seventy-five-year-old virgin.

When his mates ask why he hasn't been to the pub in months he lies, citing extra work and family obligations. They know about his father and they understand. But there is another lie Dylan tells. It's a white lie but still more dangerous than all the others, one that could get him into serious trouble. But, just as he's unable to stop listening to Walt reading, so he's unable to stop telling this lie.

Fan letters for the Night Reader had started arriving a few days after Walt began reading. His first book had been one of his own choosing, *The Life & Times of Marie Curie*. The scientific subject matter was rather dry for Dylan's taste but, wanting to soothe Walt's nerves, he allowed it and knew that his new protégé could read the dictionary aloud and listeners would still be entranced. He absolutely underestimated, however, just how entranced they would be. Within a month, Walt was receiving ten letters a day. They arrived in little piles every morning—scatterings of color and scent among the white gas and electricity bills on the mat. Dylan dutifully boxed them all up and passed them on to Walt in the evening.

"They're calling you the 'Night Reader,'" he'd joked one day when Walt had been at the station for a few months. "You should have a hotline. You'd make a mint."

Walt had blushed and handed the box back. "I don't want them," he said.

"What am I supposed to do with them, then?" Dylan asked.

Walt shrugged. "Recycling."

"All right." Dylan had shrugged in return. What did he care, after all? They weren't his letters. He didn't know these slightly desperate women. Surely it was no skin off his nose if Walt never read them or wrote replies. Yet, after dropping the box in the wastepaper bin, Dylan couldn't concentrate. He'd sat at his computer trying to focus on e-mails, advertising packages and office reports. But while he typed the box seemed to grow, expanding until it had filled the bin, until it started emanating a bitter scent that hovered accusingly in the air. Dylan continued to ignore it, holding a handkerchief to his nose for the rest of the morning and typing with one hand. At lunchtime he picked up the bin, ready to take it to the recycling spot on the second floor. Instead he'd found himself lifting the lid off the box and opening the first letter he found.

Now he reads them every day, these letters of longing, and writes back to each and every one. He writes to them of love, about which he knows almost nothing (having never had a relationship that lasted longer than six months), and desire, about which he knows considerably more. He tells them that he understands how they feel (strangely true) and that he hopes they will find happiness one day (also true). And then comes the lie, when he signs the letters with Walt's name.

Writing these replies is how Dylan fills his time between six o'clock, when he finishes work, and ten o'clock, when Walt starts to read. At midnight, when the station shuts down for the night, he goes home and tries to sleep. Although lately he's kept writing late into the night until he falls asleep on the sofa in his office. Of course, as Dylan hadn't anticipated, many of the women write back and he now has several correspondences to maintain, in addition to the new letters that arrive every day. He no longer knows *why* he must respond to them all, only that he must, that he can't leave any one unanswered. Their words, their sadness and desire, have settled into his heart and soaked into his blood. It has become his duty, his honor, his purpose in life.

Cora calls the coroner's number after running out of her parents' house. It takes her a few hours to gather herself, to stop shaking long enough to press numbers into a phone. The coroner is surprised by Cora's call and, perhaps unsurprisingly, refuses to discuss anything over the telephone, but suggests Cora come into the office the following afternoon.

The next call Cora makes is to Etta, whom she owes an update on her progress and reassurance that she hasn't fallen into the river or stepped in front of a bus. She's been putting it off, worried to tell her grandmother about the police officer and, most especially, the fire flashback—or whatever it was—that happened at the house. How can she explain it?

Taking a deep breath, with a shiver into her fingertips, Cora recalls crawling along the carpet, smelling the smoke, her own screaming echoing in her ears.

"So I understand now," she says, "what you mean about just knowing something, without having any proof."

"Well, that's good," Etta says. "I'm glad you're not being a bloody-minded scientist about this."

Yes, things are changing, Cora could say, if she'd been able to explain exactly what and how. "So, why didn't you ask the police to reopen the case before?"

"How could I, when I had no evidence?" Etta says softly, and Cora can feel her grandmother's sorrow seeping into the air and mixing with her own. "And also because I knew, somehow, that only you could solve the secret of their deaths. That, really, it was your mystery to answer, not mine."

Cora has an appointment with a coroner. A coroner. She sucks at the word, turning it over with her tongue as if it's a slice of lemon she doesn't want to swallow. She sits on a wooden chair outside a wooden door with a panel of frosted glass upon which are engraved the letters

DR. ALEX ELIOT—FORENSIC PATHOLOGIST

The hospital corridor is blank, empty, stark. There are no tiles on the floor or bricks on the walls for Cora to count, so her nerves are bubbling up and spilling out into the air. The only saving grace is a clock: a large Victorian-style clock with a circular cream face painted with black Roman numerals. Cora multiplies and divides them at random, picking out prime numbers. But she can't focus. She's still unable to quite understand the turn her life has taken. What will she say to the coroner? How does one address such a person? Dr. Eliot? *Pleased to meet you, Dr. Eliot. Would you kindly tell me how my parents died? Will you give me a copy of the autopsy report?*

Cora realizes she's chewing her fingernail and stops. Sits on her hands. She glances up at the frosted-glass panel again, and before she can look away it opens. Dr. Eliot stands in the doorway with narrowed eyes and a thin, polite smile.

"Cora Carraway?" she asks.

Cora nods.

"Come in."

—

Etta visits Fitzbillies several times a week. She doesn't come because it's her favorite café in Cambridge, though it's become so over the years, but because it borders on the edge of a street she's not allowed to cross, based on an agreement made long ago. Etta comes to remember and to hope. To remember the man she loved and hope that, maybe, just maybe, she might see him again. She arrives early, just as they open, before the students arrive with their laptops or the families with their sticky-fingered children, while the café is still and silent, except for the occasional grinding of the espresso machine.

Etta goes to Fitzbillies because she isn't allowed to go to the place she really wants to visit, to the site of first love, the church where she met him. So instead of visiting the church she makes her pilgrimage across town to the café on the corner of Trumpington Street and Downing Street and she takes her mass there: a hot chocolate and Chelsea bun. Then she sits at her pew, the wooden table running the length of the window, closes her eyes and remembers.

After Etta had lied about her sister, she hadn't been able to look the man—the handsomest young man she'd ever seen—in the eye. Sensing her discomfort, he had changed the subject as they walked. He spoke of the church, the brickwork, the architecture, but Etta hadn't really been listening. She had watched his hands hanging by his sides, his fingers long and strong. She imagined slipping her own slight fingers between them; perhaps she could hold his hand and he wouldn't notice, though he might feel the rub of her tiny diamond ring.

A jolt of shock had shivered through Etta then. How could she think such things? Sermons returned to her, the voice of the priest in her ear: *in thought as in word as in deed*. She knew that to think about adultery was as sinful as the act itself. Not that this was adultery, strictly speaking, since she wasn't married just yet. But she'd never yearned for her fiancé the way she did for this man, this stranger. Not even when she'd first met him. What was happening? She loved Joe. When he'd proposed, she'd been happy. She hadn't cried, hadn't wept with joy as many of her friends had, hadn't had goose bumps or tingles right down to her toes. But that didn't matter. They simply didn't have that sort of love. Their relationship was founded on friendship. Which was, Etta's mother assured her, what mattered most of all. This was what lasted after everything else had gone. So it was all right that when Joe fumbled for her hand in the cinema, she didn't feel a rush of illicit delight, that when he pecked her cheek after walking Etta home she wasn't desperate to kiss his lips. Because what they had together—loyalty, kindness and caring—would last for the rest of their lives.

Etta glanced across at the man. Feeling her gaze, he'd turned to her with a smile, his bright blue eyes shining with it, and she'd felt a shock of something that shivered all through her body, right down to her fingers and toes. Etta managed to smile back and he kept talking about St. Raphael, the patron saint of this church. For a moment, as they drifted out of the church together, she closed her eyes and imagined his fingers cupping her cheek, sliding up into her hair as he came forward to kiss . . .

He caught Etta as she fell, tumbling forward as her foot twisted on a raised paving stone. She held tight to his arms as she pulled herself up, their faces so close that she could feel his breath on her neck.

"I'm sorry," Etta whispered. "I—"

"Are you all right?" he asked. "Are you hurt?"

"No." Etta shook her head. "I'm fine, I'm . . . wonderful."

"Good. Me too." He smiled. "Well, now that I've saved your life I think I ought to know your name."

"I'm Etta," she said.

He had given his in response, but after that Etta just called him the Saint.

Dr. Eliot doesn't waste time with pleasantries. She doesn't offer Cora a cup of tea, a biscuit or a benign comment about the weather. She simply sits, reaches for a file, flips it open, then looks up.

"You want to know the particulars of your parents' case, is that correct?"

Cora nods.

"Specifically, why it was ruled as an accident?"

"Yes," Cora says, thinking this is what it must be like to be summoned into the headmistress's office in school. Not that she ever was.

Dr. Eliot flips over a page in the file, then another and another. She leans forward to read a few lines, squinting at the words, then mutters something under her breath. Cora waits.

"Yes, okay. Well, we carried out an autopsy on both bodies." Dr. Eliot glances up and Cora wonders if she's expected to say something. "Our findings were conclusive. We determined that their deaths weren't accidental, but—"

"What?" Cora sits up, no longer nervous. Her voice is strong and sharp. "The police told me—their report ruled accidental death."

Dr. Eliot sighs. "Well then, they clearly didn't have the specifics—"

"The fire," Cora interrupts. "They told me it was caused by a candle setting some books alight. Wasn't it?"

"No." Dr. Eliot shakes her head. "That is correct. That's how the fire started."

"So, I don't understand—"

"You would"—now Dr. Eliot's voice cuts even sharper than Cora's—"if you'd listen for long enough to allow me to explain."

Cora glances at her lap. "Sorry." She looks up. "Please . . ."

"The fire was an accident in the sense that it wasn't intentional. But it wasn't an accident in the sense that no one was to blame."

Cora opens her mouth, about to interrupt again, then checks herself.

"Your parents were found to have a blood alcohol level of nearly three times the legal limit. Thus they were too drunk to act with any rational sense. In all probability they were passed out before the books caught light and died in their sleep. Well, we can certainly hope so."

Cora gives a slight shake of her head, the screaming still echoing in her ears.

"No." Cora shakes her head. "No, it can't . . ."

"I'm sorry," Dr. Eliot says, "I'm sure that's not what you wanted to hear, but those are the facts. You can see for yourself."

She slides the file across the desk, rotating it as Cora sits forward so she can see. The pages are a mess of letters and numbers, charts and graphs, black blurring on white. Normally numbers are Cora's first language but right now they read like hieroglyphics. She follows Dr. Eliot's finger to read, slowly and steadily, a repetition of what she's just been told.

Cora looks up from the file, eyes narrowed and lips tight. "It isn't true." Her words are clipped, syllables bitten off slowly. "It isn't true." She spits out the last word as if it's poisonous.

Dr. Eliot's face darkens.

"My parents never drank," Cora snaps. "Never. Not one drop. So either you are simply incompetent or . . ."

"Excuse me?" Dr. Eliot slaps the file shut, hand and paper hitting wood. "But how dare you. I was doing you a favor, giving you access to records that closed twenty years ago. And now you are bringing my professional competence into question. I am excellent at my job. In twenty-five years I've never had a case I worked on overturned. I graduated with the highest qualifications in the university, not in my class but the entire—"

"Well, in that case," Cora says, "if you're not an idiot, you must be a liar."

Chapter Eleven

The word hangs between them for a moment. Then Cora pushes her chair back, letting it fall to the floor, turns and runs out of the room. She runs through the hospital corridors, following the signs for the nearest exit, and doesn't stop running until she's far down the street, far from Dr. Eliot. Then Cora leans against a wall and vomits.

She slides down to the pavement, not caring that anyone might be watching, and sobs. All she wants now is Etta. She wants her grandmother to hold her tight and rock her close. She wants to put on her pajamas. She wants to forget everything that's happened in the last few days and live the life she was living before all these emotions were stirred up: the quiet, dull, boring, predictable life when she was never excited by anything, not joyous or delighted but never terrified, angry or grief-stricken either.

What's happening? How could a coroner have found alcohol in her parents' blood? They never drank. She's certain of this. It was a thread of consistency woven into the fabric of Etta's stories about them. Maggie and Robert Carraway never touched a drop of drink, never smoked or ate red meat. Which isn't to say they were tedious teetotalers who looked down their virtuous noses at anyone less abstemious. It was simply a matter of taste. Maggie harbored a great passion for chocolate sundaes and if she skipped her treat one day she'd find herself very grumpy the next. Robert had a penchant for mint humbugs and was never without a packet in his pocket.

Cora has heard these things over and over again. She knows them as well as the periodic table or the gene segment coding for hemagglutinin. These tales about her parents were her bedtime stories. She soaked up every single fact and always asked for more detail. What was the color of her mother's dress when her parents met? What was her father's favorite word? What did they eat for dinner? What time did they go to bed? These were the building blocks from which Cora pieced together the picture of her parents, until she could at least imagine what they must have been like. Of course the picture wasn't even a shadow of their brightness and brilliance in real life. It was limited, one-dimensional, unchanging. But it was something, as satisfactory and reassuring as a balanced equation.

As she thinks of them, all of a sudden Cora is seized by something and stands up. Now she is awake, alert. These are her parents. This is *her* mystery to solve. She owes it to them. If their deaths weren't purely accidental, then they didn't kill themselves. She doesn't know what happened or why their case files are inaccurate. All Cora knows is that something is wrong and that she must put it right.

Cora strides along the street, heading straight for the bus station, realizing she hasn't felt so enlivened in a long time. In fact, she has *never* felt like this before. It's as if she has been set alight. Fire and fury rush through her veins, pumping her heart and pulsating to her fingertips. She wants to sprint across streets, to leap from tall buildings and fly. She wants to seize hold of strangers and look them in the eye. She wants to talk to people, to ask questions, to listen. She wants to connect. Suddenly she wants to *live*.

Four hours later, when the sky is dark and Cora steps off the bus in Cambridge, she still feels that way. She didn't spend the ride counting trees or calculating the square footage of fields. Instead she thought about her parents, the policeman and the coroner, and not in a sorrowful, self-pitying sort of way. She isn't sad anymore. She isn't lonely or grieving. She's passionate, excited. She's furious. Her parents died and either the investigation was completely botched or it was covered up. Which, of course, begs the question: Why?

As she runs along Trinity Street, her bag bumping on her back, and turns into All Saints' Passage, Cora is so desperate to see Etta she can hardly stand it. Her grandmother will know what to do next, she'll have ideas and plans. She won't be scared of anything. Together they'll decide what to do. Etta is the one she needs now.

But the person she runs into is Walt. They almost collide but stop just in time, Cora's nose inches from Walt's neck. She looks up, looks him straight in the eye.

"Hello."

"Hi," Walt says. His sleeping heart is suddenly beating hard in his chest and he's holding his breath. He takes a step back.

"How are you?"

"I'm good, thanks." Walt exhales. "You?"

"Fine. How's your girlfriend?"

"My . . . ?"

"Oh, sorry," Cora says, "the woman in the bookshop who ate my—the cherry pie. I just assumed she was your . . ."

"Yes, well, yes," Walt says, sounding reluctant, "I suppose she is."

"That's nice," Cora says, hoping to sound as if she means it. And suddenly she's feeling awkward, standing alone in the street with a man she's seen most of the days of her life but has never really known that well. It's strange, because now she wants to stand with him and talk long into the night.

Walt glances at his watch.

"Oh, sorry," Cora steps back slightly, embarrassed, "you've got somewhere to go, I'm holding you up."

"No, not at all," Walt says, "it's just work."

Cora frowns. "Isn't the bookshop shut?"

"Yes, of course." Walt flushes. "But no, it's not that. I work at a radio station, just the local BBC, I read the book at bedtime."

"You do?" Cora asks. "How wonderful."

Walt shrugs, feigning nonchalance. His heart is still beating too fast and he's starting to sweat. Why on earth did he just say that? He's never told anyone before. Only his boss, Milly and a handful of others know his secret. He certainly never advertises the fact. Not to anyone, let alone Cora.

"What are you reading tonight?"

Walt wishes he could give a different answer, wishes he didn't have to admit it. *"Sense and Sensibility,"* he mumbles. "But I don't pick the books, I—" But Cora isn't scornful, as he'd feared; instead she seems intrigued.

"I've never read it," Cora says, "so perhaps I should listen."

"No." The word snaps out of his mouth and she seems surprised. Walt quickly tries to undo his harshness. "I mean, I don't think you'd like it, it's a bit silly, a bit soppy . . . I used to read nonfiction, my first was *The Life & Times of Marie Curie* but not anymore, my boss . . ." Walt loses his words.

Cora is looking at him so closely, listening so intently that it quite unnerves him, undoing his words so they spool out into the air and drift away. He tells himself that it's nothing. He's not in love with her. He's just nervous. He's just socially inept. That's all.

"Oh," Cora says. "Yes, I love anything about Marie Curie." After that, she doesn't know what else to say. So instead Cora just looks at him.

Walt glances away, back at his watch, then at his shoes.

"I suppose I'd better go," he says, "I'll see you . . ." He starts to walk away but turns back after a few steps. "But please don't listen to me tonight, please."

"Okay," Cora promises, "I won't."

Although she knows, even as she says it, that she will. How could she not?

"My darling girl!"

Etta is waiting on the other side of the door when Cora steps inside the shop. She pulls Cora to her chest and hugs her tight. "That Old Black Magic" seeps into the air. Cora tucks her head into her grandmother's shoulder, trying not to cry with love and relief.

"How did you know I was coming?" Cora asks as they part, glancing at the floor and quickly wiping away her tears. "I didn't call."

"Don't ask silly questions." Etta ushers her through the shop, brushing aside dresses that have crept in too close, reaching out for their mistress. "You need tea and cake."

"I'm not hungry," Cora says, following Etta upstairs.

"Oh, my dear." Etta laughs, the sound humming around her. "When is cake ever for hunger? It's for flavor and, in this case, comfort."

Behind her grandmother, Cora smiles.

They walk into the kitchen and Etta flicks on the kettle. On the counter sits a large chocolate cake, icing shining and dotted with cherries. The room is filled with the thick scent of chocolate.

"It's beautiful," Cora says. "You're the best grandma a girl could hope for."

"Hardly." Etta sets out two plates and begins cutting the cake. "Anyway, it's not that cherry pie you love so much, but it will have to do." She presents Cora with a big slice. "Now sit, eat and tell me everything else."

Chapter Twelve

When Cora wakes the next morning she's in the same position at the kitchen table, head bent into the pillow of her bony elbows. She pulls herself up slowly, wincing at the pain in her neck, and yawns. It's only when she glances up at the clock, and sees the radio on the shelf above the cooker, that she remembers Walt and *Sense and Sensibility*. It's too late now. Bubbles of disappointment pop in her chest and Cora sighs, far more upset than she should be. She fidgets in her seat, rubbing the back of her neck. A restless feeling has settled over her. She tries to shrug it off like a blanket but it's in the air, thick and sticky, settling on her skin.

Cora stands, pulling herself up through molasses. It's time to go back to work. What else can she do right now, after all? She needs a plan, certainly, but can't just sit around doing nothing until she thinks of one. She hasn't been back to her flat for days, has almost forgotten what it looks like, probably because it's plain, white and utterly nondescript. Cora sighs again. She hasn't the heart to go home just yet. She remembers sitting on the pavement in Oxford, being overcome with a sudden sense of determination and purpose. She needs to *do* something now, something positive, proactive, to give her at least the illusion of control.

Thirty minutes later, unwashed, unfed and still dressed in yesterday's clothes, Cora arrives at the biology department and hurries to her tiny office, hoping not to bump into her boss. He won't ask her what she's been doing, he'll just fill her in on the latest developments in their research. Usually this would be something worth listening to, especially since she's dedicated her life to trying to realize her parents' dream. A week ago Cora still cared about doing it more than anything else. But now other feelings, other concerns, seem to be gradually superseding that desire.

Five hours later she's halfway through a particularly dry scientific paper, the top one on a pile Dr. Baxter had left on her desk (along with a note that hopes she's feeling better), and has a headache. It's nearly four o'clock in the afternoon and she hasn't eaten since too many slices of cherry chocolate cake last night. Pressing the fingers of one hand to her temples, and picking up her bag with the other, Cora squeezes out of her office, glances out to check the coast is clear, then hurries down the hall to the vending machine. As she's pulling two packets of salt-and-vinegar crisps out of the drawer, Cora hears voices behind her and curses silently.

"Cora!" Dr. Baxter calls out as she stands. "How are you feeling? Much better now, I hope."

Cora nods, not correcting his assumption. Her supervisor has someone with him, but he ignores his colleague to focus on his assistant.

"Anyhow, it's great to see you back."

"Thanks," Cora says, "it's good to be back." And she means it. Excepting the slightly tedious marking of papers, Cora loves her job and admires Dr. Baxter enormously. And not only is he brilliant, he's also tall and broad-shouldered, with graying black hair. He's excessively handsome for a scientist, Cora thinks, and looks not unlike Clark Gable in all those films Etta loves so much, which is fitting since, being born and raised in the Midwest, he sounds a little like him as well. Cora knows that half the student body harbors a secret crush on her boss. Perhaps she'd have one, too, if she were inclined to feel such things. Perhaps not. She's always thought of Colin Baxter as more of a father figure.

"Are you free for the meeting next week?" Dr. Baxter asks. "I know it's a chore, but it's with the financial department, so sadly can't be avoided."

Cora nods. "Of course." She isn't sure whether to question him in front of his colleague, but she can see a slight shimmer of concern on Dr. Baxter's face and needs to know what's going on.

"Is everything all right?"

"Yep, of course, no problem," he says. "Our funding's up for renewal next month, but I'm expecting everything to continue without a hitch."

Cora nods again. "Great," she says. And if he'd looked her in the eye when he'd spoken, she'd probably have believed him.

At the sound of the bell Etta, reluctantly putting down a tiny white cotton dress she'd been holding against her cheek, steps away from her sewing table to greet her new customer in the shop. "All Shook Up" plays as Etta walks across the carpet. Her new customer, a young woman with a mass of brown curls and a bright smile, bounds over.

"Hi, I'm Cheryl. My friend, well, my boss . . . she told me about your shop." She lowers her voice. "How it's, well, sort of special. And I need a bit of magic in my life right now."

"Oh?"

Cheryl nods. She reaches out to the closest rack of dresses and, almost without looking, plucks out a dark red ball gown and holds it out in front of her. "I'll take this one."

Gently, Etta takes the dress from her and replaces it among its fellows on the rack, where the ball gown seems to ruffle its silk folds like feathers rearranging themselves as it settles back in.

"That's not the way it works," she says. "You must take your time. You have to wait for the dress to choose you."

"But there's this guy I like," Cheryl says, not seeming to hear, "and I want him to fall in love with me. I thought that was the sort of thing you could help me with, isn't it?"

Etta smiles. "Not exactly. My dresses aren't just in the business of making women's wishes come true, though that often happens."

Cheryl looks a little crestfallen.

"But," Etta continues, "if you've lost a piece of yourself, wearing your dress will help you find it. My dresses can open your heart to love, if that's what you need. But I'm afraid they can't make anyone fall in love with you."

"Oh." Cheryl sighs. "That sucks."

"You may think so now, but—" Etta glances about the shop, then walks across the room and takes a turquoise dress of raw silk out of the window. "—when you've tried this one on, you might feel a little differently . . ."

"Really?" Cheryl asks. Her big brown eyes widen with hope. "Well, it certainly is a beautiful color." She reaches for the dress, then slips her fingers over the silk, mesmerized.

"Try it on," Etta suggests. "The changing room is just next to the counter."

Cheryl nods, walking along in something of a daze, clutching the large puff of crumpled silk to her chest.

When she steps out of the changing room, the daze has deepened.

"I don't, I didn't . . . I didn't expect . . ." Cheryl trails off.

"What, my dear?" Etta asks softly.

"I never expected to feel like this again."

Standing at the edge of the changing room, Etta leans forward to catch the quiet words.

"Like what?" Etta asks again, even though she knows the answer.

"As if I'm five years old," Cheryl says, "and the whole world is all mine and I can do absolutely anything I want to do."

Etta smiles. "And what is it you want to do, my dear?"

Cheryl grins. She smooths her hand slowly along one of the multiple folds of the magnificent turquoise gown.

"I want to be a poet," Cheryl says, "and a painter."

Etta nods. "Then that, my dear, is what you must do."

Later that night Etta is again sitting at her sewing table. She has a plan. She won't tell Cora, just in case it doesn't work. Etta has always been superstitious, suspecting that spells are more effective when kept secret from the intended recipient. This is why she never tells her customers about the dresses, together with the fact that they probably wouldn't believe her even if she did.

Since speaking with her granddaughter six nights ago, Etta has thought of nothing else but how to help Cora solve the mystery of her parents' deaths. And she's now convinced that the key lies in knowing what Maggie was going to tell her the day before she died. Unfortunately, of course, that seems impossible, especially given that Etta's never had much luck with ghosts. After her daughter died she'd spent endless hours with candles and icons and incantations, desperate to summon her daughter's spirit, to bring her little girl back. But eventually, when nothing happened after months of trying—not the flicker of a light switch or a wisp of breath on her neck—she gave up.

Etta knows better than to try that again now. It's too exhausting for one thing, it'll take too long for another and, most important, it'll probably still not work. Instead she's going to stick to what she knows best: clothes.

Although most of Maggie's possessions were burnt in the fire, Etta still has a few things from when her daughter was young: her favorite patchwork teddy bear, her first drawing (of a tree with purple apples) and a box of baby clothes. A few hours ago Etta went up to the attic and brought down three little lace dresses of white, black and blue. Now she sits at her sewing machine unstitching their seams and carefully laying out the pieces. Hours pass, jazz hums through the shop, but the door is locked. When she's done, the table is a blanket of lace.

Cora never wears dresses, so it's no use making her one. But sometimes she deigns to try a T-shirt or two. So this is what Etta will make for her now. It's already long past midnight, but she won't sleep or stop until it's done, because the air is always thicker with magic, faith and possibility at night. And Etta needs as much of all that as she can get.

At sunrise three very special T-shirts lie on Etta's sewing table: one white, one black, one blue. Each has a tiny red star hidden in a seam. They are made of cotton but edged with strips of silk and lace, and all that remains of her daughter's dresses is a scattering of sleeves and hems on the floor.

Cora had planned to go home at some point. She hadn't meant to stay in her office all day and all night. But when she looks up at the clock again it's nearly ten o'clock. About to stand up, she suddenly thinks of Walt and his books. It's true, Cora has never really been interested in fiction, especially not romantic fiction, but she's curious and has a digital radio, occasionally utilized for listening to scientific topics on Radio 4, so why not? Having no idea what frequency to tune in to BBC Radio Cambridgeshire, Cora reaches for the radio and starts fiddling with the dial. Snatches of music blast out as she turns. It's more than a minute before she finally hears his voice and stops.

"*. . . My affection for Marianne, my thorough conviction of her attachment to me—it was all insufficient to outweigh that dread of poverty, or get the better of those false . . .*"

Cora has absolutely no idea what or whom Walt is talking about but she absolutely doesn't care. Because, my goodness, his *voice*. His voice is something she could listen to forever. It wraps around her body, soft sounds encircling her limbs, and holds her tight. Cora closes her eyes and breathes deeply, sighs of deep contentment and bliss. Gradually, a memory rises up inside her: a three-year-old Cora is squeezed snugly between her parents in bed as her father tells a story about a Victorian girl called Mary who hunts for fossils and finds a very special fish-lizard. The discovery changes the current opinion on evolution. The fossil was called . . . The memory evaporates. Cora waits, calmly sinking into the softness of Walt's voice. After a while, another memory bubbles up. Now she's four years old and sitting in her mother's lap, listening to Maggie tell her about another woman named Mary who loved mathematics so much, and was so good at it that she had a Cambridge college named after her.

When Cora opens her eyes, she's crying again. When is she ever going to stop crying? Tears slide slowly down her cheeks and collect under her chin. She is so full with the feeling that she can't hear what Walt is saying anymore, her body is simply space, breath, relief—emptied of everything else. She isn't sad. For a few glorious, giddy minutes she had her parents back. She held them, smelled them, loved them. As Cora blinks, her sight a blur, a smile on her face, she isn't thinking about death and police investigations, she's thinking about life and Walt. A lightness folds over her, a shadow of joy. It's still only a whisper of possibility, a potential, a flickering at the edges of Cora's mouth. A space is opening up in her chest, a tiny crack that could let love slip in.

Chapter Thirteen

Milly has never had any grand ambitions. She doesn't aspire to be rich or famous. In fact, she'd really rather not be either. She doesn't want to work that hard and she'd hate having people watch and comment on her every move. Milly wants a simple little life: a husband, a baby, a house. That is all she needs to be happy. And, she thinks, it isn't asking too much. Surely God could give her these things and then just leave her alone. Which is why it hurt so much when her husband died so suddenly, only a year after they married, when they'd just started trying for a baby and saving up to buy a home.

Hugh had stepped into the shop where Milly worked one day and the moment she saw him she knew. It wasn't the way he looked—rather short and chubby with messy hair and slightly smudged features—but the air he carried about him. He was dependable, thoughtful, sweet-natured: a good man. He was a man who'd immediately say "yes" when you asked him to fix the kitchen light, take out the rubbish or do the washing up. He'd buy your birthday presents in advance and wrap them himself. What he wrote in the card would make you cry. He'd really listen and remember what you liked or disliked, what scared you and what made you smile. He was a man worth loving with your whole heart. Milly wasn't sure how she knew all this from just one look, but she was more certain of it than she'd ever been of anything.

Hugh had wandered around aimlessly at first, glancing at the trinkets on display but holding back from picking them up, as if they were too precious and might break at his touch. Now and then he hovered over something—a pink leather bag, a silk umbrella scattered with roses, a box lined with lace, an engraved bookend—and studied it. And all the while Milly watched him.

The Craft & Curiosity Shop on Trinity Street only sold things that were pretty and delightful. If they happened to be useful, too, that was a matter of pure coincidence. Ninety percent of the customers were female, women who visited regularly, simply to spend time among the beautiful things, to soak in the sensuality of pink silk and red roses and feel their souls sigh with joy. When a man ventured into this feast of femininity, he was shopping for one of two people: his lover or his mother. And as she watched Hugh slowly circling the shop, Milly had prayed it was the latter.

Eventually, having seen everything at least once and still not able to decide, Hugh had cautiously approached the counter.

"Um, hello," he said, his eyes flitting from Milly's face to the till to the array of pretty little things laid out in front of her.

"Hi." Milly smiled. "Would you like help picking a present?"

Hugh nodded, his face relaxing with relief. "It's for my mother."

"Okay," Milly said, unable to suppress the giggle of delight that burst out of her mouth. They'd wandered slowly through the shop together. It was early morning and still quiet. A few other customers wandered in, then out again without buying anything (for which Milly was extremely grateful), and as they walked and talked Milly discovered that everything she'd believed about Hugh was true. He listened, he remembered, he spoke kindly, he smiled when she made silly jokes. Their time together passed so quickly that the lunchtime rush, dozens of women ducking out of their offices to seek refuge in an oasis of beauty, surprised them.

"Sorry," Milly said, as chatter and perfume suddenly swirled around them, "I'd better go." She turned back to the till where a woman was already waiting with a paisley bag clutched protectively to her chest. Milly began wrapping it for her.

"Do you know what you'll get for your mother?" she asked him.

"I can't decide," he said. "I'd better come back tomorrow for another look."

When Milly arrived the next morning, Hugh was already waiting on the pavement outside the shop. He handed her a warm paper bag as she reached him.

"Pain au chocolat," he said. "In case you haven't had breakfast."

Milly smiled. She hadn't.

"How thoughtful, thank you." She jiggled the key in the lock and pushed open the door. "I want to show you something."

Hugh followed Milly as she crossed the shop. She stepped behind the counter and picked up a box from the floor.

"We had a new delivery yesterday, from an artist in Brooklyn. I don't know why I love them quite so much but I do." Milly handed Hugh a small frame containing a black-and-white photograph of a cottage, a dried crimson rose and a poem. "This one is my favorite."

He took it in his hands as though he was holding a baby bird and then read the words aloud, his voice soft and still:

I long for
a little life,
an everyday life,
a splash of sunlight
through a window
a smile from a stranger—
a heart to hold in mine

"Me too," Hugh said. And Milly had leaned over the counter and kissed him. That poem had summed up so perfectly what she most wished for in life that Milly had memorized it, whispering the words to herself when she did the dishes or swept the floor or at night if she couldn't sleep. Hugh recited the poem on their wedding day, whispering it in her ear after the priest pronounced them husband and wife. It was, far and away, the very best moment of her life.

The day Hugh died was the last day she spoke those words aloud. But for years afterward they still floated into her head, stinging so sharply they brought tears to her eyes, her heart aching with longing for the little dream that had been so cruelly snatched from them.

The first time Milly heard Walt read, she closed her eyes and remembered her wedding day, the memory so vivid that she could reach out and touch her new husband's lips and feel his kiss on her cheek. It was that night that the desire to live again had started to smolder within her. Now, as she walks down All Saints' Passage on her way to Blue Water Books, Milly begins to hum a tune and, for the very first time since Hugh died, she repeats those magic words again:

I long for . . .

Detective Dixon sits at his desk staring at the telephone. He can call her if he wants to, he doesn't need to know the number, he is a police officer after all. But he shouldn't. It isn't right. It isn't as if she'd asked him. But it is not in Henry's nature just to sit around and do nothing. He hasn't been able to stop thinking about Cora, her dead parents and the fact that he just *knows,* in the same way that he always knows—with a sense bordering on psychic—when a suspect or witness is lying, that there is something off with that case. He doesn't know exactly what it is, and can't say why, but he suspects some sort of cover-up.

Twenty years ago, when Henry Dixon joined the force fresh out of school, it wasn't because he had always dreamed of being a police officer, but because he didn't know what else to do, and because most people had been telling him all his life he was like a cop. The boys at school called him Bobby or Copper, or sometimes Pig, on account of the fact that he always knew which one of his classmates had covered a desk in graffiti, stolen someone's lunch money or hidden the textbooks from the teacher. Henry knew a guilty person even if their face never betrayed a flicker, even if they'd never done a wrong thing before in their lives. He knew the innocent from the guilty as easily as he could count to ten. And whenever questioned by the grownups, he always told the truth. Which is why he was loved (by the victims) and hated (by the bullies) in equal measure.

So when he finished school with a fistful of passable grades, Henry headed straight for the local police station to inquire about employment. After passing all the necessary tests he'd started patrolling the streets, preventing petty crimes: littering, lewd behavior, shoplifting . . . As the months passed his superiors began noticing his preternatural ability to detect liars and Henry quickly moved up the ranks to detective, where he stopped. He could easily have kept climbing, right up to chief superintendent, but by this time he was married and his wife already objected to the long unsociable hours. If they got any worse, he feared she'd leave him. Unfortunately, even though he compromised his career in a bid to hold on to her, she left him anyway. More unfortunately still, he didn't realize what was happening until it was too late.

He had fallen heart-over-head in love with Francesca Rossetti at first sight. He wanted her body and soul. She was unlike any other woman he'd ever seen: tall, dark, voluptuous and Italian. She'd been living in Oxford only a few years when they met and still had a heavy accent, one that left her sentences dripping with honey and sugar, and had Henry hanging on her every word. Francesca had reported a robbery— a student had stolen some test papers from her office at Magdalene College—and Sergeant Henry Dixon was first at the scene. He'd never believed that someone so beautiful and accomplished, a professor of Italian Literature no less, would give him a second glance. So he'd never even presumed to ask her for a date. When she had asked him, giggling in a glorious way that suggested they already shared a secret, it had taken Henry a full minute to catch his breath before saying yes.

After the most glittering, glamorous year of Henry's life, a year of book launch parties and birthday parties, feasts and fiestas, a dizzying year of cocktails and champagne, they married. Mateo was born the following year. Three years after that, by which time his wife attended the parties alone, drinking wine and sherry with her fellow academics and leaving Henry to share beers with his coarser friends, Francesca filed for divorce. The thing that most surprised him wasn't the request (he'd been expecting the end, anticipating being dumped from the day she first asked him out) but that when she told him her voice was still dripping with honey and sugar, her words still made him shiver with desire even though they were saying she didn't want him anymore.

She never explained why, and eventually he stopped asking. It wasn't another man; Henry had misused police resources to be sure of that. But he knew then and knows now, two years later still, that Francesca hadn't simply stopped loving him, no matter how often she insisted she had. Henry has always been able to sense a lie; it's a gift that makes him so good at his job, and whenever Francesca says she doesn't love him anymore Henry can tell it isn't true. So it must be something else, there must be another reason why she left him. So far, though, despite endless hours of investigation, it is a secret he hasn't been able to uncover.

Henry glances from his computer screen to the picture of Mateo, now five years old, in a gold frame on his desk. Since his divorce, his son is the only person Henry allows himself to love. Women are too unpredictable, too dangerous. If he gave his heart to a woman again she might drop it, she might throw it to the ground and watch it smash into a thousand pieces, a shrug in her shoulders, a smile on her lips. *Oops.* But his son is steadfast. His son holds Henry's heart tight to his chest, gripping it with grubby hands as fiercely as he holds his favorite teddy bear. Mateo illuminates with grins when his father picks him up from school three times a week. He jumps into Henry's open arms, giggling as he buries his blond head in his daddy's armpit, snuggling up close as if he never wants to let go. Unlike Francesca, Mateo is a safe person to love.

Luckily, the reason he wants to call Cora has nothing to do with attraction or the fear of falling in love again. He isn't drawn to her, even though she looks perfectly lovely and seems rather nice. He simply can't stop thinking about her case. Henry knew the investigating officer, Detective Nick Fielding, before he retired. Not well, but well enough not to trust him, well enough to know he might stoop to anything, well enough to know he was a liar. Which is why, after days of staring at the computer, Detective Henry Dixon decides to reopen the case himself. In private, to be investigated on his own time, with perhaps the occasional misuse of police resources.

Cora pushes open the door to Blue Water Books. She wants to read something scientific and eat a slice of cherry pie. At least, that's what she is telling herself. But it's silly. The university library has a much vaster selection of books and there are thirty-seven cafés in Cambridge offering a plethora of pies and cakes. So it's not, and perhaps has never been, about the books and pie or even the lovely little bookshop, but the one who owns it. And as she walks through the first corridor of books, quickening her step, she's even more than usually excited to see him. And has been, ever since hearing him read. Why on earth Walt didn't want her to listen Cora can't possibly imagine. True, it wasn't her favorite sort of book, at least not before *he* read it to her.

Well, not to *her* exactly, but it had certainly felt that way. Now, if Cora was intrigued by Walt before, her interest borders on desire. She wants to see him, speak with him, listen while he talks, feel his eyes on her skin . . .

Cora hurries along the corridor of books to see Walt standing at the counter alone, reading a book. 38 other books are piled up around him: 17 on the counter and 21 on the floor at his feet. It's almost as if he is sprouting from them, a human tree with paper roots. Cora approaches slowly, postponing the moment. She wants to tell Walt that she heard him last night, wants to say how much she loved listening to his voice, but doesn't want to admit to breaking her promise.

"Hi," Cora says as she reaches him.

Walt looks up. "Hello." His heart starts to speed up. She is here and Milly is here, momentarily disappeared but likely to reappear at any moment. If she sees him with Cora, she might be able to tell how he feels. Women probably have a sixth sense about these things. Walt takes a breath and glances down at his book in an effort to calm himself.

Cora looks at him, scrambling for something else to say.

"I, er, just came to . . . Do you have any cherry pie?"

Without looking up, Walt shakes his head. "Sorry. I've . . . I haven't had time but—"

Then he's silent, eyes wide, staring. Cora glances about, wondering what's going on. Into the frame steps a woman—the same woman who'd eaten her cherry pie—and Cora frowns. The woman seems to materialize, emerging miraculously from within a corridor of books to alight at the counter at Walt's side. Regarding Cora with large blue eyes, she smiles. Cora looks back, wanting to dislike her, this sudden intruder, but she can't.

These are sweet, innocent eyes, the eyes of someone kind and loving, the eyes of someone Cora might befriend if she were so inclined.

Cora watches as the blue-eyed woman slips her hand into Walt's. As their fingers touch, he gives a tiny smile. Before she can see anything worse, Cora turns and walks away.

Dylan sits at his desk at the radio station, a stack of letters and a half-eaten sandwich in front of him. Dylan's finding it hard to stay awake. Last night his father had fallen in the bathroom and they hadn't left the hospital until dawn. He hadn't broken a hip, thank God, but the doctors urged again to consider putting Ralph in sheltered housing, something Dylan knows he will never do.

Dylan rubs his eyes and chews his pen, wondering what to say to the woman who's had three husbands desert her for their secretaries. *Date a man without a secretary or find someone who's unemployed* is the first thing that comes to mind, though he doesn't want to sound callous. Reading these letters gives him an intimate perspective into the female experience, and he's saddened by much of it. It makes him think twice about asking another woman out. He had no idea they were so sensitive, so hopeful, so primed for love that they will imagine the possibility for it in every unintended gesture and word.

Dylan isn't proud of his past. Not now. It didn't used to bother him before. Before Walt's voice turned him into a soppy, silly romantic Dylan hadn't given his rather rubbish relationship history much thought, but after a steady diet of Austen, Forster and Shakespeare he can't remember those women without wincing. He'd acted like Mr. Darcy (early in the book) more than a few times, and even skirted a little too close to Wickham once or twice. The memories are enough to induce him to celibacy now. But, painful as it all is, the only benefit in hindsight is that Dylan can now write to Walt's fans with a good deal of authority on the subject of bastards and fools. And so, after a quick bite of his sandwich, he picks up his pen to write to Louise.

Dear Louise,
I'm so sorry to hear about your experiences. No one should have to suffer such heartbreak. If it was in my power to take away your pain and memories and give you back your innocence and hope again, I would. I can say this: don't give up. Not on love but, more important still, not on you. Never let yourself believe that you are unlovable or flawed in any way. You deserve to be loved. You deserve kind words and an unwavering eye. Men who can give you this are out there, trust me, I even know a few. You just have to keep looking and trust your intuition. Listen to that voice that tells you not to trust someone, even though he's deliciously charming, remember Wickham & Willoughby & all those cads. And give another man a chance, even though he's not your usual type—remember Mr. Knightly & Colonel Brandon & all those quiet heroes.

When you forget that love is good and kind, let this letter remind you. And when you're ready to fall in love again, look for a soft place to fall.

Warmest wishes,
Walt

When Dylan signs Walt's name instead, he's nervous that the lie eclipses everything else, all the truth and kindness in the letter. He really hopes not. But perhaps he should start signing his own name, calling himself "Walt's personal assistant," or something like that. But he won't, because Dylan knows that these women want Walt, the man with the magical voice who seems to sense the inner workings of their hearts and souls, and not some pretender who doesn't know his heart from his head. That is what they want, what they deserve and what Dylan will give them.

Cora slips the T-shirt over her head. "It's pretty," she says. "Thank you."

In truth, Cora doesn't care one way or the other for pretty things. But it's a gift from her grandmother and, as such, she loves it.

"Will you wear them often?" Etta asks.

Cora eyes her grandmother suspiciously. "Are they special T-shirts?"

"Of course they are," Etta says, with an offended frown. "I made them."

"You know what I mean." Cora raises an eyebrow. "Are they *special*?"

Etta shrugs, but her granddaughter can tell by the way she won't look her in the eye that these are no ordinary T-shirts. She stands with her grandmother in the middle of the shop surrounded by dresses on every side, while Frank Sinatra sings "I Get a Kick Out of You." The green-blue silk walls are slightly tinged with yellow at the edges, signaling that summer is on its way. The shop has been very quiet lately. It's April, not particularly a season for shoppers, but still Etta is a little worried. Ever since she was unable to work her magic on Milly, unable to make her see that Walt isn't the man for her, Etta's scared that she's losing her touch and somehow her customers can sense it.

Etta adjusts the T-shirt across Cora's shoulders. "A perfect fit."

Cora nods, absently rubbing the lace hem between her fingers. "Yes, I—" She stops, mouth open, blinking several times before squeezing her eyes tight shut, gripping the lace so fiercely her fingertips turn white.

The image is so clear she might be watching a film. Her father, standing by a long, deep desk entirely camouflaged with papers and books in the biochemistry lab at Oxford University, is laughing.

"This is it, Maggie," he exclaims. "This is it! We've done it, we've finally done it!" Then Robert Carraway starts dancing, holding his arms out, his features eclipsed by an almighty smile. "Dance with me, Mags." He laughs. "This is the moment. This is the moment just before we change the world!"

The scene vanishes and Cora opens her eyes.

"What?" Etta stares at her granddaughter. "What is it?"

"I'm not exactly sure," Cora says. "But whatever it is you were trying to do with this T-shirt, I think it just worked."

Chapter Fourteen

Walt stares at his mother's notebook. It seems to stare back at him. He feels himself being watched, perhaps by his mother's spirit, though that's probably just wishful thinking. Walt picks up the notebook and holds it to his chest. He hasn't opened it in weeks. The disappointment of constantly trying and failing to decipher his mother's messages hurts too much to repeat too often. Instead he uses it like a talisman, a silent oracle to inspire and guide him.

"I need help," he says softly. "Please."

Of course the notebook doesn't respond. Walt gives it a slight shake.

"I've got one woman in my heart and one in my hands. What am I supposed to do?"

The notebook remains silent and still. Finally, Walt gives up and stands. He'll have to talk to the priest, even if the subject matter is strange for someone who's celibate. He places the notebook on the sofa and glowers at it.

"One of these days," he says. "One of these days . . ."

"I'm confused," Walt says, "I don't know what to do."

"What is it now?" Father Sebastian asks, feigning a sigh.

"I suspect I'm still in love with Cora," Walt admits. "Even though I'm trying very hard not to be, it isn't that easy. But now, I think, Milly is falling in love with me. I don't know what to do."

"I see."

Sebastian's voice is neutral, bland as butter without a single hint of spice. Which is exactly why Walt comes. He could confess anything to this man and he wouldn't bat an eyelid or think any the less of him. Which is because of who Sebastian is as a man, not because of his profession.

"I care for Milly, I really do," Walt says, relieved to at last be talking about it. "But Cora—I don't know—with her it's more even than love, I just . . ."

"Ah," Sebastian says. "Well, that's the thing."

"What's the thing?" Walt frowns. He's not a fan of cryptic advice.

"Love can be tricky. The heart wants what it wants and I'm afraid there's not much you can do to convince it otherwise."

"That's just it." Walt sighs. "I thought my heart didn't want to love Cora anymore. I thought it had given up. That's why I met Milly in the first place. And now . . . now I'm in a bloody mess."

"Well . . ." Sebastian begins, drawing out the word while he tries to think of something helpful to say but fails.

Walt sighs again. "I'm a horrible person."

"I beg to differ." Sebastian can't imagine anyone less horrible than the young man currently taking refuge in his confessional, including all and every one of his genuine parishioners. "And if you were, then you wouldn't care about it, would you?"

"What am I doing here?" Walt sighs again, long and deep, so his whole body shivers with it. "No offense, Father, but I suppose you're not really qualified to give advice on love, are you? You've never been responsible for someone else's heart. You've never broken anything that didn't belong to you."

You have no idea what I've done, son, absolutely no idea. The words are on the tip of Sebastian's tongue and he has to press his lips together before they can push past his teeth. They sting his throat as he swallows them. The desire to confess his secret to someone, anyone, no matter how inappropriate, has been building up in him over the years, gathering force like a storm. One of these days he's going to blurt it out to Mrs. Collins while she confesses that she prefers her Jack Russell, Charlie, over her husband, or to Mr. Wallace who does inappropriate things with vegetables, or to the phantom parishioner who sits in his confessional for twenty minutes every Sunday, breathing rapidly and coughing occasionally but never confessing.

"I think Milly's falling in love with me," Walt repeats over Sebastian's thoughts, "and, if I could love her back, I know I could make her happy. Cora's even—"

"Sorry, what?" the priest asks, realizing he's drifted off into his own past.

"I don't know what it is exactly," Walt says. "Lately she seems different somehow . . . But, anyway, it doesn't matter. The point is she doesn't love me and Milly might. That's the point. And, in order to be worthy of Milly, I need to sweep Cora out of my soul. I must. Do you see? It's just—I'm trying and I don't know how."

Father Sebastian feels an ache in his chest and touches his wrinkled palm to his heart. If he'd ever had a son, he would have wanted him to be just like this young man. He wishes now, as he often does when a wounded soul seeks comfort in his confessional, that he could just rip out the wire-mesh window separating them and pull Walt into a tight hug. He's tired of this artificial separation from his fellow human beings. Sebastian once believed that becoming a priest was the best and most beautiful way he could serve humanity but, though that may be true for some, it's not true for him. Not anymore. He has nothing of real value to say to those who ask, no wisdom to impart, no inspiration. Indeed, Sebastian wonders sometimes why he still has the job, why his superiors, or God, haven't thought to take it away from him.

"My dear boy," Sebastian says softly, "if I could help you, well, I'd do it without a second thought. But if I could help with that sort of thing then I'd probably have a queue down the street of people wanting my advice."

"Yes," Walt says halfheartedly. "I suppose you would."

Though that doesn't help him at all.

Cora lies in bed, waiting. In a few minutes he'll be continuing *Jane Eyre* and she can't wait. She wants his words now, more than ever. She wants to remember her parents, she wants to . . . She hasn't been into the lab. She's just been worrying about what to do next, trying to suppress her rising panic, counting everything she sees: cigarette stubs, bottle tops, leaves, cars . . . Behavior that, of course, is creating absolutely nothing constructive.

Cora fingers the edges of her special T-shirt. Big Ben strikes the hour of ten and, after the program is introduced, Walt begins to read from where he'd left off the night before:

"For one thing, I have no father or mother, brothers or sisters . . ."

Her mother. Cora closes her eyes, her hand resting on the lace trim of the T-shirt. All Cora can see now is the past. Her parents stand side by side in the laboratory doorway, heads bent together, whispering. Cora tiptoes across the Formica, until she's close enough to hear them.

"We've got to be careful who we tell," Robert says. "We can't trust anyone. Not until we've published our findings. Not until we've got a company on board."

"Yes, but how will we do that without telling anyone?" Maggie asks. "We have to make inquiries first. We have to find out the best way to do this."

"I know, I know." Robert nods. "We've just got to be careful, that's all. We have to protect it. We have to make sure it's in safe hands."

Maggie giggles. "You sound like someone in those silly spy books you love so much." She kisses him. "Don't worry. We'll be fine. And we'll do something absolutely wonderful with what we've discovered."

"I hope so," he says. "I hope so, I really do."

"Oh, my darling." Maggie kisses Robert again. "You worry too much."

Cora blinks and her parents disappear.

Milly has invited Walt for dinner. He hasn't been to her place before. They've always met in the bookshop and ended up at his flat in the evenings. But today she wants to be at home. She needs to be on her own territory for this; it's time to tell him how she feels and what she wants.

"What's wrong?" Walt asks. "Are you okay?"

Milly looks up at him. She's cooked spiced chicken and sweet potatoes with chocolate mud pie for pudding. They eat on the sofa, the plates on their laps, since Milly's flat is too small for a dining table. It's a studio flat with a bed in the corner, a minuscule bathroom, a fridge, cooker and countertop. She doesn't earn much managing the Craft & Curiosity Shop but what she misses in wages she makes up for in a staff discount at 75 percent. She's bought so many beautiful things, cushions, throws, bags, pictures, that stepping into her house feels like stepping into the shop.

Milly opens her mouth. It's time. She'll tell him. Right now.

"Yes," she says softly, "I'm fine." Though of course she isn't, she's a coward. She loves, though, that he notices how she's feeling and that he cares.

"You haven't eaten your pie. Don't you like it?" he asks.

"I'm afraid it's a bit burnt on the bottom," she says. "Sorry."

"No," Walt says, "not at all. It's delicious."

So thoughtful, so kind. Milly smiles, in spite of herself. "Thank you."

Walt sets his empty plate on the floor. Gently, he takes Milly's plate from her hands and puts it on top of his own. The china clinks—a bell sounding the start of something. Cora pops into his head and, gently, he pushes her out. He opens his arms.

"Come here."

Milly shifts closer, discarding a silk pink cushion between them, and rests her head on his chest. Walt's breathing is slow, soft, and it soothes her. He holds her, stroking her hair, until her eyes close and she feels herself falling asleep. Walt whispers words into her ear. At first she doesn't realize what he's saying and then she hears:

"I long for, a little life, a splash of sunlight . . ."

Milly sits up, eyes open. "How do you know that poem?"

"I don't," Walt says. "It's framed on your wall." He nods toward her bookshelves (mostly adorned with pretty boxes, origami stars, white feathers and bouquets of dried flowers instead of books) where the poem hangs alongside a garland of purple paper butterflies.

"Oh, yes, of course," Milly says. "I forgot." She thinks of days: the day they met, their wedding day, the day he died.

"Did you write it?"

"What?"

"The poem."

"Oh, no," Milly says, returning to him. "I found it. It arrived at our shop the same day my husband did. It became something very special to us."

"Tell me about him." Walt brushes a strand of Milly's hair from her face. He wonders if Milly's heart broke at the loss of her husband in the same way that Cora's did at the loss of her parents when she was a girl, though this isn't something he can ask either of them.

"Are you sure?" Milly asks.

"Of course, I want to know all about you, not just who you are now but who you were before I met you." Walt sits up. He can do this, he thinks, he can learn to love her, he can. "Everything. All of it."

Milly smiles. "Okay," she says, "if you insist. But it's mostly very boring, I warn you."

"I'll be the judge of that."

"It'll send you to sleep."

"You forget, I'm a creature of the night. Nothing sends me to sleep," Walt says with a cheeky grin, "not even Jane Austen."

"Hush!" Milly exclaims, glancing around the room.

Walt laughs. "I don't think she heard me."

"I don't understand how you can read so, so beautifully, like you're in love with every character, every word," Milly says, dropping her voice to a whisper, "when you don't even like the books."

It had been a huge disappointment to her when Walt had confessed he didn't like *Sense and Sensibility* or, indeed, any of Austen or anything similar. She's still trying to pretend he didn't.

"Hugh loved Jane Austen, you know," Milly says. "He read them all, even *Persuasion*. Sometimes we'd read them aloud together, as if they were plays."

Walt is about to raise an eyebrow in mockery, before remembering they are talking about a deceased husband. Milly is a *widow*, he realizes. The word makes him think of wineglasses so delicate, so fragile you fear they might shatter in your grasp. She's to be handled with extreme sensitivity and care. Walt glances down at his hands, probably too rough and clumsy for the task. Cora, the thicker-skinned sensible scientist, would probably be a perfect fit, though he mustn't think of that.

"That's . . . sweet," Walt says. "He must have loved you like crazy."

"Yes." Milly smiles. "Yes, he did."

She falls silent and Walt wonders what to say next. A dozen platitudes about love, life and death pop into his mind but they all seem too cheap and silly to say now. Walt had thought that tonight might be the night he finally stayed over, but now he isn't sure he's ready. Milly turns to look at him then and before she even opens her mouth Walt can hear the words in the air. *I love you.* She wants to say it. He can feel it vibrating off her skin, evaporating in waves of cinnamon and nutmeg. He breathes it in. Then he sees the doubt in her eyes. He sees that she's scared to say it; she probably wants him to say it first. But he can't. Not yet. He cares for Milly. He could love her, he thinks, or at least something like love, if only he could give up the ghost of someone else. But these tentative, possible, maybe feelings pale in comparison so greatly to what Milly's husband gave her that he can't offer them now. However, he needs to give Milly something, to offer a piece of himself, a little slice of his heart. So Walt reaches into his back pocket and takes out his mother's notebook.

"What's this?" Milly asks as he hands it to her.

"It was my mother's," Walt says. "My father found it the night she died. She wrote it for me."

"Oh." Milly touches the notebook as if it were the most precious thing she's ever held, as if it might crumble to dust in her fingers. "Oh."

"Open it."

Very slowly, Milly turns the first page. She studies it for a few minutes, squinting and frowning at the letters and numbers streaked and swirling across the paper. "What does it mean?"

"I don't know," Walt says. "I've spent most of my life trying to figure it out."

"It's like a code. Like Sudoku or something like that."

"Yes, I suppose so. But I've never been good at those sorts of things."

"I'm okay," she says. "I like doing *The Times* cryptic crossword."

"Hey, that's pretty impressive," Walt says.

Milly shrugs. She wants to ask more about his mother, about his father, about his past. She wants to know everything about him, but she'll wait.

"Thank you," Milly says.

"For what?"

"For showing me."

She leans forward and kisses him. She'll save the confession for another day.

They slept together for the first time that night. Just slept, in each other's arms, on the light blue velvet sofa with the pink silk cushions, and everything unsaid circling in the air around them.

Chapter Fifteen

Etta chews her Chelsea bun slowly, plucking off pinches of dough while she gazes out of the window. Every time she sits here Etta hopes to see him, though she knows that, if not impossible, it's improbable. For, fifty years ago, when she and the Saint parted, they'd agreed never to see each other again. And since Cambridge is too small a place for two people not wanting to meet accidentally on its streets, they decided to split the city in half. Now Etta waits at the boundary line, wishing she'd never made that promise and wishing she had the courage now to break it. With a sigh, Etta sips her coffee. It's an especially quiet Sunday morning so her memories can play out perfectly, unrolling in her mind without interruption.

When Etta met the Saint, she'd only been engaged to Joe for six months though they'd known each other almost all their lives. She'd lived in the flat above the shop with her mother and he'd lived just around the corner from All Saints' Passage on Portugal Place. They had grown up together, cycling their bikes and kicking balls and playing tag. He was a handsome boy, with dark hair, beautiful skin and a tiny triangular birthmark in his left iris. Most of her girlfriends had enormous crushes on him, but Etta had never felt the spark. She liked him very much, as a best friend or a brother, but catching a glance of the mark in his eye didn't make her quiver like all the other girls. It was to everyone's surprise then that, when it was time for childhood friends to start falling in love, Joe chose Etta.

At first, she fobbed him off. She ignored the looks he gave her. She didn't reply to his notes. She even encouraged him to give her girlfriends a chance. And then, one day, he did. On Valentine's Day he showed up on her doorstep with a card but, before Etta could say anything, Joe opened it up.

"I was going to give this to you," he said. "Now I'm giving it to Alice Mychik instead." And he pointed to the place where her name had been crossed out and replaced with Alice's. His handwriting was surprisingly small and neat.

Once Etta couldn't have Joe anymore, she wanted him. She watched Joe holding hands with Alice and began to wonder if she hadn't made a mistake. He became like the prettiest dresses in her mother's shop, the ones that she wasn't allowed to touch. Of course those were the ones she coveted most of all. When she tried on other dresses, ones not made with silk and lace, she'd only look in the mirror for a moment before turning to the prohibited racks and begging her mother. All her friends fancied Joe, after all, so he must be something special. With the forbidden dresses Etta didn't even stop to consider whether they'd fit her figure or complement her coloring, and it was just the same with Joe.

So Etta set about trying to win him back. She gazed at him during classes, she sent notes, she offered to hold his hand, to let him kiss her cheek. At first Joe wasn't interested, at least he didn't seem to be. He ignored her notes, pretended he didn't see her staring at him, and continued to flirt with all the other girls but her. Then one day, perhaps after deciding she'd been punished enough, he offered to walk Etta home. She glided along, every step as light as lace and as smooth as silk, barely able to stop smiling, fueled by joy, triumph and delight. When they turned the corner onto her street, Joe offered his hand and she took it. Their fingers didn't fit together, knuckles rubbing awkwardly. Without saying anything, they tried different positions but nothing quite worked. Finally, Joe let Etta's hand go and offered the crook of his arm instead. When he walked her to her door, Etta thought he might try to kiss her, but he didn't. And she thought that as the years passed the awkwardness between them would soften and relax but it didn't, not really. Etta simply became used to it and better able to smooth out the rough edges.

The Saint, on the other hand, was a perfect fit. From the first moment they touched, Etta knew it. The fact that she had to sit on her hands after that, to stop herself from reaching out and touching him again, confirmed it. And it wasn't just that she wanted to touch, kiss and do all sorts of things she really shouldn't be wanting, she wanted to talk with him as well. All the time. They met every Sunday afternoon at the candles under the Virgin Mary, said their prayers, then went for a long walk around the neighborhood. They talked about everything: flower power and feminism, their favorite Beatles songs, faith, the state of the world and what they wanted to do to make it a better place. He told her about the theology degree he'd just earned and she told him about the dress shop, though not entirely everything about it.

Etta told herself she wasn't doing anything wrong. They were just friends who talked a lot and made each other laugh. She wasn't being disloyal to Joe and, to prove it, she never took off her engagement ring. For his part, the Saint either didn't notice or pretended not to.

The first time the Saint told Etta she was beautiful, she knew they'd started skirting a dangerous line. It was fairly easy to tell yourself a friendship was innocent if nothing was ever said to indicate otherwise—what went on under the surface of things could be put down to imagination and fancy. But once an attraction was admitted, no matter how tentative, innocence was harder to feign.

"You shouldn't say that," Etta had said at first.

"Why not?" the Saint had asked. "If it's the way I feel."

He looked at her with bright blue eyes. It was an earnest look, full of sweetness and hope. And when she looked back into his eyes for a little too long, Etta entirely forgot she even knew a boy named Joe.

Henry waits a moment before knocking. When he tells Nick Fielding why he's really here he'll probably be chucked out on his ear. His superior officer, before retiring a decade ago, was known for having one of the worst tempers in the department—several times accused of assaulting suspects, though none of the charges ever stuck or held him back from promotion. He'd completed his career as chief superintendent probably because, Henry thought, the powers that be were as scared of him as the criminals were. And because he got results. Conviction rates went up 38 percent and crime fell by 23 percent while Nick

Fielding headed the Oxfordshire Constabulary. Figures so good for publicity that no one asked exactly how he achieved it.

Henry grips Cora's case file tightly in one hand and reaches up to ring the bell. He waits for nearly a minute before he hears scuffling in the passageway and someone fumbling with the lock. When the door opens Henry tries hard not to show his shock. The man who'd scared the life out of him on several occasions has, in the last ten years, shriveled and shrunken into something rather resembling an overgrown goblin.

"Get inside then," Nick snaps, "or you need me to hold your hand?"

Diminished in stature then, but not in spirit, Henry thinks.

"Thank you," he says, and follows the old man down the hallway. They step into a living room with frayed gray carpets underneath an orange-and-green-striped three-piece suite, still wearing its plastic protection, clustered around a glass coffee table. Nick eases himself onto the sofa and regards Henry, who lingers in the doorway, suspiciously.

"Are you going to sit or stand there like a lemon?" Nick asks.

Actually Henry would love a cup of tea, even a glass of water, to help take the edge off what he's about to do, but since he's clearly not going to be offered either, he sits gingerly on the edge of the nearest chair. They sit in silence for a moment. Henry studies the faded yellow wallpaper.

"Well, what's this about then? Get on with it. I haven't got all day."

"Yes, of course," Henry says, though he can't imagine what other pressing engagements are pushing him out the door. "I came to see you about a case I'm working on—"

"So you said on the phone," Nick interrupts. "If you're going to repeat yourself we'll be here all day."

"Okay, well, it was an old case of yours," Henry blurts out, "two Oxford academics died in a house fire: Maggie and Robert Carraway."

"Doesn't ring any bells."

Henry opens the file and slides it across the coffee table. "It was ruled accidental. But I have reason to believe it might have been arson."

"Do you now?" Nick says. "And what do you care about a twenty-year-old case?"

"Their daughter came to me a few weeks ago. She wants to reopen it."

"Does she now?" Nick sits back into the sofa and the plastic covers scrunch slightly under him. "Pretty girl, was she?"

Henry doesn't like the way Nick looks at him, doesn't appreciate the implication of the question. It makes him think of Francesca, who could stop the words in his throat with just one look, but for a different reason. Then he thinks of Cora.

"No, not especially," Henry says, perched on the edge of the plastic-coated chair, slightly afraid he might at any moment slide off onto the floor. "So, can you tell me what you remember about the case? Anything unusual, anything out of place?"

Nick Fielding shakes his head and shrugs. "You're barking up the wrong tree. There was nothing unusual about that case. Open and shut. I've nothing else to tell."

Oh, but you do, and you just did, Henry thinks. *You just don't know it.*

"They must have made a great scientific discovery," Cora says. "I don't know what it was, but the way they were talking . . . it could only be that."

Etta nods. They sit on the banks of the river on the lawns of

Trinity College, snuggled in their coats. It's a cold morning and the river is empty of punts, the paths empty of tourists. Etta persuaded her granddaughter to venture out for a walk, citing fresh air as good for the brain cells, knowing Cora forgets to exercise unless forced.

"So that's what Maggie was going to tell me." Etta says, her breath puffs of clouds in the air. "If only I'd stopped long enough to listen."

"Unless it's just a figment of my imagination," Cora says.

"No." Etta takes her granddaughter's cold fingers and rubs them between her palms. Cora looks up into her grandmother's gray-blue eyes and, in that moment, she no longer *thinks* what she saw was true, she *knows.* It's still a strange experience, having faith instead of facts. It's odd the way her heart has been triumphing over her head lately. Having spent her whole life ignoring it, prizing facts over feelings, Cora's surprised it still works at all.

"But what will we do now?" she asks. "We've got no proof, no empirical evidence. I can't go back to the police and tell them I'm having visions."

"Why not?"

Cora can't tell whether or not Etta is serious.

"Well, for a start, I'd rather not lose my reputation as a scientist," Cora says. "I still have hopes of doing something . . ." She trails off, too embarrassed to admit the full grandiosity of her desires to another person, even her adoring grandmother.

"What about that nice chap you saw in Oxford, the policeman?" Etta asks. "The one who helped you before."

"He was probably just taking pity on me." Cora shrugs. "And however nice he is, I doubt he believes in investigating cases based on intuitive whims without corroboration. And he shouldn't, I wouldn't. At least, not before . . ." She trails off, unable to articulate just what's been happening to her lately.

"I could never be a scientist. No imagination, no fiction, no magic." Etta sighs. "I don't know how you don't die of boredom."

"How can you say that?" Cora exclaims. "There's incredible imagination in science. It's what matters most of all. Einstein said, *'Imagination is more important than knowledge.'* That's how all the great leaps are made, when a scientist thinks of something she can't yet prove, then dedicates her life to trying."

Etta regards her suddenly impassioned granddaughter curiously. "Are you speaking from experience? Because I always thought you were rather suspicious of imagination and all that is plucked out of the air, unmeasurable, untestable, unquantifiable."

"Maybe." Cora smiles, realizing how much she's changing. "I don't believe in imagination that doesn't undergo rigorous tests. At least I didn't used to, before . . . Anyway, 'unmeasurable' isn't a word."

"Come here." Etta wraps her arms around Cora and they sit together, nestled up close in the cold, watching the ducks dipping their heads into the river as they drift. 7 ducks, Cora notes, a prime number, the square root of 49.

"I'd hate to be a duck in winter," Etta says. "Their feet must freeze."

"Not really," Cora says. "At zero degrees ducks lose only five percent of their body heat through their feet. They have a counter-current heat exchange system between the arteries and veins."

Etta laughs. "What are you talking about? Speak English."

"Their blood keeps their feet cool so they don't lose heat in cold water," Cora explains. "Because the smaller the temperature difference between two objects, the more slowly heat will be exchanged."

"You had me until 'water,'" Etta says. "You lost me after that. How I, such a free-spirited artist, produced two mad scientists like you and Maggie, I really can't think."

"I don't know. But I'm glad you did."

"Me too." Etta smiles. "Me too."

Cora finds her grandmother's hand and holds it. She isn't used to the way she feels. She doesn't want to go back to the lab or stare into microscopes, she doesn't want to think about policemen or anything else. She just wants to sit and hold the hand of the person she loves most in the world. The ice around her heart isn't just thawing now, it's melting fast. It's a bit unnerving but rather lovely and she probably can't do much to reverse it now. And so Etta and Cora sit by the river, until their fingers and toes are numb, and for a while the question of death and police investigations and what they are going to do next is forgotten.

Chapter Sixteen

Milly lies in Walt's arms. She has to position herself just so in order not to slide off the sofa. But she doesn't want to move, she doesn't want to wake him. Walt snores softly, the tips of his ears wiggling with every exhalation. Milly smiles. She watches Walt while he sleeps, craning her neck back to get a better view. He sleeps so peacefully, so openly, so completely, like a child: arms and legs flung out, tummy exposed, open to the world. He shifts in his sleep and a little smile opens his mouth. Milly gazes at him and realizes then, clearly and absolutely, that she's kidding herself. She will never tell him she loves him to his face. No. It'll have to be done a different way. She could call him. But that wouldn't be very elegant, and she'll still be waiting to see whether he'll say it back.

Then she remembers the way they met: a letter. A letter is perfect. She'll write it now before she chickens out. Gently lifting Walt's arm from around her waist, Milly slides off the sofa onto the floor. She sits on the cream carpet for a moment, glancing about for paper and pens in the moonlight. Walt's notebook lies a few feet away on the floor, illuminated, almost glimmering in the light. She picks it up.

Turning the pages very gently, Milly traces her fingers over the jumble of letters and numbers. She thinks of Walt's dead mother and the cryptic memento she left him. What on earth is it? What does it mean? She'd love to be able to decipher it for him, to bring a piece of his mother back. She's sorry that Walt's parents are gone, sorry for him and sorry that she'll never meet them. She'd love her parents to meet Walt. They've worried about her since Hugh's death and she'd like them to see her happy again. They'd also long ago given up on grandchildren, and Milly, seeing how Walt loves babies, is rather keen to give them hope on that front, too.

Holding the notebook, Milly stands and walks across the room. She lifts a pad of paper, the pages embedded with rose petals, off the bookshelf. It's the paper she wrote her first letter to Walt on, which might bring luck. It's also her best, reserved for such special occasions. Milly picks a pen, one with magenta ink to match the roses, from a tiny china pot. She walks back to the sofa and sits on the floor with the notebook and paper in her lap. The notebook will infuse her words with power and potency. So, as the moonlight fades and the sun slowly rises, Milly writes, the lines of her letter ebbing and flowing with the rise and fall of Walt's snores.

Etta slept with the Saint a month after he told her she was beautiful. Right up until the moment they fell onto his bed, her dress already unzipped, Etta promised herself it wouldn't happen, they were only friends, they would resist. But really she had known from the moment they met that—if he wanted her—she would give him everything, every inch, every part and piece of herself. And when she finally did, making love with the Saint was the most heart-expanding, mind-eclipsing magical night of her life. Every moment, every touch—even the fumbles and the first initial flash of pain as he pushed inside her—was infused with delight and joy.

When Etta thought about that night afterward, and she did so often, she tried to compare it with other experiences in her life, though the similes never quite matched up. Sex with the Saint was like falling into a pile of enchanted dresses; like chocolate cake, cherries and cream; like sunlight on bare skin; like dancing, singing and laughing. Except that it wasn't, not even, not hardly, nothing she'd ever known before could touch it. Etta was sometimes shocked to remember that she'd been so consumed with pleasure and passion that night, she hadn't even had the decency to think of Joe or to feel guilty. Not even a little. Not once.

When they woke the morning after, his head pressed to her breasts, his foot clasped between hers, Etta told herself that it was the first and last time. But she knew that it wasn't. Given the chance, she knew she'd do it all over again, that night and every night for the rest of her life.

During her lunch hour Milly usually wanders around town eating her sandwiches and window-shopping, leaving her assistant, Cheryl, in charge of the Craft & Curiosity Shop. Since meeting Walt she's often gone to Blue Water Books and shared the hour with him. They sit behind the counter, eating and talking, watching customers wandering in and out. But today she's got something else to do; today she has to post a letter.

Milly had considered simply giving Walt the letter, then scampering off to be somewhere else while he read it. But that'd be silly. She also thought of leaving it at his house, or in the bookshop, but finally decided on posting it to the radio station, just as she did with the first one. It might bring her luck, she hopes, since the last time she sent a letter there it brought Walt to her.

In addition to the letter, Walt's notebook nestles in Milly's handbag. He'd left it at her flat that morning as he rushed off to work. Intending to restore it to him later, she'd spent the morning trying to make sense of something, anything, in the pages full of puzzles. She dips into it now and then as she walks through town.

Drifting in and out of shops, buying a few things here and there, a hopeless attempt to postpone the posting, Milly finds herself, like a lovesick homing pigeon, at the corner of All Saints' Passage. But she's not ready to see Walt yet, she hasn't let go of the letter. It still sits in her overflowing handbag, underneath boxes of vitamins, face cream, fragrant tissues, an empty can of ginger beer and an empty packet of chocolate mints—fortification for the job at hand.

Before turning out of the street, Milly stops at a bin to empty her bag of clutter. When she looks up again she sees the window full of dresses. They shimmer and sparkle, sequins and beads glimmering, flashing and winking, inviting her in. Milly shakes her head. Now is not the time for beautiful dresses. But she still remembers the way she looked in that mirror—the image seared like the sun on her eyes, she only has to blink to see it. Would it hurt to step inside again? Would it invoke fate too strongly to try the dress just once more, to touch the silk and lace between her fingers?

Dinah Washington belts out "Is You Is or Is You Ain't My Baby" as Milly steps inside. She doesn't see Etta until she's standing right beside her.

"You came back."

"Yes," Milly says, surprised she's so memorable since it's the last thing she imagines herself to be. "I thought . . . I hoped maybe I could try on the dress again, if it hasn't been sold."

"Oh, absolutely," Etta says. "It's been waiting for you."

"Really?" Milly smiles. She's missed it, too, though is rather embarrassed to admit it.

Ten minutes later, clothes and handbag discarded on the floor, Milly stands in front of the mirror staring at herself wearing the red dress of silk and lace. Milly had thought her memory of the dress had been gold-tinted, a wish fulfilled in fantasy. But it wasn't. If anything she's more beautiful now than she was before.

"You're glowing," Etta says softly.

Milly nods, still unable to believe the way she looks: like a prom queen, an actress, a supermodel.

"It's too fancy, too fabulous," she murmurs. "I'll have nowhere to wear it."

"What nonsense." Etta laughs. "And anyway, what does that matter?"

"Well . . ." Milly struggles on, feeling she should at least seem to put up a fight against such a frivolous, unjustifiable expense.

"Well, what?" Etta asks.

"I'll take it," Milly blurts out.

"Perfect," Etta says. "Just let me make a few adjustments." She pulls a needle laced with red thread out of her pocket and begins sewing six little stitches at both the hem and waist. To see her own beauty, this woman needs more than just the usual single star. "I can always do alterations after this," Etta says while she sews. "Bring it back anytime, free of charge."

"Oh, okay," Milly says, wondering if Etta's suggesting she's going to get fat. "Thank you."

Etta looks up from the hem of the dress, a clutch of dark red silk in her hand. There is so much she could say to Milly, she's not sure where to start. She sees into Milly's quiet heart. Unlike many of her customers, she has no great dreams, but some of them are impossible nonetheless. It's a shame, Etta thinks, that such a sweet young woman won't get the simple joys she so desires. At least, not yet. But perhaps she'll be all right in the end. Etta can't see that far ahead, she can only hope.

"Remember," she says, standing, "if life is ever less than lovely, put on this dress and it'll help you to remember that you are loved. And that will see you through everything."

"Okay," Milly says, though she's hardly listening.

When she walks out of the shop, she swings her new bag back and forth, high into the air. The most beautiful dress in the world is wrapped up, safe and snug, sparkling in gold tissue paper. She can't wait to show it to Walt. It's then that she remembers the letter. Perhaps she should post it now then nip into Blue Water Books and debut the dress, before it's too late.

Milly hurries out of All Saints' Passage and stops in front of the bright red postbox sealed into the wall of Sidney Susset College. She sets the new bag carefully on the pavement between her feet, then rummages around in her chaotic handbag for the letter. When she picks it up the envelope is so thin, so insignificant between her fingers she wonders how it can hold such a weighty message within. When she drops it into the mouth of the postbox, Milly holds her breath. She glances at her watch. She still has ten minutes left of her lunch break, just enough time to visit the bookshop.

As she walks, Milly sticks her hand in her bag for the notebook, so she can give it back before she forgets. When her fingers don't immediately touch it, she doesn't worry. She pauses on the pavement to take a closer look. It's only after tipping the contents of her bag into the street that she realizes Walt's notebook has gone. She has lost it. Somewhere among all the shops and supermarkets, she has lost it.

When he started working at the radio station a decade ago, Dylan was always the first in the office at six o'clock. Nowadays he feeds his father breakfast, makes the day nurse a cup of coffee and aims to arrive just in time for the post. Unlike most people in media, Dylan didn't consider it his dream job. He hadn't captained the school radio station, hadn't done stints as a producer, interviewer or anything like that. He'd fallen into it at university after his best friend, who presented a Saturday morning show called *Bangers, Mash & Beer,* was still too drunk from the night before to go in. Dylan, knowing absolutely nothing about anything, covered for him. That first show was slightly disastrous but Dylan had done well enough to hold it all together. When the producer asked if he wanted to cohost the show for the rest of the term he'd shrugged and agreed. After leaving university, unable to find a job, he'd started temping at BBC Radio Cambridgeshire and stayed. He'd never met anyone he loved enough to settle down with, no one he loved enough to introduce to his father, and now he finds himself pushing forty and wondering what he's done with his life.

Years ago, like most introverted teenagers, Dylan had dabbled in poetry. He'd even written half a novel that he didn't have enough life experience to finish. He'd completely forgotten about both those things until recently, when he started writing all these letters. Dylan loves writing them. He puts his whole heart and soul into each one. He finds the writing lifts his spirits, so at the end of the day he's invigorated instead of drained. Slowly, the letters have been encroaching into his working day. He used to wait until lunchtime and evening to write them; now the letters linger on his desk, in his drawers, in boxes on his floor and he replies to them whenever he can.

This morning Dylan walks through the lobby just as the postman is dropping the daily pile of post with the receptionist, a pretty woman with a flirtatious smile. They dated for a few weeks a while ago but, like the rest of Dylan's relationships, it never went anywhere. She hands him his own post, along with the stack of Walt's fan mail, and winks.

"Have a good day," she says as he walks away, riffling through the letters.

"Yeah, you too, Helen."

Dylan throws the words behind him, hardly hearing them himself. He recognizes one of these letters—the envelope embedded with red rose petals—and opens it as he's walking upstairs. Before reaching his office door, before he's even finished the first paragraph, Dylan realizes that this letter is one he shouldn't be reading. But, now he's started, he can't stop. He drops his bag to the floor and stands in the middle of the room until he reaches the last line.

This isn't fan mail. This is a letter from Walt's girlfriend, someone Dylan didn't even know existed, writing to tell him what is in her heart. It's like holding her diary in his hands. Her words are so sweet, so gentle, so true, that they bring tears to his eyes. He feels his own heart contract with longing. Very carefully, Dylan folds the letter again and slips it back into the envelope. He stands in his office without moving. Then he goes to his desk, sits and scrambles about for a piece of paper and a pen. Quickly, before he can change his mind, before he can fully acknowledge that he really shouldn't be doing what he's about to do, Dylan begins to write back.

Sebastian, in his long career as a priest, has heard every confession he could have possibly imagined and a great number he couldn't. But, among all the adultery, coveting and stealing, he's never heard anything unforgivable. Sebastian has always hoped that absolving other sinners of their own crimes will help him forgive his own, which is why he hears confession as often as he can. For the most part, these are silly minor sins. Every Sunday his middle-class parishioners tell him they've sworn, taken the Lord's name in vain, thrown snails from their gardens over their neighbors' walls . . . Even when the crimes are bigger, adultery, fornication, some sort of sexually deviant act, Sebastian still found them easy to pardon.

"Say thirty-five Hail Marys every night, stop sleeping with your wife's sister, and you're absolved. The stain on your soul is cleaned." Done. If only Sebastian could believe the same about his own sin. But, after fifty Hail Marys every night for the last fifty years, he still hasn't forgiven himself. Sometimes he wonders how many confessions he'll have to hear, how many souls he'll have to save, before he's off the hook. But he knows the answer to this: an infinite amount. Because who is he to decide that? Only God can decide such things and, as yet, Sebastian hasn't had any sign that he can step down from his penance and live out the rest of his life in peace. And he's been looking, every day he looks and hopes and prays. Then this Sunday, something strange happens. It's not a sign, sadly, but a strange little gift from God (in lieu of the one Sebastian wants) perhaps, to throw things into perspective.

The man steps into the confessional after Mrs. Allen, who let her dog poop in the park last weekend without picking it up. Sebastian doesn't know the man personally, but he knows he's the one that comes every Sunday to sit without speaking. It's been the case for the last twenty years and, every week, Sebastian says his line: *May the Lord be in our heart to help you make a good confession* and the man says nothing. Sometimes he sits for five minutes, sometimes ten. Sometimes he sighs. Sometimes he opens his mouth. Every week he leaves without saying anything.

Sebastian waits. It's not his place to urge, to prod and pry. He is only supposed to listen, even to someone who doesn't speak. While he waits, the priest mumbles a prayer, an Our Father, something to bring solace to this clearly troubled soul. It's then that the strange thing happens.

In the silence, even though Sebastian can only really hear the man's slow breathing, all of a sudden he hears something extraordinary: a confession, the words a whisper in his own head. At first Sebastian wonders if the man did speak aloud, though he's quite certain he didn't. He feels the man next to him, still silent, separated only by wood and wire. He presses his hands together and whispers his own prayer, for help, answers, assistance. He tips his head back and looks heavenward.

Nothing happens except that Sebastian is now absolutely certain that he silently absorbed this man's confession, as if he'd just snatched the thoughts from his head. Which is a shocking enough experience in itself, and would count among the most startling events of Sebastian's life so far, if the confession itself hadn't been even more alarming than the method in which it was delivered. It wasn't murder, but it seemed close enough.

Chapter Seventeen

The night Etta at last made love with the Saint, when they had finally, reluctantly, pulled themselves apart to lie side by side, he had given her his confession. A little later they sat together on a bench in a secluded park beside the river. They sat a few inches from each other, their hands resting on the wood, nearly touching, just a moment apart. Etta could feel the warmth of his skin in her fingers as if she was already holding his hand but they hadn't yet touched.

"I have something to tell you," he said.

"Yes?" Etta turned to him, smiling.

"I'm sorry, I'm more than sorry," he said, "I should have told you before. I meant to, I meant to every day, but I knew I'd lose you when I did. I was selfish, I—"

"What is it?" Etta asked, thinking, with her own stab of guilt, of Joe. "Are you married?"

He laughed. But it wasn't a bright, light sound. It was low, bitter and heavy with regret. "I suppose I am, in a way, at least I'm going to be."

"You're engaged?"

It was nearly a minute before the Saint spoke again. To Etta it felt like forever, time that opened up a pit for her to fall into, every second an infinity of despair and dashed hope.

"No," he said softly. "I'm going to be a priest."

Strangely, Etta wasn't too shocked. She wasn't sure why. Surely she should have been. It wasn't as if she'd predicted it, as if she knew. Etta wasn't psychic, unlike her mother, grandmother, sisters and nearly all of her other female relatives, back to the dawn of time. She had a different gift. Etta could see when something was right and when it was wrong. She could feel if it *fit*. And, if it did, then she accepted it, surrendering to the rightness of life and embraced it as she did the seasons and the sunrise and the sunset.

But even though Etta could feel the pure rightness of Sebastian's choice reverberating right down to her bones, for the first time in her life she had trouble embracing it.

"Yes," Etta said, at last. "Yes, I can see that."

"I'm sorry," he said. "I'm sorrier than I've ever been about anything . . ."

"I know," she said, and she did. He looked and sounded sadder than she'd ever experienced anyone to be before. Even her mother when her father died.

"I didn't tell you when we met because, it didn't seem . . . I mean, I didn't know we would become—"

"I know," Etta said again. "It's okay, you don't have to explain."

"I do," he protested. "I've done something for which I shall never forgive myself. I should have told you before—but I wanted to touch you, more than anything, I wanted to feel you. And I thought, while we were together, that I could give up God, I could . . ."

Etta put a finger to Sebastian's lips, though she couldn't quite yet look him in the eye. She'd never be able to stop her tears from falling then. "Don't say that," she said. "You won't and you mustn't. It's what you're meant to do. It'll make you happy, it'll—"

"I hardly deserve that."

"Oh." Etta looked at him then. She reached up to touch his cheek. In spite of what he'd done she still saw in his eyes that he was one of the purest, truest souls she had ever known. "You're going to do so much good," she said softly, "you're going to heal so many hearts."

Sebastian shook his head. "Not yours," he said. "Not mine."

"That's not the point."

"Why not?"

Etta shrugged slightly, unable to explain exactly what she meant.

Then he took her hand and held it to his chest. "Tell me not to do it," he said. "Tell me to choose you and I will."

Etta wanted to do that, more than anything in the world. She wanted him more than she had ever wanted anyone or anything in her life before. But she couldn't. It wasn't right. It would be like trying to rip the moon from the sky or changing the tides, destroying a delicate balance, taking something perfect and making it imperfect. Nothing good would come from that, only suffering. So Etta shook her head. But she couldn't speak, she couldn't answer his question with even a single word, because then Sebastian would hear the break in her voice and see the break in her heart. And when they made love again, for the second and the last time, Etta wept though she didn't make a sound.

Milly hurries along the street on her way to work. On the outside she looks like her ordinary, boring, nondescript self: fluffy brown hair, baggy blue dress, oversized coat and flat black shoes. But inside she is shining. Every nonvisible cell of her is alight, her body a container brimming over with delight: bottled sunlight and bursts of stardust. In her pocket is a letter. The loveliest letter she has ever received: the sentences so sweetly simple, the sentiments so heartfelt, the words exactly what she wanted to hear. That morning the post arrived before she left the house, an unusual thing in itself, and instead of the usual bank statements and bills, the letter lay on the mat. Milly read it five times after opening it; the first few times gobbling up the words like chocolate cake, then savoring it slowly like soft caramels coating her tongue. As a result Milly is late to open the shop. It's the first time that's happened in the twelve years she's worked there so she doesn't feel too guilty about it, but still she rushes along the pavement, panting. In her head the letter replays on a loop . . .

> *My dear Milly,*
> *Thank you so much for your letter. I can't quite put into words how it made me feel to read your words, but I will try. No one in my life has ever been so honest, so bare, with me. No one has ever entrusted their heart to me before. You told me things that, had they happened to me, I could never imagine telling to another living soul. But you did and now I feel I can tell you anything. I only ask that you*

don't speak of these things, not when we are together in person at least, only on the page. Would that be all right? Can we have two relationships, one in person and one on the page? At least until I'm confident enough to write and speak the same words. Now I am too shy, sorry to admit, and I think it will take my tongue a little while to catch up with my pen . . . Write again. Until I receive more words from you I shall simply read the ones I have over and over until they are as close to my heart as my own.

With love,
Walt

He loves her. He loves her. He loves her. The smile is so wide on Milly's face that her cheeks hurt. So happy is she, so bright is her joy, that she almost—almost, but not quite—forgets she hasn't yet told Walt that she's lost his mother's notebook.

Cora has been wearing one of her grandmother's T-shirts every night and every night she has dreams so vivid and bright that they seep into her days. She doesn't only dream of her parents, but also her childhood, of her grandmother and Walt. Perhaps, in his case, it's because she also listens to his readings on the radio before falling asleep. Though she suspects it's more than that. It's incredible though, the things she had forgotten, the events with Walt that didn't seem significant at the time, the words he'd said that didn't touch her heart then because she'd lived life in her head.

Last night, after hearing, to her great relief, Marianne Dashwood recover from her illness, Cora dreamed of how she'd used to sit sometimes on the doorstep of the bookshop with Walt on Saturday afternoons. Etta had been busy with her customers and, after feeding her a breakfast big enough to last the day, told Cora it was time to play outside and fill her lungs with fresh air. Cora, having never been a big fan of fresh air, would wander up and down All Saints' Passage doing sums with the number of leaves on the trees or cigarette stubs on the street, and imagining how she might one day save the world. Would she cure a disease that killed millions? Would she invent a drug that halted the aging process? Would she create a miracle plant that could feed starving populations? One Saturday while Cora paced she'd glanced over at Walt hunched over a book, shoulder blades bent together like birds' wings. As a general rule Cora avoided people but for some reason, perhaps because he was a few years younger and small for his age, Walt didn't scare Cora. She said things to him that she'd never for a moment even consider saying to anyone else.

"You've got a hundred and eight stripes on your shirt," Cora said as she stopped at the step and looked down at him. "That's only if the back matches the front. Does it?"

Walt looked up at her, awestruck. "I don't know," he apologized, "I've never looked."

"Oh," Cora said, glancing back in the direction of her grandmother's shop, then down at her feet. "Did you know there's a wine cellar underneath the street?"

"No," Walt said, "I didn't."

"Yes." Cora sat down on the step beside him. "It belongs to Trinity College. Apparently the cellar is made of caves six hundred and eighty-nine feet long containing over twenty-five thousand bottles worth over two million pounds."

"Really?"

"Allegedly. I've never seen it with my own eyes, so I can't promise, but I think it's true. My grandmother told me. I'd like to count it myself, to check on the number of bottles, but I'm not sure how to get down there."

Walt closed his book. "I like your grandma. She said she'd make me a scarf. She said I could pick any color I want."

Cora smiled. "You'd better be careful. She's always trying to make things for me, too, but she doesn't know how to make anything without frills and sequins and sparkly bits. You'll end up looking like a Barbie doll."

"Yuck." Walt pulled a face. "Do you want to hear a story?"

"Okay, sure." Cora shrugged. "What's it about?"

"A boy called Pip who falls in love with a girl called Estella, but she doesn't like him because he's a poor orphan and—"

Suddenly Cora stood, stuffing her hands deep into her pockets. "Actually, I can't, sorry. I just remembered, um, Etta wanted some help in the shop. I'd better get back or I'll be in trouble."

"Oh," Walt said, "okay. Maybe later."

"No thanks." Cora shook her head, not wanting to run the risk of hearing that particular story. "I don't think I'll have time for stories. I've always got important things to do."

Walt looked at her as she spoke and, just as she finished speaking, Cora caught his eye. She didn't know what it was she saw in his gaze but she knew it made her uncomfortable.

"Bye," she said, and turned. She felt him watch her walk away and, though she wanted to change her mind, to go back and sit with him and ask him to read her a different story, one that wouldn't make her sad, she didn't. It was easier just to keep walking, so she did.

—

Sebastian can't count the number of times he's wanted to go back to Etta, to find her, beg her forgiveness and ask her to reconsider. How many moments in over fifty years? Perhaps 250 times a day for 18,611 days, nearly five million . . . But each time he's slipped on his coat and hat, stepped out of the church and begun heading in the direction of All Saints' Passage he has always turned back. He does this a few times a year, on the anniversaries of the day they met, the night they made love and the day they parted.

He stops himself because of their promise, on parting, not to see each other again. And when Sebastian read her wedding announcement in the local paper six months later, he was relieved and grateful for it. When, thirty years later, he'd read of her husband's death Sebastian decided it was too late to go back. Etta would have forgotten him. He didn't want to stir up old regrets and pains long since buried. He knew her heart would have healed and he could deal with his own broken self. It would be simply selfish to do anything else.

Sometimes he thinks he sees her, on the street or in a shop. Cambridge is a rather small town, especially when the university students leave at the end of term, so if she's forgotten their promise long ago, it wouldn't be such a surprising thing to happen. Sebastian hopes for it. Sometimes a woman will catch his eye and for one eternal second his breath balloons in his chest and he floats above the floor, until she turns to show her face. Then he falls and exhales again, deflated. Occasionally Sebastian wonders if Etta might have changed so much that he wouldn't recognize her now, that perhaps he's passed her in the street many times and just hasn't noticed. But, deep down, he knows this can't be true: he will know Etta anytime, anywhere, no matter what. It's not just her face he can see whenever he closes his eyes, but the way she walks, holds her hands, the very air around her. If Sebastian were standing in the corner of a darkened room and Etta stepped silently through the door, he would know it.

Of course it's never happened, he's never been lucky enough to see her, not once, and for this Sebastian isn't surprised. Indeed, he's almost grateful. He's being punished for his sin, properly and completely, which is exactly as it should be. The fact that he'll be tied to Etta for the whole of his life yet never be able to speak with her, to unburden himself again, to lighten the load on his suffering spirit, is perfect punishment for what he's done.

Henry stands on the doorstep of his ex-wife's house with Mateo tucked into his chest. After a heady day of laughter and play, his son finally fell asleep, nodding off in the car and not waking when Henry gently unbuckled his seat belt and lifted him out into the cool autumn air. Now his soft blond hair brushes Henry's chin and his smooth, sleep-heavy fingers are curled against Henry's coat.

As he waits for Francesca to come to the door, Henry glances down at his son, still unable to believe he's played a part in creating this miniature person, this strange and inexplicable creature so exquisitely beautiful and perfect. His life is so steeped in the worst that mankind has to offer—death, destruction, and general devastation—that sometimes, in the darkest hours, he forgets that anything else exists at all. And then Henry remembers Mateo and, no matter the situation he's standing in, no matter what awfulness is currently soaking the soles of his feet, he thinks of his son and smiles.

As Henry nestles his nose in Mateo's soft curls, Francesca opens the door and he quickly glances up.

"Hi, Fran," he says, wishing that she wasn't so bloody beautiful: even without makeup or sleep, with red rings around her eyes. Maybe it would be easier not to pine for her. Then again, maybe not. Because Francesca isn't simply beautiful, she's seductive. Before Mateo they went to parties every weekend and Francesca had always been the life and soul of them, showering everyone with the glitter and sparkle of her laughter, wit and charm.

"Hello, Hen," she says, her voice perfectly flat, every molecule of emotion ironed out. But Henry knows it's there, that love lingers underneath her words even if so deeply buried he can barely hear it.

Francesca doesn't look at him when she speaks but gazes at her son, a flicker of absolute delight and adoration on her lips. This is the thing that will always connect them, no matter what: their shared love for this little boy. It gives Henry some comfort to know that, even if Francesca no longer wants to share her life with him, this invisible thread will tie them together forever.

Henry leans forward as Francesca reaches out for her son. The two adults dip toward each other and carefully transfer their sleeping child from one parent to the other. Mateo emits a soft sigh as he snuggles into his mother's arms and Henry suppresses the urge to reach out and stroke his hair one more time. He still remembers how it felt to press his own body into his ex-wife's arms, to smell her scent: sweet and rich, deep and earthy. Each time he'd pick up a different fragrance: roasting coffee, expensive red wine, baking bread, verbena soap, rose face cream . . . And each time he breathed her in he thought of Italy and imagined them lying together in an olive grove in Tuscany with the sun slowly heating their skin, as they had the afternoon Mateo was conceived.

"He ate all his dinner," Henry says, shaking himself free of the memory. "He only slept for an hour after lunch, so he'll probably go down for the rest of the night now."

"Perfect, thank you." Francesca smiles and Henry glances away. When she opens her mouth to him like that, no matter how innocently, he only wants to kiss her. It is a desire he can't control, can't reason himself out of, no matter how many devastating words have been spoken to him from those same lips. The night Francesca told him she didn't love him anymore, that she wanted to leave him, Henry thought that would be it, that he'd never want to kiss her again, but sadly it wasn't so. The withdrawal of her heart has done nothing to quell his desire. It is, as he stands on her doorstep, just as strong, if not even stronger, than the day he stood on the doorstep of her office at Magdalene College, the day he first saw her.

"You want to come in? I have a fresh *caffè*."

Henry suppresses his surprise. Francesca rarely invites him into her home. He only passes over her threshold if he's carrying something heavy and unwieldy that she couldn't easily manage herself. He finds Francesca's thick black Italian coffee virtually undrinkable, but that isn't going to put him off. He'd swallow turpentine if it gave him the chance to spend an hour with his wife once more. *Ex,* Henry reminds himself, *ex-wife*. But a lot can happen in an hour. Lives can change, love can resurrect. Especially if that love never died, despite Francesca's claims to the contrary. Henry knows a liar at a hundred paces and he knew, even when she looked him in the eye and said she didn't love him anymore, that she was lying.

"Yes, please," he says now, "that'd be lovely."

While Francesca is putting Mateo to bed Henry waits in the kitchen. It's the kitchen they shared as a couple, then a family, for four years before Henry moved out, but now he doesn't feel able to sit down at the table, even though he was the one who built it out of oak one sunny weekend three summers ago. He steps over to the wall to study a collection of pictures of Mateo. In some he is alone, in some he's with his mother, in all he is smiling his sublime little boy smile: eyes bright, face and heart thrown open to the world. Henry runs his finger gently over the photographs, remembering the ones he'd taken himself, exactly where and when and how happy he'd been.

"Would you like biscotti?"

Henry turns to see Francesca standing by the stove, pouring two cups of coffee. He's shocked that he was so caught up in the photos that he didn't even hear her come in. It hardly speaks well of his policing skills.

"No, thanks, I'm fine."

"I made them." Francesca opens the wooden cupboard above her head. They are made of pine, painted white with blue trim. Henry's first project when he moved in three months after they met. "Toffee and pecan."

His favorite. Henry feels the blood pumping in his throat. It is a loving gesture, an overture of friendship at the very least, a meaningful beginning, the start of something significant. Why else would she bother to make him his favorite biscuits unless she cared?

"Yes, please then, I'd love one."

Henry turns away from the wall and lingers at the edge of the table. As he watches Francesca twist the lid off a glass jar of caramel-colored biscuits, her long thin fingers effortless and elegant, her thick black curls falling over her shoulders, Henry tries not to get too excited, too hopeful. When she lifts the cups of coffee off the counter and onto the table, he pulls his eyes away from her jumper, the shape of her breasts, the tuck of her waist, the soft curve of her belly. She'd always been self-conscious about her stomach, wanting to subdue its gentle bulge, to starve it into submission until her body was flat and shapeless. Fortunately, she'd always loved food and wine too much to be able to forgo it for very long. Henry steps forward, hesitant, toward the table.

"Sit down," she says, "I've got something to tell you."

Chapter Eighteen

Dr. Baxter has summoned Cora to his office. He'd actually called her that morning at home, waking her at seven o'clock, to make sure she'd be coming in. It's the first time he's ever done that so she knows it's important and she knows why. Consequently she's putting off the moment for as long as she can. To be a scientist, to make a significant contribution to the world, is all Cora has ever wanted to do with her life. She's dedicated nearly every hour of her life to it, save for sleeping, eating and those other few annoyingly obligatory things one must do in order to survive.

Cora knocks tentatively on Dr. Baxter's door, half-hoping he won't hear her, so she can pretend that everything is okay, that nothing has changed. But in addition to his excessive handsomeness and chronic messiness, Dr. Baxter also has hearing like a bat.

"Come in," he calls.

Cora pushes open the door and glances around her supervisor's office. If she thought Etta's sewing room was untidy, her grandmother is a neat freak compared to Dr. Baxter. Stacks of papers, toppling towers of books, science journals and assorted newspapers cover every surface from floor to ceiling. Cora stands in the doorway, unable to step inside without treading on anything. "So," she says, "I'm here."

Dr. Baxter nods. He doesn't say anything but reaches into the sea of papers on his desk and pulls out a letter. He holds it out toward Cora, who now has no choice but to walk across fields of scientific research to get it. When she takes the letter gingerly between her fingers, Cora summons a wish, a pleading prayer, from the depths of her thawing heart. Then she opens her eyes again to read it.

The letter is a single page. Cora scans it in a few seconds (only 143 words, 607 letters) and feels that pesky heart plummet as if she'd just stepped into a lift. She swallows several times and takes deep breaths. But it does nothing to calm her. It's no good. It's all over. Their funding has been pulled. She's lost her job. And the chances of finding another one, of winning another grant to fund their research, are about 278,976: 1.

"What are we going to do?" Cora asks at last.

Dr. Baxter shakes his handsome head. "I don't know. I really don't know." He sighs. "I was hoping we'd be safe, given the importance of what we've been working on and the progress we've been making. But you know what it's like out there, how hard it is to get grants for independent research, how easy it is to lose them."

Cora sighs. "I take it you've already investigated all the alternatives?"

Dr. Baxter nods. "Yes, of course. I'm afraid we've reached the end of the road on this one. It's a dire shame, this financial stranglehold on scientific research nowadays. Finding funding in this economy is a nightmare. It's a war against . . . Anyway, we've got other options. I happen to know that Dr. Eric Marsden is expanding his project in Angola. I'm sure he'd—"

"Angola?"

"He's looking for a new field assistant. I've put in a good word. The job is yours if you want it."

"And what about you?"

Dr. Baxter smiles. "Don't worry about me, I'll find something. I won't give up fighting the good fight."

Cora nods, not yet comprehending that this means they won't be working together anymore. The thought makes her sadder than she might have expected.

"Eric's running a two-year project researching nutritional alternatives for infants with mothers too malnourished to feed them. It's not such a significant detour from what we've been working on. You'd have a great deal to offer."

"But I'd be working in Angola for two years?"

"Yes. And working with Eric—you couldn't hope for a better step up in your career."

She should take it. She should go to Angola. She'd be absolutely mad not to. A month ago she wouldn't have thought twice. She'd have gone around the world, across the Sahara or to the North Pole for science, for the chance to do something of significance. Of course she'd have missed Etta, but that wouldn't have stopped her. But now it's not only her grandmother Cora would miss. No longer listening to Walt every night on the radio, she couldn't bear to lose that. Though that's silly, she realizes, since they surely have digital radios in Angola she could tune in whenever she wanted. So perhaps that's not quite the point . . .

"So," Dr. Baxter gently interrupts Cora's thoughts, "shall I call Eric?"

"I'm not sure," Cora says. "Can I think about it?"

Francesca fingers the rim of her coffee cup, studying the delicate china as she speaks. "I'd like to take Mattie to Italy."

"Okay," Henry says, wondering why she'd bake his favorite biscuits to tell him this. Mateo goes to Tuscany twice a year, in August and December, to visit Francesca's family for a few weeks. Of course Henry misses him, but he knows it's important for his son to know his family, culture and history. And then Henry makes the connection. It's April 15. "Why now?"

"I don't think you understand," Francesca says softly. "It's not just for a holiday. I want to take him there to live."

It's perhaps a full minute, though it feels like fifty, before Henry can say anything. He just stares at the woman he loves, and now suddenly hates in equal measure, terrified.

"What?" His voice is soft, barely audible. "Why? I don't, you can't . . ."

"I've been thinking about it for a long time," Francesca says. "Not forever, just for a year. I've been given a sabbatical by the college. It's not such a huge thing. I know it'll be hard at first, for you both, but flights are so cheap and quick, and you can visit whenever you—"

"Hard?" Henry shouts. *"Hard?"* He wants to pick up his coffee cup and hurl it against the wall. He wants to smack his hand against the table so it shakes. So strong are his feelings, in fact, that they scare him. "I see Mattie all the time. I'm a good father.

He loves me. He'd be devastated. Don't you care? Don't you care about that at all?"

Francesca is nodding, tears running down her cheeks. "Of course I do, of course, more than anything in the world. Please don't—"

"You're a liar," Henry says, his voice sharp and sour as vinegar. "You wouldn't even think of doing this if you did. Mateo needs me. He needs to grow up with his father."

"Don't be so dramatic, Hen," Francesca says, though she can't look him in the eye as she does. "It's only a year. You can visit as much as you like."

"I can't fly to Tuscany every other day," Henry snaps. "I could probably make it over once a month, if that."

"That's not too bad then, is it?"

"Not too bad?" Henry is incredulous. "Have you talked to Mattie about this? Have you told him what you want to do?"

Francesca stares down into her coffee cup and nods. "He's . . . happy, he's excited to see his *nonna* every day."

"Bullshit. He doesn't understand what it means. He doesn't know."

"He does. I've explained everything to him."

"You shouldn't have spoken to him first," Henry says, his voice and hands still shaking with rage. "How long has he known? He hasn't said anything to me."

"He was probably protecting you," Francesca suggested softly. "He didn't want to upset you."

"Bullshit," Henry says again, though his voice wavers this time.

It sounds just like his son. When he and Francesca had separated, when Henry had finally moved out, Mateo had seemed to know that his father's heart was breaking and did everything he could to soften Henry's sadness. He stroked Henry's hair, patted his cheek and spoke in whispers. He put himself to bed at night and curled up waiting for sleep. He offered to keep his daddy company "if he was lonely without mummy" in the early morning hours. One day Mateo had heard Henry crying behind the locked bathroom door and had given Henry his favorite bear, Piglet, to cuddle because "every time he makes me feel better" and Henry's heart had sighed with love for his son. So he knows now that what Francesca is saying is probably true, and he hates her for it. He glares at his ex-wife, at her olive skin and long dark hair. All of a sudden a memory of the last time they made love rises up and flips his hatred over on its head, exposing the soft belly of love underneath it. And so, because he wants to get down on his knees and cry into his ex-wife's lap, he curses her instead.

"You're a selfish bitch," Henry snaps. "If you do this you'll damage him, you'll ruin his life." *And mine,* he wants to say, but doesn't bother since he knows she clearly doesn't care either way about that.

"No," Francesca says, "you're wrong. We need to do this. And Mattie's going to be fine, he's going to be wonderful. I'd die before I let him suffer."

Henry pushes his chair away from the table and stands.

"And I will die before I let you take my son away. I know some nasty people, lawyers that'd rip your life to shreds if I paid them, and I will. I am going to—"

"Please."

Her voice is so soft that Henry barely hears it. He stops to look at her, the swell of his anger subsiding, and waits.

"Please," Francesca says again. She reaches out across the table toward him, her long fingers trembling. "I have to do this. I need to."

"Why?"

Francesca shakes her head, the black curls falling over her face. "I can't—"

"You have to, Fran, I'm not even going to think about it, not without an explanation."

"I will," she says, "I will one day, I promise."

"No, that's not good enough, Fran, it'll have to be now."

Francesca fixes her eyes on Henry and holds his gaze. As he looks at her he sees, for the first time, how haggard she seems: her skin pale, sallow and blotched, her hair dank and unwashed, her eyes red and swollen.

"I'm doing this for Mattie, too, I swear it is the best thing for us both, for us all, I promise you."

Francesca speaks slowly, clearly choosing each word carefully. She doesn't glance away and Henry, before she's even finished, understands absolutely that she's telling the truth. This isn't a decision she's made on a whim without a thought for their little boy. This is something she's doing for him as much as for herself. Henry only knows that she's telling the truth. He has no idea why she wants to go, only that it will be best for Mateo, and that is really all he needs to know.

"Okay." Henry nods, though he can't believe he is, even as he's saying it. "If you need to do this then I won't stop you. But it had better be only for a year. And I'm allowed to visit as often as I can. And I want to hear him on the phone at least three times a week, and see him over the internet. I don't want you changing the rules on me once you're out there."

Francesca gives him a weak smile and the gratitude and relief on her face are so overwhelming that Henry instantly knows he's done the right thing. He hates doing it and hates not knowing why he must. But sometimes acts of faith are called for in life, especially in love, and Henry understands that this is one such time.

"When will you go?" he asks.

"At the end of next month," Francesca says. "If that is okay."

No! Henry wants to scream. *It's dreadful. It's terrible. It's awful. It's heartbreaking.* But he doesn't. Instead he nods and turns and walks slowly out of the kitchen and out of the house. It's not until he's reached his own home and closed the front door behind him that Henry slides to the floor and allows himself to cry.

Dylan sits on the sofa in his office, composing another letter to Milly. The words flow out of his pen so fast he can hardly keep up. He usually has to think and carefully choose which thoughts to commit to paper. But his letters to Milly are entirely effortless and easy. It's as if he's talking to her, as if she's sitting at his feet and listening, smiling and hanging on to his every word, just as he hangs on to hers. They've exchanged half a dozen letters in the last two weeks and every day he asks the receptionist, Helen, for Walt's post before she's even sat down at her desk. She's started giving him suspicious looks lately so Dylan knows he'll have to start playing it cool, lest she bump into Walt and let something slip.

Dylan tries not to think of Walt while he writes to Milly, which wasn't easy at first but once he gets caught up with the words he can't think of anything else except her. If a herd of elephants crashed through the room while he was in the middle of a letter he'd be hard-pressed to pay attention. Sometimes he can't quite believe that they've actually never met. She's so honest in her letters, so open with her feelings, so willing to expose her heart and soul that he needs to remind himself they haven't known each other all their lives. He feels as if he knows Milly better than he knows anyone else.

Dylan finds it hard to look Walt in the eye nowadays and he's relieved that his employee had never responded to any of Dylan's previous overtures of friendship. He already feels guilty enough at the betrayal and if Walt was less standoffish then Dylan's conscience might have won the battle with his desire and held him back. If Walt had been a friend, then Dylan would have given him Milly's letter after it arrived, or he would have torn it up and pretended it never had. At least, that's what Dylan tells himself. But once Milly's words had seeped into his head and wrapped themselves tightly around his heart, he was already unable to think straight, unable to remember right from wrong, unable to act in a rational, decent, moral manner. If Walt had been his own brother he probably would have gone straight ahead and replied to her letter, betraying his own flesh and bone in good conscience and cold blood.

Now Dylan writes:

I believe that soul mates will always find each other, that true love will weather all storms, that people who want to be together will always find a way, that once our hearts find a home in another then they will stay, that false love will fade away and be forgotten in time, that a free heart is happier than an unloved one.

Dylan isn't simply being self-serving, he believes all that and more. He believes that if Walt and Milly are meant to be together then a few letters from him won't stand in their way. And that if they're not (as he hopes), Walt will find someone else to love. But he tries not to think too much about what the fallout could be and how he's going to explain himself once his epistolary identity fraud comes to light. Because it will, that much is clear.

One day Milly is going to say something to Walt about all these letters he's supposedly sending her and then all hell will break loose. Although Dylan entertains fantasies of a fifty-year romance of letters, conducted while Milly and Walt get married and raise children, continuing until she dies, he knows that such things are not possible. Husbands and wives tend to talk about the intimate details of their lives, including the love letters they're secretly sending each other. And of course there is the small matter of the fact that, once they're sharing the same address, postal privacy would be rather harder to maintain. So Dylan knows that, sooner or later, the end must come. Until then, however, he will keep writing . . .

How many times have you read Sense & Sensibility? *It sounds as if you know it by heart. I must confess I've only read it once but I loved it, deeply. The moment when Elinor realizes Edward isn't married after all, and sobs, it brought tears to my eyes. I'm not saying that any of those tears actually fell down my cheeks (that would be too much for me to confess, I think) but I was significantly moved. I watched the film a few days ago, the one Emma Thompson won an Oscar for, well-deserved I think. She did that sobbing scene justice. Hats off to her. I don't know how these actors do it, really. Are they really just pretending, or are they really feeling what they seem to*

> *be feeling, just in that moment? It seems so real to me. If someone acted like that with me, I'd believe them. If Emma Thompson sobbed for me the way she sobbed for Hugh Grant, then I'd think she loved me too. Is* Sense & Sensibility *your favorite book of all? If not, what is? And why? And your film, what film do you love more than any other? And, if you can't pick one (I can't) then pick many and tell me what and why for each of them. Tell me that, tell me everything . . .*

Milly sits next to Walt in the darkened cinema. Robert Redford and Mia Farrow declare their love for each other onscreen and Milly blinks, trying to concentrate. *The Great Gatsby* is one of her favorite books and she loves the film, but she's finding it hard to focus. All she can think about is Walt's latest letter. She knows they agreed not to talk about the letters, to keep that part of their relationship separate, secret, private, so she won't mention them aloud but that promise can't stop her thoughts.

It's a strange thing, Milly realizes, that she feels closer to him while she reads what he writes than when she listens while he speaks. She feels closer to Walt thinking of his letters than she does sitting next to him right now. In his letter he admits to things he denies face-to-face—like his love of Austen—and she wonders why he holds back in person. It's even true of when they kiss. As their lips touch, she lets his sentences collect and curl in the air between them. She seeks comfort in his written words when she feels alone, when they've run out of things to say to each other, which happens more often than Milly would care to admit. Which is why, slightly silly secret though it is, she will keep writing to Walt at the station and never mention aloud what they're doing.

Walt leans across the seat and presses his mouth close to her ear. "Shall we go for a drink in the café afterward?"

Milly nods, not taking her eyes off the screen. He's as distracted as she is and he hasn't even seen the film a dozen times; he clearly isn't enjoying it.

"I need caffeine," he whispers. "I'm falling asleep."

"You're bored."

"No, no." Walt shakes his head. "I've just been having trouble sleeping lately, that's all."

"Oh?"

"It's nothing," Walt says. "It's not—"

"Shush!" A voice from the row behind admonishes them. Walt and Milly exchange a silent smile, drawn together by a common enemy. He reaches for her hand and squeezes it. She snuggles down in her seat and nestles into his shoulder. While Mia Farrow cries onscreen, Milly closes her eyes, remembering Walt's last letter:

Thursday, 30th April

I don't need to address you anymore. I know who you are, you know who I am. I don't write to anyone else. I don't think of anyone else. It is you for breakfast, lunch and dinner. And I often snack on you in between. I never knew that love is so substantial, so nourishing, so all-encompassing. I must admit I always thought all those poets and writers were exaggerating, dipping into hyperbole for dramatic effect. Either that or they just felt things differently to the common man. But I was wrong.

I can't put things as well as you. When you write about love, I feel as if I'm holding you in my arms and you're whispering every word into my ear, your breath warming my skin. But when I try to explain myself, I feel clumsy, reaching for explanations, searching the English language for adequate sentences to reflect my feelings. And nothing will ever do. It's all a shadow of what's in my heart, it's a muddled, muddy mess of striving and searching and failing. I'm sorry. I only hope you can feel how I feel, even though I'm doing a thoroughly appalling job of saying it.

You wrote before of how your father never told you he loved you, never actually said the words. It seems silly of me to assure you that he did, since we've never met, though I can't imagine how he couldn't, so I'm convinced he did. Still, every person should be told, if they are in any doubt. Perhaps in the closest relationships people never say it, since they don't need to, if it's within every look, inside every gesture and underneath every word. I'm not sure if that is true of us yet, so let me step in and say: I love you, I love you, I love you . . .

Milly strokes her fingertips along Walt's hand. It should be enough, she thinks, that he writes the words, she shouldn't need to hear them out loud, too. But it's no use telling herself that, since she can't help wanting it anyway, every minute of every day. Milly turns her head up to his face and he looks down at her.

"Tell me you love me, please," she says. "I want to hear you say it."

Walt feels something tighten inside him. He knew this day would come soon, he knew it wouldn't be long, he'd only hoped to delay it a little longer, to give his heart a chance to catch up with his head. He didn't want to lie to her, he wanted to wait until he could tell her he loved her and it would be pure and true. He wanted to wait until he could at least stop thinking of Cora twenty times a day. But now Milly is looking up at him with wide eyes full of hope and desire and, not wanting to hurt her, there is nothing else Walt can say.

"I . . . I love you."

Chapter Nineteen

"It's okay," Etta says, "it'll be okay."

"How will it be okay?" Cora says. "I turned down Angola. I haven't got a job. I haven't got a purpose. I don't know what to do."

"You'll find another firm to fund your research, you'll be able to complete it, you might just have to take a break, that's all. But you'll do it in the end, I'm sure."

"Are you?" Cora asks. "Do you know how hard it is to get scientific funding nowadays? Do you know how many other research groups we had to beat out to get that Royal Society grant? Six hundred twenty-six."

"Gosh," Etta says. "Well, yes, I suppose it won't be easy, but you'll do it. You're brilliant. You're the most brilliant scientist I know."

At this, Cora can't help but smile, even in her sorry state.

"And how many scientists have you known in your life, Grandma?"

Etta shrugs. "Including your parents and you? Probably three."

"Yes, I thought as much."

They're sitting on the floor in A Stitch in Time, surrounded on all sides by dresses of every imaginable color. Cora realizes as she glances around, her gaze flitting quickly from one wall to the next, that Etta has arranged them like the seasons: sparkling whites, grays, blacks for winter; shimmering greens and blues for spring; pinks and purples for summer; reds, oranges and yellows for autumn. Together they are breathtaking, almost too bright if stared at for too long, like falling through a rainbow lit by the sun.

"You can always swap this science stuff for sewing," Etta suggests. "I think you might enjoy working here. I can't say you'll save the whole world here, admittedly, but I do believe I help it along a bit, one dress, one life, one heart at a time."

Cora glances down at her clothes—faded blue jeans and a green jumper—then looks pointedly at her grandmother's red velvet dress, purple tights and violet bolero.

"I don't think the customers would trust my taste, do you?"

Etta smiles. "Perhaps not now, but we could always spruce you up a bit."

"Of all the things I could ever imagine doing, of all the fields I could work in, I'm afraid couture isn't one of them," Cora says. "I think I'd probably make a better waitress than a seamstress."

"Maybe," Etta says, "but then maybe you don't know what you're capable of until you try it and see."

Cora rolls her eyes, settling her gaze on the white dresses sparkling like fresh snow in sunlight. "What I *can* do isn't really the point, it's what I *should* do, which is do the thing my parents never got the chance to. They gave me the ability to do it, to do something that will actually save people's lives."

"Yes, but—"

"No," Cora says, "I don't think you understand. If I don't do it, then it's like . . . it's like I'm letting someone die when I have the power to let them live."

Etta sits up a little straighter, smoothing the red velvet beneath her palms. "Well then, there is only one thing for it."

"What?"

"It's time to get you into the changing room."

Miraculously for Milly, Walt still hasn't asked the whereabouts of his mother's notebook. It's been a while since he lent it to her and she'd expected him to want it back after just a day or two. But perhaps he's giving her a bit more time, hoping that another miracle might happen and she might decipher it. Sadly, there is next to no chance of that. In her rare free moments, those when Milly hasn't been reading and rereading Walt's letters and writing her own, she's been trying vainly to make sense of the few pages she'd copied out of the notebook before losing it. It's the strangest code, random jumbles of letters and numbers, one that makes absolutely no sense at all. Milly's always been good at cryptic crossword puzzles and sometimes even dabbles in Sudoku during dull periods in the shop. But this code is impossible. As impossible, it turns out, as confessing to Walt that she's lost it.

Milly still listens to Walt every night without fail. When she wakes the next morning, his voice echoes in her head, the sentences of the stories he reads mixing with those of his letters. She wonders how many other women are listening, imagining him lying next to them in bed, making love . . . Lately Milly has been having rather wicked thoughts that won't leave her alone. She tries to push them away, she tries to think of other, better and purer things, but she can't, no matter how hard she tries she can't.

Milly has wanted a baby for as long as she can remember. Since she first hugged a doll to her chest and stroked her blond hair while whispering soft words in her china ear. When other little girls imagined their weddings, wearing pillowcases over their heads, Milly imagined what it would be like to feel a being growing inside her, tiny arms and legs kicking, until she gave birth and could finally hold the new life she'd created, wet and warm and screaming in her arms.

Incredibly Hugh had wanted a child too, as soon as possible. They'd even discussed it on their first real date (dinner in a pizza restaurant followed by a walk along the river from Clare College to Trinity) and had agreed on three to start, with an option to add another after further consultation. They'd begun trying after they married four months later. Twelve barren months after that, Hugh died, and the only two dreams of Milly's life (for a husband and children) died with him. Grief had buried hope and desire for ten years, until she met Walt.

They haven't talked about babies yet, not specifically at least, or written about them. Milly doesn't quite dare put her most desperate and precious of dreams into words yet, because she isn't sure he'll echo her feelings, but perhaps soon. He's said he wants to be a father. Walt is friendly with babies and children when encountering them in public places, tickling their chubby fingers and making them explode with giggles. This gives Milly hope.

They haven't made love yet, Walt has been curiously cautious physically, but Milly hopes it won't be long now. She's thirty-nine, after all, she doesn't have that much longer to wait. When they finally start having sex, would it be so very bad if they had an "accident"? After the initial shock, everything might work out beautifully. They love each other; they would love their child. But, of course, however hard she tries to convince herself, Milly knows it'd be a dreadful thing to do. She can't betray his trust so completely. She can't take a baby from a man without first asking him to give it. And yet . . . is her desire greater than her devotion? Perhaps. Once the thought seeded itself, she couldn't stop thinking about it. In the beginning she'd thought only of him but now this imagined being has snatched much more than its fair quota of love from the heart Milly has handed to Walt.

As the two emotions fight within her, Milly already knows which will win. She's too old to wait. It took ten years before she fell enough in love with another man to want to have a child with him. And after a year with Hugh they still hadn't gotten pregnant, though after being checked by doctors it was found that the difficulty lay with him rather than her. So Milly has the possibility and she knows she'll take it. She'll hate herself even as she does it, certainly. Guilt will cut into her desire, regret will taint her joy. But the shame won't stop her, what's in her head won't be able to hold back her heart. Milly almost wishes it would, but she knows it won't. And then Milly has an idea. She doesn't have the courage to ask him to his face, so she'll take advantage of their little secret and write to Walt and ask what he thinks about having a child . . .

It took Etta three months to be certain she was pregnant. She put the first missed menstruation down to her body being overwhelmed with sadness and stress. The second, she started to suspect but was too scared to visit a doctor. The third, she no longer needed a doctor to tell her what she already knew.

When they parted Etta told Sebastian that they wouldn't see each other again, that it would be easier that way. He was already marked to take over from Father Isaac Harrison who, after hanging on to his parish for sixty-seven years, was ready at last to see heaven himself after rhapsodizing on it for so long. It would be too hard for him, she felt, to commit to the church if she was always lingering in the background. They couldn't be friends, of this they were both certain, the temptation to touch each other would always be too much. So it would have to be out of sight and out of mind, if that was at all possible. Sebastian hadn't wanted to promise but she'd persuaded him. That was when they agreed to divide the city in half. Etta would stay at the north end, within a mile circumference of her shop, and the Saint would stay at the south end, centering on the Catholic church at the crossroad of Regent Street and Lensfield Road. The line that divided them, Downing Street, would be no-man's land. Of course, it was understood that certain eventualities might necessitate encroachment into each other's territory, but at least the possibility of chance encounters was drastically reduced.

Etta had told Joe she couldn't marry him before she'd slept with the Saint. It was too much, she thought, after all she'd done, to betray him in this final way. She'd told him everything and he'd taken it remarkably well.

"I always knew," he said, still holding the hand she'd rested on his knee when it looked like he might cry.

"You knew?" Etta felt shock, followed by shame. "How?"

"No." Joe shook his head slowly. "I don't mean I knew about

you and him. I just knew that it would end like this, I knew I couldn't hold on to you forever. I knew you'd leave me in the end."

"Oh, Joe." For some reason this confession made Etta feel sorrier than all the rest of it. That her fiancé held himself in such slight regard, that he'd been resigned to the inevitability of her betrayal even before it'd happened, that he seemed to hold his own inadequacies and inferiority responsible for everything, rather than her own inconstancy and immorality, made Etta regret it all more deeply than anything else. "I can't believe you'd think that. I wanted to be with you, it wouldn't have happened if—"

"If you loved me," he said softly. "But you don't, you never did. That's why you fell in love with him."

"Oh, Joe," Etta said again. Tears sprang to her eyes. "It's not like that."

He turned to face her then so her hand fell awkwardly from his knee. "Do you love me? Did you ever love me?"

Etta looked into his wide, wet eyes and felt her heart rise up to hold him. "Of course," she said, "of course I did. I still do." It wasn't a lie. She did love him, just not in the way she was supposed to.

They bumped into each other again, a few days after Etta was certain she was carrying Sebastian's child. They stood in the street chatting awhile, both surprised by how easy it was, how comfortable they felt together. When Joe suggested a cup of Earl Grey in the teashop on King's Parade, Etta found that she wanted to go. Her body was sick with the baby growing inside, her spirit battered since her separation from Sebastian, and being with Joe felt like being wrapped in a rug and warming your toes on an open fire. She told him her news before she'd even taken a sip of tea.

He'd given her a wry smile. "Well, I know it's not mine."

"No," Etta admitted, "that would've been something of a medical miracle."

"What will you do?"

Etta shrugged. "I haven't told my mother yet, though with the looks she gives me sometimes, I think she might just be waiting for me to confess. Dad will be upset, of course, but they won't throw me out, or anything like that. I won't be banished to a place for girls of easy virtue."

Joe laughed. It was such a fresh and welcome sound, like a light in the dark or water in the desert, that Etta laughed, too. She needed this. She needed someone not to react with deathly seriousness to her dreadful situation. She wanted to pretend, if only for a few minutes, that everything was fine and normal, not life-shatteringly awful.

"Thank you," she said, after they'd fallen into silence again. "That felt good."

Joe smiled and leaned forward across the table, his tie hanging over his teacup. "Marry me," he said.

"Do you love her yet?" Sebastian asks.

"No," Walt admits to the priest. "I think I'm closer every time I say it, as if my heart follows my words, or something like that. I really like her, I care about her, I do. But . . ."

"But?"

Walt sighs. "But whatever it is I feel it doesn't even begin to touch how I feel about—" He shrugs, unwilling to say her name.

"So, why are you still trying?"

"What do you mean?"

"Why are you trying to love someone you don't love and trying not to love someone you do? Why don't you just go with the woman your heart chose, wouldn't that be easier? Rather than trying to force it to take a hand it doesn't know how to hold."

"It'll learn. And I no longer want to be alone all my life," Walt explains. "Now I have the chance to be with someone who loves me, who I can learn to love . . . I'll let go of Cora one day, I'm sure I will—"

"I wouldn't be so sure of that."

Walt turns toward Sebastian, looking at him through the wire mesh of the confessional. Walt doesn't need its protection anymore, but they still sit and talk through it out of habit, which Sebastian thinks is a shame though he doesn't say anything. Walt regards the priest curiously.

"How do you know?"

"I know more than you might imagine," Sebastian says. "I know that a heart can hold on for a lifetime, hoping for the impossible, loving, wanting what it will never have."

The priest falls into silence for a long time and Walt waits.

"I used to wonder why it would hold on," Sebastian says at last, "why it would cause such suffering. Then one night I had a vision, or something like it . . ."

"What?" Walt asks, impatient now. "What was it?"

"I'm not so sure you'll want to hear it," Sebastian says, "since you're set on doing the opposite."

"Tell me," Walt insists.

"It was just a feeling I had many, many years ago. But a feeling so sharp, so strong that it shook my spirit and I knew it was true."

"What?" Walt asks, so impatient now he could rattle the mesh and shake the priest by the shoulders.

"My heart holds on because hers does, too," Sebastian says softly. "That's what I know to be true."

Walt frowns. "What does that mean? What do you mean?"

"If two hearts truly love each other then they always will, even when they are apart. Unless they both let go. But if one holds on then it's because the other one hasn't yet let it go either."

"But that's not true of us," Walt says. "She's never loved me, so—"

"Really?" Sebastian asks. "Are you quite certain?"

Walt sits up straight. "Why do you say that?"

"I don't know," Sebastian says with a shrug. "It's just a feeling I have."

"Are you sure about this?" Cora frowns at herself in the mirror. She's wearing a dress of bright red silk with a black net petticoat and feels like a chorus girl. "Is it a trick to convince me I should be a seamstress?"

Etta casts an appraising eye over the outfit. "It's not quite right," she admits, "the red is slightly too bright. You need something deeper, more of a maroon." She turns and walks to the wall of dark winter gowns. "And you should know I never need to resort to tricks."

Cora waits in the changing room until Etta returns with two dresses. "Try this one first," she says, handing Cora a simple column of dark red silk.

"I can't believe I let you talk me into this," Cora says, taking it.

"I can't believe it took you so long."

"Only twenty years." Cora smiles, slipping the dress slowly over her head. It falls to her feet, folding her body in silk.

"So?"

Cora brushes her hand across her belly and along her hips. "It feels like sex," she says quietly, then clamps her hand over her mouth in shock.

Etta laughs. "Really?"

Cora flushes. "I can't—I don't know why I said that."

"The dresses do have rather surprising," Etta says with a giggle, "and sometimes rather delightful effects on the women who wear them."

"Well," Cora says, pulling the dress back over her head and letting it float to the floor, "I don't think I want that particular effect."

"Are you sure?" Etta winks while she offers her granddaughter the other dress: a red velvet so dark it's nearly purple, with a neck so low it falls over Cora's shoulders and a hem so short it barely touches the tops of her thighs. From the fabric hangs a curtain of jet black beads reaching her knees. The delicate strings of glass swish and shimmer as she walks.

Cora stares at herself, open-mouthed, in the mirror, turning one way and then the other. "It's . . . obscene," she says, not wanting to admit that it's quite the most beautiful thing she's ever seen, still less willing to admit that it makes her feel more beautiful and powerful than she's ever felt in her life.

Etta claps. "It's magnificent."

"Well, yes," Cora admits, unable to deny the truth of such a fitting word. "I suppose it is."

"How does it make you feel?"

Cora closes her eyes to search for the perfect words, but can't find any more apt than the one her grandmother chose.

"Magnificent," she says with a sigh. "It makes me feel magnificent."

"Perfect." Etta laughs. "And what does it make you want?"

Cora considers. She gazes at the dress and swishes the beads slightly from side to side. As she strokes her fingers around her waist, an answer slips into her heart. Walt. Her eyes widen in surprise.

Etta smiles. "What is it?"

But Cora can't say his name. She can't say it to herself, let alone her grandmother. So instead she says something else, something that at least makes some sort of sense.

"I want to know what happened to my parents," Cora says. "I need to know the truth."

"Well," Etta says, "I suppose that will have to do for a start."

Chapter Twenty

Cora sits on her sofa in her T-shirt and pajama pants. It's ten o'clock in the morning and she's got nothing important to do. She doesn't have a lab to get to, a scientific breakthrough to make, a chance to save the world or at least make it a bit better than it was before. She's not exactly sure how she's going to go about solving the mystery of her parents' deaths. What's the next step? She needs to think about it from a scientific viewpoint; solving a suspicious death can't be any harder than solving world hunger would be, in fact one would imagine it'd be decidedly easier.

Cora glances at a box at her feet, a box of cream linen edged with gold and on it, in colors that change whenever Cora looks again, are embossed the words A STITCH IN TIME. Inside the box is the red velvet dress, a talisman, an amulet, a charm, quite the most magical thing Cora has ever owned. She hasn't tried it on again since last night but she can feel it lying folded in its special box, waiting, calling to her, whispering promises of possibilities, of what might be to come.

Cora hasn't had the courage to even open the box and touch it without Etta there. What she felt when she wore it was so startling, so incredible, it hit her with such electric force that Cora needs to wait awhile before submitting herself to it again, stepping into the power of that particular whirlwind.

Last night she dreamed of her parents again, and of Walt. When Cora woke she realized they hadn't been just dreams but memories. Walt was ten years old, she was twelve. She'd stepped out of her grandmother's shop to see him waving at her from the bookshop doorway.

"What is it?" Cora asked as she reached him.

"I've got a surprise for you."

"What?"

"We're going on an adventure," Walt said. Then, seeing the spark of fear ignite in Cora's eyes, he reached out his hand. "It's okay, you'll love it, I promise. We won't be going far. It's just under our feet."

Cora smiled. "The tunnels."

"Exactly."

"But how did you—?"

"My dad knows someone at Trinity College." Walt sat a little straighter and grinned. "He's going to show us the caves."

"When?"

"Today, if you like."

"Really?" The idea of more than twenty-five thousand bottles of wine, of counting as many of them as she could, rose inside Cora and she was barely able to contain her excitement.

"Sure." Walt stood up. "Come with me."

Less than an hour later Cora and Walt were standing at the entrance, gazing down at a deep hole in the ground, a flight of wooden stairs—13 visible steps—that led down into darkness. Next to them stood the Trinity College sommelier, a man whose name, in all the excitement, they'd both already forgotten.

"So kids," he said, "you ready to follow me?"

"Yes," Cora piped up. Now that she stood just on the edge of adventure all her fear had evaporated and she bubbled over with excitement to enter this cavern of counting, all these rare and precious bottles simply waiting to be categorized, computed and calculated.

"Yeah," Walt said softly.

Cora glanced at him, then slipped her fingers through his. He looked at her with surprise. The man looked at them both.

"Come on then," he said, hurrying down the steps, "what you waiting for?"

Walt hesitated, his toe on the top step. Cora felt his nerves tingling on her fingertips.

"Will you hold my hand?" she asked. "I'm scared of the dark."

"Are you?" He looked hopeful, relieved. "Okay, sure."

And together they walked hand in hand down the steps and into the dark.

Then the dream shifted and, instead of stepping into a secret grotto of alcohol, Cora found herself in the lab with her parents. They wore white coats and held tongs while Cora, now four years old, sat cross-legged on the wooden laboratory table in front of them. At first she thought she was watching them conduct some important scientific experiments but then glanced down at the tong she was holding and realized they were roasting marshmallows over Bunsen burners.

Cora pointed to the bag of remaining marshmallows. "Fifty-six left," she said, "Eighteen point six each. I'll have the extra two, then it'll be even."

"Oh, really, will you now? My tiny, greedy genius," Maggie said with a smile. "Okay, so now we need chocolate. Marshmallows need chocolate."

"Do they?" Robert laughed. "Is that a fact?"

"It is. The low-frequency call of the humpback whale is the loudest noise made by a living creature. A quarter of the world's plants will be threatened by extinction by 2010. In five billion years the sun will run out of fuel. And marshmallows need chocolate. All very well-known scientific facts."

"Well then, it's lucky I happen to have a little something of that nature in my pocket," Robert said, pulling out a small chocolate bar with a flourish and breaking it up into pieces.

"Daddy?" Cora said, taking three pieces of chocolate. "Tell me how you met Mummy."

"We were at a lecture on molecular biology at Corpus Christi," Maggie said. "And your father didn't know the molecular structure of flerovium."

"Professor Conway called on me and your mother turned to look. Our eyes met and my mind went blank. If he'd have asked me how many electrons were in helium I couldn't have told him. I didn't know my own name."

Maggie laughed. "Blaming your ignorance on my beauty, not a bad strategy, Dr. Carraway."

"Why, thank you, Dr. Carraway," Robert said, "I'm glad you approve."

Munching on a cube of chocolate, Cora watched her parents kissing and giggled.

"One proton of faith, three electrons of humility, a neutron of compassion and a bond of honesty," Robert said, winking at his daughter.

"What's that?" Cora frowned, confused.

Maggie laughed. "That, according to your father, is the molecular structure of love."

"Indeed it is, little girl, so you remember that, okay? It'll help you out when you're older and looking for a man to marry."

"Okay, Daddy, I will." Cora glanced up from her melting marshmallow.

"Perhaps a bit early in life for such advice, don't you think, darling?" Maggie laughed again. "Shouldn't we at least wait until she starts dating?"

"The girl's a genius, Mags, she's an early starter. She'll probably win the Nobel at eleven and be in love by twelve. You mark my words."

"I already know who I'm going to marry, anyway," Cora says, "I'm just waiting till I'm old enough."

"Oh, yes?" Maggie smiled. "And who might that be?"

"Francis Crick." Cora carefully balanced a cube of chocolate atop the marshmallow and held it over her Bunsen burner. "Or, if he's dead, then James Watson."

"An older man, eh?" Robert nodded. "I can't argue with their pedigree, that's certain. Only the best for my girl."

"When I'm old enough I'm going to do something really great like . . . Rosalind Franklin discovering DNA," Cora explained. "And you both will be very proud of me."

"Oh, my darling girl." Robert grinned, cupping his hand to her cheek. "We couldn't be prouder of you right now than if you saved the world."

—

The bell above Etta's door rings and "Mack the Knife" fills the shop. Etta, having been lost in thought, drops the hem of a blue lace dress she'd been adjusting in the window. She looks up to see a shy woman in her mid-fifties, pretty but clearly not believing herself to be. Etta waits, giving her new customer space to slowly investigate the shop. Ten minutes later the woman takes a soft pink shift dress off the rack and clutches it close to her chest.

"It's the perfect complement to your complexion," Etta says. "Would you like to try it on?"

The woman nods. "It's for a blind date tomorrow night," she blurts out. "The first date I've had in twenty-five years. I'm feeling slightly terrified."

Gently, Etta takes the dress from her hands. "Don't settle on someone too quickly this time," she says softly. "You need longer to recover from your last relationship. You need to learn to love yourself first."

The woman stares at her with wide brown eyes. "How did you know that?"

Etta just smiles. "This dress will help you to heal. Every time you want to swallow a box of chocolates or a bottle of wine, just put it on. It won't take long. A month, that's all you'll need."

"Really?"

Etta nods and the woman, now flushed bright with hope, flings open the curtain to the changing room. To sounds of surprised delight, Etta allows her thoughts to drift again, back to her own marriage and the man she lived with for nearly thirty years but only half loved.

Etta never told her daughter that Joe wasn't her biological father. She's never told her granddaughter either. Sometimes she wonders how Cora might react, knowing that she has a grandfather living in the city. Of course, Etta does know, which is exactly why she's kept it a secret. Cora would demand to see him, just as she'd have every right to do. But, given that Etta promised Sebastian she'd never see him again, it would be a tricky thing. She sometimes wonders how he would react if he knew she'd had his child all those years ago. Unlike the reaction of her granddaughter, the reaction of her ex-lover is harder to gauge.

Etta was happy with Joe, not blissful or ecstatic, but quite content. They were married for thirty years, until he died of a heart attack a few months after Maggie died, and they were happy together. Joe loved Etta and told her so twice a day, in the morning when they woke and at night just before they fell asleep. He would smile and she would kiss him and tell him she loved him too. Which was true. Etta didn't feel for Joe even a flicker what she'd felt, and continued to feel, for Sebastian but that didn't mean it wasn't love. If Sebastian set fireworks alight in her belly then Joe kept a candle burning: constant, consistent and true. He was kind to Etta and loved her daughter with joyful devotion.

They never spoke of Sebastian but he was always there, in Etta's mind and on Maggie's face. Sometimes she'd catch her daughter's eye, and for the briefest second, she'd be looking into his eyes again on the last night they spent together. It was unnerving at times, how much she looked like her father. But since no one knew, there was nothing to say. People see what they believe, so they'd tell Joe how his daughter had his nose/mouth/eyes and he would just nod and smile and give Maggie a kiss. People pointed out parts of Maggie they thought resembled Etta, too, but she could never see it. Sometimes she'd stand at the mirror with Maggie and search their faces for matching features but it was only ever facial expressions and certain mannerisms they had in common: the way they both chewed their lip when thinking or raised a single eyebrow when concentrating.

Maggie was so different from Etta in every other way it was almost as if Joe and she had adopted the little girl together. Maggie could count before she could walk. Her first word was *three*. She counted to ten before saying *mummy* or *daddy*. As a teenager she preferred solving complex chemical equations to listening to punk music, which suited Etta just fine though she still couldn't understand it. With every new and unusual trait her daughter exhibited (reciting the periodic table while boiling an egg, counting the steps from the shop to the supermarket, collecting crickets in shoeboxes and dissecting dead frogs), Etta wondered if these were things that Sebastian had done as a child or, with the exception, she hoped, of the crickets and frogs, still did. In this way she kept her lover alive in the present moment, almost as if he'd never left her.

Lately, as she watches her granddaughter unfold, her heart gradually opening up, Etta wonders more and more often whether she should break her promise to Sebastian and take Cora to meet him. The thought is a slightly terrifying one, since it would mean first telling them both that she'd kept this gargantuan secret from them all these years. Perhaps they wouldn't speak to her (which wouldn't really matter in Sebastian's case, she supposes) or perhaps the revelation would cause heartbreak, which certainly would matter. What is the right thing to do? Etta isn't sure. Just as the magic of her divine dresses has never worked on her, so she's never been able to give herself good advice. She can see what another woman needs to do as easily as she can stitch a dress, but when it comes to herself Etta has always been blind.

Now Etta sits at her sewing table with a piece of green velvet between her fingers and a piece of matching silk on her lap. Etta often isn't sure what she's creating until she actually starts to sew; the fabric guides her as much as she shapes it, and it's always the most exciting moment when the dress shows Etta what it's going to be. As she slips the velvet under the needle Etta pauses to place her palm on the soft green.

"What should I do?" she whispers. "Tell me what I should do."

Etta doesn't know why she asks. It's never worked before, so there's no reason why it should work now. But Etta isn't a quitter. One can't be in the business of opening thousands of women's hearts, bringing them wisdom and inspiration to change their lives, without being a character of particular stubbornness and determination. So, when nothing happens, when no answer comes, Etta simply decides to wait and believe that it will come soon enough, in one way or another.

Cora is still sitting on her sofa, an hour later, counting the nails in the wooden planks on her floor boards (189, a number that unsurprisingly hasn't changed since the day she moved in) when the phone rings. She sits up. The only person who ever calls her is Etta, but never during the day when she's busy in the shop. Unless something is wrong. Cora leaps up from the sofa and hurls herself toward the phone on the kitchen table.

"Hello? Hello?"

"Is this Dr. Cora Carraway?"

"Yes." Cora is breathless with relief. Etta is okay. She knows instantly who it is: the policeman, but can't remember his name.

She racks her brain. Why is she so good with numbers and so bad with people?

"Yes," she says, "speaking."

"This is Detective Henry Dixon."

"Oh, hello," Cora says. Yes, of course, Henry. She wonders briefly how he found her, then realizes that, as an officer of the law, he can probably find out the color of her underwear if he so desires. Cora flushes at the thought. Perhaps not. He's silent now and she waits for him to speak.

"Anyway, well," he sounds nervous, "I'm calling to tell you, or rather I suppose to confess, that . . ."

"Yes?" Usually she'd take advantage of the quiet to count the seconds and subject them to beautifully intricate long division sums, but she wants to hear what he has to say. "Is everything okay?"

"Well, I've been looking into your case. And—"

"Yes?" Cora's fingers tighten around the phone.

Henry takes a deep breath. "And . . . I believe you're right. I don't think your parents' deaths were simply accidental."

Now it's Cora who is unable to speak. She's not simply incoherent, she has no words at all. Her mind is completely blank, barren, baffled. It's an unusual and rather extraordinary experience but not, Cora realizes, an altogether unpleasant one.

"I spoke with someone—a little while ago, I'm sorry it's taken me so long, I had a personal matter . . . Anyway, he was the investigating officer on the case," Henry explains. "He didn't admit to a cover-up or anything like that. It was more what he didn't say than what he did, really. I'm probably not making any sense—"

"Yes, no," Cora finally finds her words, "it doesn't matter. Does it mean you're going to reopen the case?"

"Well no," Henry admits, "not exactly. I'll investigate your case, but not . . . I'll do it in my own time, without officially utilizing police resources."

"Oh."

"And of course I'll let you know everything I discover, as soon as I do."

"Thank you," Cora says, not quite understanding what Henry's going to do but grateful anyway. "Thank you."

"Okay then." Henry hesitates. "Well . . ."

The box with the red velvet dress sparkles by the sofa and Cora feels it, whispering to her, coaxing her on. And then, in that split-second of opportunity, Cora takes a leap of courage. "Can I join you?"

Chapter Twenty-One

"Wait."

"What is it?" Walt has his arms around Milly. They lie in bed, kissing. It seems as though tonight might be the night, until Milly sits up.

"I have to tell you something." She wants to ask why he hasn't yet replied to her question about having a baby, why he hasn't written back. But she doesn't quite dare. Just in case he says something she doesn't want to hear. So instead she'll make her other more pertinent confession.

Walt sits up, too, pulling the duvet over his knees and looking at her, nervous now. "What?"

There is only one way to do it, fluid and fast, ripping the plaster off the raw skin. "I lost your mother's notebook," she says softly, but loud enough for him to hear. "I'm so sorry. I searched everywhere. I couldn't find it. I must have walked around town twenty times, staring at the pavement. I went back into every shop twice, I—"

"When?" Walt tries to keep his voice calm and steady, though panic and fury fire through his body and sizzle at his fingertips. "When did you lose it?"

"Two weeks ago." Milly mumbles the words into her lap.

"Two weeks?" Walt repeats, only just managing not to shout. "So why the hell didn't you tell me two weeks ago?"

"I'm sorry," Milly says softly. "I'm so sorry, I was scared, I was hoping I'd find it, I was hoping I wouldn't have to tell you."

"Bloody hell, Milly, you just wanted to cover your tracks, you weren't thinking about me. All this time I could've been looking for it, too. We might have had a chance. Now there's no chance." Walt stands and starts pulling his clothes off the chair, falling over his feet and yanking his jumper on inside-out. "The only piece of my mother I had. And you lost it. I can't believe you!"

"Please." Milly reaches toward him. "I'm so sorry. I'll do anything to get it back, I'll do anything to make it better, I'll—"

"I think you've done enough already," Walt snaps, stuffing his feet into his shoes. "I think I'll sort it out myself now."

"Are you going home?"

"No, I can't sleep," Walt says. "Tell me where you were when you lost it, tell me everywhere you went."

"I've been over and over every place," Milly says, "I couldn't find it. It's two o'clock in the morning, it's pitch-black, you'll never find it—"

"Don't tell me what I can and can't do," Walt says, "just tell me where you went, that's all I want from you."

"Don't go, don't go now, please," Milly begs, reaching out to him. She can't bear the look on his face, the distance between them. She can feel the desolate hole that swallowed her when Hugh died beginning to tear open under her feet. "Please . . ."

When Milly starts to cry Walt feels his chest tighten as if all the air is being squeezed out of him. The sound that comes from her isn't soft sobbing or even heavy, throaty cries but a wail so high it's almost inhuman and so deep it's almost from another world. The sound rips through the room, scratching his skin and shredding him. For a moment he's frozen to the spot but then he steps toward Milly and has her in his arms before two seconds have passed.

"It's okay, it's okay," he says, pressing his lips against her ears, the words a lullaby and a love song. He speaks in his reading voice, in his most soothing and seductive tones. "I'm here, I won't leave you, I promise, I won't leave you. I'm here, I'm here . . ."

Milly rocks back and forth, arms wrapped around her legs, face pressed into her knees, while Walt holds her tight. As he whispers his promise to her, over and over again, her wail begins to wane, peeling away from the ceiling, dropping its pitch and strength until it sags to the floor and falls flat. When the air is still and silent again they sit holding each other until they fall asleep.

Cora finds the notebook while helping Etta in the shop, just before leaving for her trip to Oxford. It's tucked between the wall and the purple velvet chair in the changing room (146 matching purple roses are stenciled on the walls) and Cora's surprised she didn't notice it before. Then, of course, the last time she was inside she'd been too busy gazing openmouthed into the mirror to notice stray notebooks on the floor. When she picks it up, Cora's surprised to see Walt's name on it, embossed in gold. It's *the* notebook. His mother's notebook. But why would he be in the changing room of Etta's shop trying on dresses? Cora smiles at the thought. And then she remembers the woman, the one who was eating the cherry pie. They must have been here together, finding something beautiful for a special occasion.

Cora feels a twist in her chest. The more she dreams of Walt the more she realizes how deeply she cares for him, though that doesn't mean she's *in* love with him. Does it? She can't be. She's never been in love with anyone. Of course, the scientist part of her points out, that means she wouldn't know what being in love feels like, since she's never felt it before. No experiments to evaluate, no variables to adjust, no results to contrast and compare.

Cora opens the notebook. If it's a diary, she won't read it, even though the scientist side, remorseless in its desire to investigate, urges her on. But it isn't a diary, or a book of any kind. Instead of words across the page a glorious carnival of numbers and letters dances before her eyes. Cora smiles. It's a code, a puzzle, a mystery, which is far, far better than a simple diary. A moment ago she had thought to hand it back to Walt, to drop in at the bookshop before catching the Oxford bus. But now she can't possibly do that. Cora knows it's wrong to do what she's about to do yet she can't help it. Refraining from reading a man's private thoughts is one thing, as a woman she can do that. But desisting from deciphering a mathematical enigma, as a scientist she can't possibly do that.

"When will you be back?" Etta calls from the sewing room.

Cora glances up from the notebook. "In a few days I think, I won't be long." She hears her grandmother's footsteps on the carpet and quickly tucks Walt's notebook inside her jacket.

Etta seems to give Cora a slightly suspicious look as she pokes her head around the purple velvet curtain draped across the entrance to the cramped changing room. "What will you be doing there?"

"I'm not sure," Cora admits. "Henry's investigating their case on the side, sort of, and since I'm currently unemployed, I'm going to see if I can help at all."

"Oh, I see." Etta smiles. "And who is Henry?"

Cora frowns. "Detective Dixon, I told you."

"I know. I just didn't know you were on first name terms now."

"Stop being so seedy," Cora says. "It's not like that."

"I'm glad to hear it," Etta says, "since he's not the one for you."

Cora frowns again. "What?"

Etta turns, lifts the velvet curtain and ducks out of the changing room. "You heard me," she calls out, the words floating behind her as she walks away.

Cora absently multiplies and divides the numerals on car number plates as they pass, waiting until the bus is bumping gently along the M25 before she opens the notebook. It has been sitting in her bag, safely squashed between two T-shirts, waiting to have its code cracked, until Cambridge and Walt were far enough away from the scene of the crime. Cora's fingertips tingle as she opens the notebook, blood pumps fast in her veins and her heart races. She reaches back into her bag for a piece of paper and a pen, then shuts out all sound around her to focus on the delicious task.

Three hours and thirty-seven minutes later, just as the bus joins the standstill traffic on the Woodstock Road into Oxford, Cora has deciphered the first line. And it is quite the most shocking, surprising, life-changing line of anything she has ever read. The bus comes to a stop in the station, all the other passengers file out, and Cora is all alone save for an impatient driver before the implication of the words has sunk in.

"Oh," Cora whispers. "Oh my God."

Chapter Twenty-Two

Cora taps her finger against the coffee cup, beating out her nervous thoughts in Morse code. She's agreed to meet Henry in a café on Walton Street, one far from the police station and heavily populated by chattering Oxford University students, so they won't be noticed. Not that it should really matter one way or the other, since no one is watching them, but, being professionally paranoid, Detective Dixon thought it best to be cautious anyway.

He's already five minutes late and Cora, always so precise with timing, is starting to worry that he won't show at all. Why should he, after all? Why should he investigate a case on his own time and possibly jeopardize his position in the process? She certainly wouldn't blame him if he changed his mind. Cora takes another gulp of coffee. It's too sweet. In her nervous haste she'd added six sugars to the cup, so distracted she couldn't even count.

If she didn't have the more imminent matter of her parents' deaths to address, Cora would be obsessing instead about the startling revelation she read in Walt's notebook. Though to claim she simply *read* it is perhaps slightly misleading, suggesting a casual innocence absent from the dedicated attention applied to cracking a cryptic code. She can hardly hand it back to him and claim that the first page fell open and she just happened to glance down . . .

The café door opens and Cora glances up. But, instead of Henry, a gaggle of giggling students tumbles through. They aren't wearing their matriculation robes or carrying textbooks, but Cora knows they are students nevertheless, the odds are 98:6: 1:4. She'd bet her life on it, or at least her laptop. Oxford students carry that same air that Cambridge students do, the affected casualness thinly veiling the self-conscious sense of superiority at being among the top 2 percent of the country. At least in terms of intelligence, if not modesty and grace. Of course, the odd exception wasn't unknown but unfortunately Cora didn't meet the exceptions while she studied at Trinity, only those that proved the rule.

Shaking off the sorrow always accompanying memories, Cora focuses her thoughts on Walt and her mood lifts. Before Etta released Cora's heart she'd been feeling a sort of numb sadness all her life, almost as if it was part of her genetic makeup: the double helix of her DNA being composed of the usual nucleic acids, atoms of hydrogen, oxygen, phosphorus, carbon and nitrogen with additional molecules of sorrow woven into the cells. It's surprising to Cora to realize that she's never noticed this before. Probably because it had been her permanent state;

she'd had nothing to contrast it to, no comparative experiments with alternative variables to analyze and identify. She'd simply been sad. The feeling imbued her body, lay in her lungs so she breathed it in and out all day long. And it's only now another element has entered her life, something a little like happiness, that Cora can see she'd been breathing in smoke and only now she was getting a taste of crisp, fresh air.

Cora considers her past now, with objective eyes. The sadness was a dark, dense fog clouding crucial things she might have seen. This new happiness is a light, a torch that is beginning to shine through the fog and illuminate those things, especially throwing her thoughts of Walt and memories of their childhood into sharp relief.

Moments she'd forgotten float up through the fog, popping to the surface of her subconscious and emerging into the air. Cora thinks of the times Walt read snippets of stories while she sat under the willow tree in the summer, counting its leaves. He'd pretend he was just reading aloud to himself and she'd pretend she wasn't listening. She remembers when she'd sit with him on the doorstep of the bookshop and attempt to explain complex chemical equations. She'd be effervescent with excitement, exploding with neurons, electrons and atoms. He would nod along with an enormous grin, pretending he loved and understood numbers as much as she. But whenever Cora asked Walt questions at the end, it was always clear he hadn't really understood a thing. Once, when she was ten and he was eight, Walt had asked what it was she loved so much about numbers. No one had ever asked Cora this before, not even her grandmother, and she was surprised by both the question and the earnestness with which it was asked.

"I don't know," she'd replied automatically, then realized that in fact she did. "I love them because numbers are black and white, pure and clear. You can't mess and muddle them about, you can't fake them. They fit together or they don't. When I balance an equation I've done something right and good, like balancing the world a bit," Cora said. "That sounds silly, I didn't mean . . ."

"No," Walt said. "It isn't silly at all, it's beautiful."

Cora smiles at the memory. And, all of sudden, the imbalance between her heart and head finally aligns. *She loves him.* She does. She absolutely does. She has always loved him. It's clear and simple, black and white. How this fact, so pure and true, could have gone undetected by her brilliant mind for the last twenty years, Cora is at an embarrassing loss to explain.

As Walt steps into Etta's shop a piano starts to play and the air hums with "Crazy Little Thing Called Love." He smiles, used to this particular quirk of the place, having stepped through the door more times than he can remember. As children he and Cora played hide-and-seek among the puffed skirts of the ball gowns and the beaded hems of the flapper dresses. It had taken Walt a while to win her over, to extract more than a few words from Cora's lips, but eventually she had deigned to pass the odd hour in play when she wasn't working on solving string theory or dissecting dead frogs. On rainy afternoons when the shop was empty of customers they sometimes sat together in silence watching Etta sew or making endless inquiries about the great mysteries of life: Why is the sky blue? How was the Earth made? When did the dinosaurs die? It was usually Walt who asked these questions and Cora who provided answers to them with Etta merely the onlooker, soon discarded as a potential source of knowledge once it became clear that she didn't really know the answers to anything.

"Hello, Walt." Etta smiles as she sees him. "It's been a while."

"Yes." He nods, walking to where she stands next to a rack of blue dresses in every color and hue: cornflower, cerulean, cobalt, navy . . . "I'd forgotten how beautiful it is in here."

"Thank you," Etta says, smoothing her hand over the skirt of a ball gown, a waterfall of silk the color of the Pacific Ocean on a sparkling summer day. "What was it that chap said? *'Have nothing in your houses that you do not know to be useful or believe to be beautiful.'*"

"William Morris."

"Right, him. Well, I try to combine the two, of course, but things don't always work out the way one plans."

Walt regards Etta wondering exactly what she means by this. There is a lilt in her tone that suggests she's not simply talking in generalities but means something specific that he might be expected to understand. He wants to ask, but it has been so long since they've spoken properly that Walt is slightly embarrassed to presume such intimacy so quickly.

"So, what can I do for you?" Etta asks. "I'm guessing you haven't come to buy a dress."

Walt smiles. "No, I don't suppose you do any in my size. Though maybe I should give one a try, one of those sparkling pink numbers might at least take attention away from my nose. No one would be staring at my snout if I was dressed like Ginger Rogers, would they?"

Etta laughs and winks at him. "No, I suppose not. Though I think you have a particularly handsome nose, so perhaps they would." She has always rather adored this young man, always believed absolutely that he and her darling granddaughter would marry and have a million babies. Sadly, despite all her efforts to this end, things aren't looking as if they will work out the way she wanted.

"I've—well, my girlfriend has lost a book, a notebook, and I'm looking for it. I've been in virtually every shop in town and she told me she came here that day."

"Oh?"

"She bought a dress here," Walt explains. "It was two weeks ago, on a Tuesday. Her name's Milly. I hoped—"

"Ah, yes, I remember."

Walt brightens. "You do? Excellent. Did you find it?"

Etta shakes her head. "I'm sorry. She came in looking for it herself, but I told her then I hadn't found it."

Walt's face falls and his shoulders slump forward, even his ears seem to droop. "Bugger," he says softly. "She didn't tell me. You were my last hope."

Etta reaches out and rests her fingers lightly on the sleeve of his woolen coat. "In my experience even inanimate objects have a will of their own, and they won't be found until they want to be, until they're good and ready," she says. "When your notebook wants to come to you, it will."

Walt starts to scowl at this particularly unhelpful piece of information then remembers his manners. "I hope you're right," he says. "It means more to me than . . . anything I own."

"Well then, I'm sure it feels the same way about you," Etta says, "and I'm sure it'll come back, don't you worry about that."

Walt gives Etta a sideways glance, wondering whether she's making fun of him. Despite her little smile, she doesn't seem to be. "Okay, well, thanks." He turns to go but Etta still has her hand on his sleeve.

"Wait," she says, "I wanted to thank you."

"For what?"

"I listen to you reading on the radio," Etta says. "I must have heard every book since you started. You bring me a lot of joy."

Walt frowns. "I'm glad, but—"

"I've known you all your life, Walt. How could I not know?"

Walt lets out a sigh.

"Don't worry." Etta smiles. "I'm not going to drape myself all over you. I only wanted to say that you have a wonderful gift, the ability to fill people with a sense of possibility, make us believe in everything, most of all in ourselves."

"Do I?"

"Oh, yes," Etta says. "Most people think this world we live in is mundane, but you remind us that it's magical. You wrap reality in the wonder and joy of fiction, until it infuses us and becomes true."

"Well, I . . ." Walt falters.

Etta smiles. "You're one of life's magicians. You simply haven't realized it yet."

Walt contemplates her words. He'd dismiss this notion, coming from anyone else—from any of his fan letters, even from Milly or Cora—but he's looked up to Etta since he was a boy so he pays her the compliment of considering what she says.

"I've never thought about it like that," he admits. "I know people are moved by my voice, when I read, but I've never experienced it, I've never heard—"

"Of course you haven't," Etta says. "Unfortunately most magicians are immune to their own magic. We see behind the veil, we live inside the nuts and bolts, the element of surprise is lost on us. But we can help each other. Last night, when you were reading *Cyrano de Bergerac* I started thinking again about something, a secret I've been keeping for a long time. Now I've decided at last to tell him, and Cora, as I should have done years ago. That's thanks to you."

Etta sees the look of sorrowful longing that passes over Walt's face at the mention of her granddaughter's name.

"Why Cora?" he asks. "What secret have you been keeping from Cora?"

Etta takes a deep breath. "Her grandfather. He's . . . It's complicated, but he's a priest now, at the Catholic church on Regent Street—at least he was, nearly fifty years ago—I actually have no idea if . . ."

"Sebastian?" Walt asks. "Is he Sebastian?"

Etta's heart quickens at the sound of his name. She nods, unable to speak.

"He's there," Walt says. "I, um, I talk to him quite a lot."

In her surprise, Etta finds her voice again. "You're Catholic?"

Walt glances at his feet. "Not exactly, no. But he's a really good listener."

Etta smiles. "Yes," she says. "Yes, he is."

A little sigh of relief escapes Etta's lungs. She'd always believed that Sebastian was still alive and still in the same church. She'd counted on it, she'd imagined him for so long, felt his presence all the way across town. She'd have been stunned to learn he'd moved or—God forbid—died. But it's a relief nevertheless to have her faith confirmed.

Etta looks at Walt, waiting for him to catch her gaze and hold it. "You need to talk to Cora," she says. "You need to tell her how you feel."

"W-what?" Walt splutters. He gazes down at the floor, the tips of his ears turning red. "I can't. I tried. I couldn't—"

"You can," Etta says, "and I can help you. Follow me."

With an alacrity that belies her age, Etta scurries across the velvet carpet and into her sewing room. Walt follows considerably more slowly, dragging his feet until he reaches the doorway.

"I won't wear a dress, no matter what you—"

Etta giggles. She slides open a drawer, rummages through a rainbow of fabric swatches then pulls out a piece of maroon-colored velvet, an off-cut from the hem of Cora's dress. Then Etta takes her needle and thread and sews six quick stiches in the shape of a star at the corner.

"Here you go," Etta says, handing the velvet to Walt.

He examines the cloth. "I don't understand."

"Just keep it in your pocket. And make sure you've got it when you talk to Cora. It'll give you courage."

"No, I can't," Walt protests, "I can't—"

But even as he's speaking he can feel a surge of courage rise in his chest, making him stand slightly taller. Cautiously, Walt rubs the velvet between his fingers as he wonders at what he might be about to do. What about Milly? How would it be fair to her? Surprisingly, as he holds the fabric tight, Walt feels the answer to a question he hasn't asked tug at his heart and whisper in his head. *Faith,* it says. *Have a little faith.*

Cora sits in the passenger seat of Henry's car. He speeds around a bend and she grips the handle of the door, trying not to gasp. A traffic light ahead turns red and they slow, having just screeched past 14 cars, 21 pedestrians and 3 dogs. Cora exhales, fingers still tightly clasped, and stares at her feet, silently praying to St. Christopher that they reach their destination in one piece.

"Sorry." Henry glances over at the rigid figure next to him. "I'll go slower."

"It's okay," Cora says. "I'm fine."

"There's one thing you might want to know about me," Henry says, "since we're working on this together. I can tell a liar at a hundred paces."

Cora glances over at him. "You can?"

Henry nods. "Not just in a cop way," he says. "I don't just have a feeling in my gut, I don't just suspect, I *know*."

"Really?" Cora says. "So, just then, you—?"

"Well, it didn't take much of a sixth sense to see that you weren't fine. Your white knuckles were a bit of a giveaway." Henry smiles and nods at the door handle around which Cora's fingers are still wrapped.

She rests both hands in her lap as the car glides along the road. They are heading to the house of Nick Fielding to pay him an impromptu visit. They had been sitting in the café when, gulping down her second espresso, Cora found herself telling Henry everything: about her parents, Walt, Etta, losing her job and the dreams she had for her life.

"Do you find people often confess their entire life stories to you?" Cora asks.

"Not as often as I'd like. I tend to find that hardened criminals and corrupt police officers are usually tougher nuts to crack than scientists. But yes, I suppose I have a way about me that encourages people's confidences." Henry thinks of his ex-wife. "Except in some cases."

"Oh," Cora says. "I see."

"You're in love with that guy, Walt, right?"

Cora sits up straighter, hands now clasped together, knuckles quickly turning white. "I didn't say that. What makes you say so?"

Henry shrugs. "Some things are just obvious."

Cora glances out of the window as they turn into a street of terraced houses. "Maybe," she admits. "But it wasn't to me."

"Yes, well," Henry says, "that's usually the way, isn't it? We can't see what's closest to us. I have no idea what's going on with my ex-wife. I think once the heart is tangled up in something we lose all sense of perspective."

Cora nods. With a half smile she thinks of Walt and wonders again how, given that she knows and understands some of the most complex subjects conjured up by man and nature, she could have failed to see something so simple. Henry has already revealed his own painful tale, a generous offering to reciprocate the flood of personal information she'd poured out on the table. Somewhere during her third espresso Cora had told him about visiting the coroner, and the fact that her parents had never drunk alcohol, so it was impossible that they'd been drunk that night and set the fire themselves. At this point Henry had almost leaped up from the table, and dragged her out of the café and into his car.

"Are you really sure I should come with you?" Cora asks as they pull up outside Nick Fielding's house and Henry starts reversing into a rather tight parking space.

"Yes," Henry says. "You're going to tell him what you told me, while I watch him for clues. He's a bit of a bastard, so he's not going to tell us anything, not out loud at least, but that doesn't matter."

"It doesn't?" Cora asks as they push open the car doors and step onto the street. "Why not?"

"Because he'll give himself away anyway, then we'll know what to do next."

Dylan chews the tip of his pen. He's been writing and rewriting the same sentence for more than an hour but just can't find the best way to say what he needs to. He knew this time would come sooner or later. His conscience would catch up with him and he'd have to put a stop to the crazy thing he'd started. He should have done it days ago, weeks ago, he never should have let it get this far. He never should have written to her in the first place. But, of course, once he'd begun it became harder and harder to stop. With each letter he fell a little more in love with Milly, and Dylan found that letting go of love wasn't an easy thing at all.

Dylan has every one of Milly's letters, eighteen in total, stored away in a dark oak box lined with green velvet and locked in the bottom drawer of his desk. He rarely takes them out to reread, since he learned them by heart on the day they first arrived, and he can't risk anyone finding them, but he certainly can't burn the letters, and having the pages, inscribed with her handwriting, close to him brings Dylan comfort. He will always have them, at least, even if he won't have her.

Dylan puts his pen to the paper again. In truth he knows that he's finding this final letter so hard to write not because he doesn't know what to say but because he doesn't want to say it. He's never been in love before, never imagined what it would feel like to want another person more than anything else in life, so much so that you'd be willing to compromise everything in order to be with them, if only on the page. And Dylan desperately wants to keep going, to exchange written words with Milly until the day he dies. But he can't, unless he tells her who he really is. But, if he does that, she'll probably tell him to go to hell anyway, as well she should.

Yesterday Dylan, who tells his father everything, finally confessed his crime. He waited for a lucid moment one night and began reading Ralph the letters. The sun was rising by the time Dylan finished and both men were wiping tears from their eyes.

"I'm sorry, son," Ralph said at last, "but you must stop."

"I know."

"Write to her one last time," his father suggested, "to say good-bye."

"Yes." Dylan nodded. "I will."

"Good boy." Ralph patted his son's knee. "You're a good boy. Now, what are we having for lunch?"

At dawn Dylan had absolutely promised his dad he'd stop writing to Milly but, ultimately, it was listening to Walt last night that finally pushed Dylan into forgoing the whims of his heart and doing the right thing. As part of a compilation of plays, Walt read the last act from *Cyrano de Bergerac* and, at ten minutes to midnight, his voice had stuck a knife into Dylan and sliced him clean through:

"How obvious it is now—the gift you gave him. All those letters, they were you . . . All those beautiful powerful words, they were you! . . . The voice from the shadows, that was you . . . You always loved me!"

The burgeoning guilt, the feeling Dylan had been successfully suppressing for the past few weeks, suddenly rose in a wave and crashed down upon him. It wasn't just for Walt, but for Milly, too. They deserved a chance to be happy together, without Dylan standing in their way with his own selfish love and his letters. So now Dylan takes one deep breath, summons up the words in his throat and starts to speak them softly as his pen scratches across the page.

My dearest Milly, this will be my last letter to you. I don't think we should write anymore. I've loved every one of your letters, and will treasure them always, but I think it's time to stop . . .

Cora and Henry sit perched on the edge of Nick Fielding's plastic-covered sofa. Cora's fingers tremble under the old man's angry gaze of pure hatred and she slips them under her knees, the palms of her sweaty hands squeaking as they stick to the plastic. Cora counts silently to herself. 68 green stripes on the sofa. 12 pictures on the walls, 5 paintings and 7 photographs. 9 silver trophies for golf tournaments. Zero books.

"So," Nick snaps, "what the hell do you want this time? You've got less than five minutes before *Countdown* is on so you'd better bloody well hurry up."

Cora glances at Henry, who gives her a slight nod.

"Go on," he says, "tell him what you told me."

A surge of panic floods through Cora's chest and her palms sweat. She stares at the coffee table just beyond her feet and speaks to that, doing her best to pretend that she's alone in the room, merely voicing her thoughts.

"My parents never drank, not ever. So if there was alcohol in those blood samples then either it wasn't their blood or their drinks were spiked . . ."

It's several seconds before Cora can look up again and, when she does, she glances over at Henry, who hasn't taken his eyes off Nick Fielding. The old man shrugs.

"So? They made a mistake at the lab. It wouldn't be the first time that happened. Bunch of bastard boffins," Nick says, "with their chemicals and science, thinking they're better than the rest of us doing the real police work."

"Nice try, Nick." Henry's voice is sharp as glass. Next to him, Cora shivers. "But you're lying."

"What the hell do you know?" Nick barks. "You never even worked on the case, it was twenty years ago."

Henry stands and walks slowly over to the plastic-covered chair in which former chief superintendent Nick Fielding is reclined. Cora watches him walk, a man suddenly transformed into someone hard and cruel and ruthless, someone who might threaten to snap an old man's neck in order to get a piece of information he needed. Cora can't see his face but she knows he must look like an entirely different man from the one she shared coffee with less than an hour ago. She can tell by his walk, by the way he holds his shoulders. This is a man who could terrify someone into a confession.

"What do you know?" Henry stops at the chair and leans in so close that Nick Fielding shifts away until his back is pressed against the chair.

"I don't know what you're talking about."

"You're lying."

"I did nothing wrong."

"You're lying."

"Fuck you."

Henry leans in closer still, dropping his voice so low that Cora has to shift nearer to hear. "The blood samples are still on file, I checked. And with her blood to compare them to—" Henry nods in Cora's direction. "—I can reopen the case based on corrupted evidence. You'll be dragged through the mud. Your reputation, for what it's worth, will be ruined. You may even go to prison. So tell me what you know."

Nick Fielding stares at the man standing above him. He spits out his words, firing them into Henry's stomach.

"I'm not saying anything without a lawyer."

"You don't have to, I've got everything I need," Henry says with a smile. "Thank you."

Chapter Twenty-Three

"What do you know?" Cora hurries alongside Henry as they walk down the path toward the car. "He didn't tell you anything."

"Oh, yes he did," Henry says, opening the car door and sliding inside. He's himself now, soft and gentle again. No longer someone Cora would be scared to meet in a dark alley, but someone she'd confide all her secrets to over coffee. Henry starts the engine, pulls out of his parking space and does a U-turn in the road. Cora slides across her seat and scrambles for her seat belt.

"Where are we going?"

"To the scene of the crime."

Etta can't quite believe she's about to do this. It has been nearly fifty years since she last saw the man whose heart she's held in her own all this time. She's wearing a dress she has made especially for the occasion: dark blue velvet to the knee with patterns in emerald green beads around the hem, collar and cuffs. A scarf of shot silk, green and gold, drapes over her navy coat. Red patent-leather shoes complete the outfit.

Once Etta had made the decision to go to Sebastian she wasn't able to wait. She stayed up all night sewing, finally finishing the dress just before dawn, and has now closed the shop in order to complete her mission, even though it's a Wednesday, which is usually her busiest day. As she walks along King's Parade, hands tucked deep into her pockets and head down against the wind, Etta smiles at the silliness of her urgency. She's been sitting on her secret for nearly half a century and now, all of a sudden, she can't possibly wait another minute before seeing Sebastian.

When Etta reaches Downing Street she stops. Fitzbillies stands at the corner. Now she can hardly believe that she's spent the last fifty years sitting in the café three times a week gazing into no-man's land, on to the street that divided her territory from his. How many hours has she wasted at the window, drinking tea and consuming near-deadly doses of sugar and hoping she'd one day see Sebastian? How had she never broken their pact, how had she had the willpower to never before cross over into his side of town?

With a single deep breath, Etta walks past Fitzbillies and turns onto Downing Street. She walks slowly now, taking her time to look at everything, anxious to see how it has changed in such an age. Surprisingly, excepting the addition of a rather soulless hotel and multistory car park, Etta finds the street hasn't changed much at all. Though perhaps she shouldn't be shocked since university buildings take up most of the space and it is an institution that holds hard and fast to tradition, avoiding change. Etta walks past the Museum of Archaeology and Anthropology, past the Zoology Department where she once saw the skeleton of a finback whale. When Etta turns onto Regent Street she begins to hurry, almost breaking into a run, the landscape now forgotten as she's overcome by the desire to see Sebastian again. Right now.

Etta can see the Catholic church before she reaches the end of the street. She has to stop and lean against a lamppost for a full minute before she can keep walking. When she reaches the crossroad leading to Hills Road, Etta lets the traffic lights change three times before she finally scuttles across the road on a red light, narrowly missing a car that honks at her as it screeches off. When she's standing outside the open door to the church, Etta waits with her hand pressed against the wall. Perhaps Sebastian is saying mass or giving a service. Etta leans forward, poking her head halfway into the open doorway to listen for a voice she hasn't heard for so long she wonders if she'll remember the sound.

Just then, a man hurrying out of the church brushes roughly past Etta, almost knocking her over. For a second, as she stumbles, Etta imagines it is Sebastian. But when she looks up into the face of the man who now holds her elbow she's disappointed to see that he's far too young and doesn't look like Sebastian at all, though of course Etta has no idea what Sebastian looks like anymore.

"Are you okay, madam?" he asks. He's American, she notes, and looks not unlike Clark Gable.

Etta nods and feels herself flush just a little. Of all the film stars she loves to watch, Gable is hands down her absolute favorite. "I'm fine, thank you."

"Thank goodness for that," the American says, smiling a charming smile, and hurries off along the street before she can say anything else.

Taking a moment to collect herself, Etta turns back to the open door.

Milly hasn't had another letter from Walt since he wrote that he wouldn't write again. She wonders if he's purposefully avoiding the topic of children, since he didn't mention the matter in his final letter, or punishing her for losing his mother's notebook, withholding his written words while not admonishing her aloud. He hasn't said anything about it since that night she cried. She hadn't meant to cry, hadn't done it on purpose to deflect his anger, hadn't wanted to show him so much of her soul, but it all just came pouring out.

They've seen each other every day since then. Nothing is different that Milly can put her finger on and point to and, at the same time, everything is different. A gap has opened up between them, tiny at first, barely big enough to slip a blade of grass through. Now though, less than a week later, Milly could wiggle two fingers through the gap and it's only getting bigger and bigger. She's aware of it when they sit together and she wonders how he's feeling, when they talk and everything they say seems hollow and meaningless, when she tries to catch Walt's eye and he doesn't quite meet hers. Now Milly definitely doesn't have the courage to ask him, face-to-face, about having a baby.

So Milly has a plan. Sex. She's going to seduce him. She's going to bring them together again. It is time to wear the dress. The red dress of silk and lace has been hanging in Milly's wardrobe since the day she bought it. Occasionally she will take it out and hold it close, stroking its soft, silky folds against her cheek, breathing in its beauty, burying her face in the lace and allowing the scent of delight and joy to soak into her skin. But she hasn't worn it yet. She's been saving it for a very special occasion, not knowing what, when or where that would be. Until today.

Walt is coming over for dinner. She's cooking him his favorite foods: fish, chips, mushy peas and flourless chocolate cake. She's bought posh candles that smell of verbena and vanilla, a bottle of ten-year-old Merlot and a box of bitter mints to finish it all off. Of course, Milly knows that all this pales in comparison to the dress. It is the dress that will reunite them, the dress that'll mean Walt, finally, won't be able to keep his hands off her, the dress that'll lead them to bed. Milly hopes, with such fervency she almost scares herself, that the particular powers of this undeniably magnificent and quite possibly enchanted dress will bring a particularly special magic to the bed when they finally fall into it.

"I've been here before," Cora admits as they step out of the car. "I mean, not just when I was a child, but recently."

Henry glances at her as they cross the road. "You have?"

"The day I first met you."

They stand together on the pavement outside the house, both pausing in front of the steps and looking up at the door instead of at each other.

"Did you find anything?"

"No. At least nothing you could call evidence. I just . . ." Cora remembers her vision—the fire, the screaming—and then running out of the house. It isn't something she wants to relay to Henry, though she suspects somehow that he won't judge her for it. Cora shifts her feet, now thinking of the lady of the house, flushing with embarrassment at the thought of seeing her again.

"Right, then." Henry starts walking up the steps. "Let's go."

Cora follows behind him, holding back. "What are we hoping to find? It was twenty years ago. There won't be evidence left of anything—"

Henry stops on the top step and turns back to her. "You never know what you'll find anywhere, even when you think you do. Solving mysteries is as much about having an open mind as keeping your eyes open. Isn't it the same in science?"

"Yes," Cora admits, feeling chastised, even though she knows he doesn't mean it that way. "I suppose it is."

Henry is knocking on the door when a ringing vibrates from his coat. He pulls the phone out of his pocket. "Hello?"

Cora steps away to give him at least the illusion of privacy. She busies herself observing the environment: 16 parked cars on the street, 28 roses growing in the neighbor's garden, 5 cigarette butts on the pavement.

"Fran? I can't hear you. Are you okay? What's wrong?" Henry says. "Are you at home? I'll be right there." He turns to Cora, who's gazing fixedly at her feet. "I've got to go."

"Okay," Cora says, secretly rather relieved. "Well, we can come back another time."

"It looks like they aren't in anyway," Henry says. "So I'll call you later."

She nods. "Okay."

Henry dashes across the road to his car. When he's turned on the ignition and Cora has one foot on the pavement, the door to number 25 Walton Street opens. Judith sticks her head out to see the young woman she thought she'd never see again, the one who'd been screaming, who hadn't been able to run out of her house fast enough.

Henry parks illegally and sprints along his ex-wife's driveway. When she opens the door, Francesca is red-eyed and white-faced, but Mateo is in her arms, reaching out to his daddy.

"Papa, you've come home."

Francesca holds her son out for Henry to take. As the boy snuggles in his father's arms, Henry buries his head in the soft black curls, breathes in his smell and tries not to squeeze too tight.

"Mattie," he whispers, "Matt-Matt. My little Matt-Matt."

Francesca turns and walks slowly back down the corridor. Henry follows her into the kitchen. Francesca slides into a chair and Mateo wriggles out of Henry's arms. Henry waits for his ex-wife to speak. When it's clear she isn't about to, he starts making coffee. Francesca rests her head on the table, long black tangles of hair spread out like tentacles, as her son shifts magnets into new shapes on the fridge and her ex-husband pours steaming water into a French press, setting it down with two cups and a bowl of sugar between them.

"I shouldn't have called you," Francesca says softly, from beneath her hair.

"Why not?" He pushes down the plunger and pours the coffee, adding two sugars to each cup. He glances over at the wine rack—rather at the space by the fridge where it usually stood—wondering if she might prefer alcohol to caffeine. Francesca drinks grappa whenever she gets bad news.

"Would you like something stronger?"

Francesca shakes her head.

"Well, I'm glad you called me. And whatever's wrong, I'll do everything in my power to help." Henry sips his coffee and flinches. It's far too strong for him, but it's exactly how Francesca likes it.

"It's not really right," she says, dragging the drink toward her. She sits and stares into it, both hands wrapped around the cup. "But thank you for coming."

"I told you I always would, if you needed me."

While Mateo slides magnets across the fridge, mercifully oblivious to his mother's sorrow, Francesca stares into her coffee, and Henry wonders what dreadful thing has undone her. He's never seen her like this before. She's the sort of woman who always remains calm, even in the midst of situations that would cause other people to panic. Apart from the last time, he can't remember ever seeing Francesca looking anything less than entirely gorgeous and glamorous, even after giving birth to their son. So what's happened? It's nothing to do with Mattie, he's certain, or she'd never have let him out of her arms.

"What's wrong, Fran?" he says gently. "What happened?"

Francesca mumbles words into her coffee cup. Henry leans forward, trying to snatch up the echo of the words, but they evaporate too quickly into the air. Not daring to ask her again, Henry waits. When she starts to cry he pushes his chair back, skirts around the table in three steps and gives her a tentative hug, leaning his chest into her back, wrapping his arms around hers, resting his face against her head. As she cries Henry tightens his hug so she can sink her weight into him, dropping her head into his hold. As Mateo plays a few feet away, Henry stands in the kitchen he built, wondering what's happening, while his ex-wife sobs into his arms.

Henry holds Francesca for a long time. When she finally wipes her eyes she won't look at him.

"Thank you for everything," she says. "You've been very kind."

Henry just nods. He senses she's on the edge of telling him something of great significance, a secret, *the* secret perhaps, the reason she left him, and so he waits, saying nothing. When she finally speaks, it's in a rush so fast he has to grab each word as it falls then play it back in his head.

"I hurt Mattie."

"What?"

"I slapped him, hard." Tears slide down her cheeks. "It's not the first time."

"What?" Henry says again. "I don't understand." His head is spinning as she speaks. He feels as if he's slipped down the rabbit hole into an inverted universe where nothing makes sense anymore. Francesca loves Mateo, more than anything, he knows this for certain, so why would she hurt him?

"What happened?" he asks.

Francesca takes a deep breath. "I'm an alcoholic."

"Hello again," Judith says, rather wary. "Did you just knock on my door?"

Cora looks up slowly, inwardly cursing Henry, while wishing she'd evaporate, seep quickly and silently into the air. Sadly, since to run away again would be unforgivably rude, she has no other choice but to look up.

"Hello," Cora says, trying to sound light and bright, quite the opposite from someone who breaks down screaming in strangers' houses. "Yes, well, actually my friend did, but he's—"

"Your friend?"

Cora can see Judith getting more suspicious by the second.

"Well, sort of, but he's a policeman."

"A policeman?"

"Yes, but it's nothing bad, we just—"

"What did he want?" Judith asks, her voice getting a little high-pitched.

"We just wanted to, um . . ." At this point Cora wonders what exactly they had been going to do in this woman's house. "I guess, look around for clues."

"Clues to what?"

"Um . . ." Cora can see her chances of getting back into the house, even accompanied by Henry, fading rapidly. There's only one thing to do now: tell the truth. She walks slowly up the steps, smiling in a way she hopes suggests both sanity and friendliness. "My parents died in your house, twenty years ago," Cora explains as she walks. "I had a bit of a . . . flashback last time I was here, that's why I—anyway, I was talking to the police about it and the investigating officer, Detective Dixon, he thought it would be worth checking your house, to see if we might see anything." Cora thinks it best to avoid words like *blood samples* and *fire* and *police cover-ups*. Stick as close to the facts as possible without causing undue alarm.

Judith frowns. "Like what?"

"I don't know," Cora admits.

"But this happened twenty years ago?"

"I know. It's ridiculous, but he just thought—"

"Okay, well . . ."

Cora sees a tiny window of opportunity opening up. "It'd mean an awful lot to me. I wouldn't take up too much of your time, I promise."

"All right," Judith relents, "I suppose it won't hurt for you to have a look. Unless . . ."

"Don't worry," Cora says, offering another reassuring smile as she reaches the top step. "I absolutely promise I won't scream again."

"Wow," Walt says when Milly opens the door. "You look, you look . . . Wow."

"Thank you." Milly smiles.

Walt shrugs. "I'm at a loss for words." And he really is; at the sight of this dress he's forgotten everything he had been meaning to say (something about their relationship?) and can only see just how breathtakingly beautiful Milly looks.

"Good." Milly takes his hand and leads him into the living room. He's early, she hasn't even started dinner yet and had of course been planning on taking the dress off while she cooked. But now, seeing Walt's face—his glazed eyes and open mouth, as if he's been drugged or enchanted—Milly wonders if she might not need to bother with food after all.

"Is that the dress you bought from Etta's shop?"

"Yes. Do you like it?"

"Do I like it?" Walt laughs. Something snags at his subconscious, thoughts of Etta, of mystery and magic. But none of these thoughts forms a coherent sentence in his head. "No, I hate it. It's hideous. Ugliest dress I've ever seen. Destroy it immediately."

"Why don't you rip it off me?" Milly smiles. It's a seductive little smile, a suggestive smile.

For a second Milly almost stops. She shouldn't be doing this, she should at least talk to him about it first. But it's the right time of the month, her biological clock is ticking so loud it's drowning out her rational mind and surges of hormones are making her dizzy. Gazing into Walt's enchanted eyes, in this moment Milly has never been happier. Not in ten years. The gap between them has gone. Evaporated, disappeared, vanished in a flash of silk and lace. Now, when she looks into his eyes he is gazing back at her, when she touches him she feels him closer than he's ever been. When they reach the sofa Milly stops walking. She draws Walt's hand around her waist and, when he's holding her tight with both hands, Milly stands on her tiptoes and kisses him.

Cora is following Judith down the corridor of her childhood home when she stops. Hanging on the wall in a silver frame is something she has seen before, a long time ago. She must have missed it the first time—in the daze and the screaming—she'd visited the house.

"What's this?"

Judith turns back. "What?"

Cora points to the frame. Inside, mounted on a background of cream and gold, is a page ripped from a notebook. The page is covered with annotated equations drawn in a thick, black pen.

"Where did you get this?"

Judith walks back down the corridor until she reaches Cora.

"We found it a few years ago," she says, "well, my husband did. In a safe downstairs, hidden behind some hideous wallpaper. Anyway, we thought it was compelling somehow, not that we could understand it, being rather like hieroglyphics . . ."

It's then that Cora remembers where she has seen these same equations before.

Chapter Twenty-Four

When she steps inside the church Etta glances around, half expecting Sebastian to be hiding behind a pew or behind a statue. Not that he would be, since he has no idea that she is even coming. But how will Sebastian react when he sees her? Will he recognize her? Will he hold out his hand or will he hug her? And how will he react when she tells him her secret? Will he cry? Will he slap her? Will he hate her forevermore?

Etta walks slowly along the aisle. This is the first time she's walked down an aisle, or indeed been in a church, since she met Sebastian, because she married Joe in a registry office a few weeks before she started showing with Maggie. When Etta has peeked into every nook and cranny of the church but found neither priest nor parishioners, she sits on a pew and waits.

It's nearly an hour before Sebastian shuffles out of the vestry. He passes the votive candles and is almost at the pulpit when he sees Etta. Sebastian stops. He stares at her, bringing a hand slowly to his chest. For a moment she thinks he might be about to suffer a heart attack but then Sebastian slowly walks forward until he's only a few feet from Etta.

"It is you."

Etta nods.

"Every day I've imagined you sitting there," Sebastian says softly. "I wasn't quite certain if you were real."

In one sentence he has brought Etta more joy than she ever imagined possible. She smiles. "I am."

"May I?" Sebastian nods at the pew and, when Etta nods in response, he sits down next to her. After a few moments he reaches out and slowly slips his hand over hers. He closes his eyes, drops his chin to his chest and breathes quietly as tears roll down his cheeks. Etta closes her eyes, too. For a full thirty minutes they sit together, not saying anything. There seems to be nothing to say. Until, at last, Etta remembers that there is, that she came here for a reason.

"I have something to confess," she whispers.

"Then you've come to the right place." Sebastian squeezes her hand and offers a little smile. "You are more beautiful than I've ever seen you," he says.

Etta laughs. "I can hardly imagine that's true," she says. "I was nineteen when you met me, I'm sixty-nine now, so—"

"—so, you've lived a whole life," Sebastian says. "I can see it on your face and it's beautiful."

Etta smiles. "You always were a charmer."

"I'm a priest," Sebastian says solemnly. "I never lie."

"Thank you, you're very kind."

"I mean every word."

And Etta can tell he does, though she still can't quite believe it. This reunion, the possibility that she has been thinking about nearly every day for fifty years is so easy and uneventful. She feared there might be drama, anger, rejection or, perhaps worst of all, that Sebastian simply wouldn't be moved to any emotion at all, that he'd greet her as he might any old friend. But, incredibly, the reunion is surpassing all her happiest fantasies. Although, Etta realizes, that might be about to change.

"You may hate me for it," she says, wanting to prepare them both for the worst.

"I doubt that."

"Well . . ."

Etta glances at Sebastian and he gives her hand a gentle squeeze.

"Try me."

Suddenly Etta has the urge to talk about anything and everything else but that. She can tell him all about her life, all the things he doesn't know, all the good and loving things she's done. Maybe then he'll forgive her this one sin.

"It seems to me," Sebastian interrupts Etta's thoughts, "since you're here, that you may have forgiven me for what I did to you. The thing I have never forgiven myself for. Can this be true?"

Etta frowns. "Of course it is. But I never felt I had anything to forgive, so—I didn't blame you. I understood. Of course I understood."

Sebastian releases his breath. "I feel . . . I feel as if you have blessed my soul."

Etta smiles.

"Whatever it is," Sebastian says, "whatever you've done, I will forgive you. I can promise you that."

"I, I . . ." Etta closes her eyes again. "I had a daughter," she begins.

Cora stares at the framed page on the wall. She last saw these equations four years ago, when she stayed up for two days straight reading the entire collection of papers that Dr. Baxter had published over the last twenty years of his illustrious career, a career that had skyrocketed on the back of his world-changing creation, the discovery for which he'd been awarded a Nobel Prize in Biochemistry. The paper describing that startling inspiration and creation had been the first he'd published in *Science* and the first Cora had read. It had centered around one set of chemical equations that had been replicated for the reader. Cora had stared at them in awe then and she was staring at them now.

"Is there something wrong?" Judith interrupts Cora's thoughts.

Cora pulls herself away from the page with every ounce of will she has.

"This is my father's handwriting. These are his initials." Cora points to a scribble at the bottom right-hand corner of the page. "My parents wrote this," she says. "They must have been working on it before the fire."

"What fire?" Judith asks, sounding slightly nervous.

"The fire they died in," Cora says without stopping or thinking, no longer caring about concealing anything. "The fire we thought destroyed all their research."

"Really?" Judith says, nerves now erased by curiosity. "Gosh, I didn't know they were famous scientists."

"Did you find any other papers?" Cora asks, trying hard not to get her hopes up too high.

Judith nods.

"You did?" Cora's eyes are wide. "Really?" She uses all her

remaining willpower to resist shaking Judith hard and demanding more information. "Do you happen to still have them?" she squeaks, with a failed attempt at nonchalance.

"I'm not sure," Judith says, "we may have. I don't know if Don threw the rest of them out or not."

Cora suppresses a rush of panicked fury and swallows a scream. Her hands start shaking at her sides. "If he didn't, do you know where they might be?"

Judith considers this, brow furrowed in concentration. Cora watches, trying desperately to keep her promise not to scream.

"Well . . . I suppose, if he didn't recycle them, then they might be stashed somewhere in the mess of my office," Judith offers. "But goodness knows where. The place is a mess, it'd take an age to find them, if we ever did."

Cora understands the subtext of this statement and knows that her only response should be to nod, smile, thank Judith for her time and excuse herself without any further impositions. Under any other circumstances she would. But this means too much, the stakes are too high, she will simply have to bite the bullet and be rude.

"Could we just take a look?" Cora asks in her gentlest voice. "It'd mean an awful lot to me if we might find them." She still can't quite make sense of the implications of what she's just found. Does it mean that her employer, her mentor, her hero, has stolen her parents' work? Does it mean that he killed them for it? She can't quite believe that. Not now, not yet. But she needs to know the truth. And, most important of all, secure her parents their rightful place in the history of great scientific discoveries.

Judith glances at her watch. "I'm hosting the bridge club this afternoon," she says. "I've still got the guacamole dip to make. My guests will be arriving in a few hours. Rita is always annoyingly early."

Cora flushes with embarrassment. "We could just take a few minutes, then if we don't find them . . ."

Judith sighs. "Couldn't you come back another day?"

You don't understand! Cora wants to scream. *I can't wait another second, let alone another day!*

"It's just, well, I don't live in Oxford," she offers instead. "I came up on the bus. I left my grandmother at home and—"

Judith huffs again. "All right then, we'll just take a peek." She turns in the direction of the stairs. "Come on, be quick."

"Thank you, thank you, thank you," Cora says, scampering up the sixteen steps after her.

"If you'd told me about her I would have left the church," Sebastian says. "I never would have left you alone. Didn't you know that?"

Etta nods. "That's why I couldn't tell you."

"But, I don't . . ."

"You were meant to be a priest," Etta says softly. "I could see that, as clearly as I could see anything. We couldn't take you away from your greatest passion, the meaning and purpose of your life. It wouldn't have been right."

Sebastian scoops up Etta's hand and holds it between his own. "I wouldn't have cared if I'd had you instead, and a baby, I wouldn't have missed it—"

Etta gazes up at Sebastian. His blue eyes are nearly gray now and misty, as if he's looking at her through a fog. His jaw is softer but still strong. With the hand that he's not holding Etta reaches up and cups his chin.

"Perhaps not at first," she says softly, "but you would have, sooner or later. When you'd been working ten years in a stuffy office, when the glow of love had become commonplace, the spark in your spirit would have gone out."

Sebastian shakes his head. "You both would have been more than enough."

"No," Etta says, her voice firm. "I've seen it before. I saw it in my own father. Some men are meant for marriage, some aren't. I couldn't have done that to you, it wouldn't have been right."

Sebastian gives a sigh of surrender. "I can't convince you," he says. "It's too late now to show you how I would have loved you, but I know it's true. And anyway, I haven't been the priest I hoped I would be. I wanted to serve God and help humanity. Now I think I would have done a better job of it as a husband and father. I certainly would have been happier."

Etta, having been about to say something else, is stopped by his words. She had been so convinced of her choice, had believed so strongly that she'd saved Sebastian from a life of regret. But he sounds so certain of his feelings that now Etta wonders if she'd made the right choice after all, or if she sacrificed a lifetime of love for no reason at all.

"Can I see her?" Sebastian asks. His voice is tentative, as if he has no right to such a thing. "Do you have a photograph? Or perhaps I might maybe meet her one day . . ." His voice is so cautious, yet so full of hope, that Etta feels her heart break all over again that she has to tell him such a hideous thing.

"She died. Twenty years ago. In a fire," Etta says, so quietly she can hardly hear herself. These facts are enough for now, she thinks. Talk of suspicious circumstances and the like can wait. "I'm sorry, I'm so sorry to be telling you this."

Etta takes her hand from between Sebastian's, buries her face in her palms and starts to sob. Her shoulders shake.

"It's not your fault," Sebastian says. "Please don't speak of it anymore. I don't want you to suffer like this."

"But," Etta's voice is muffled, "I took your daughter. You never knew her. That *is* my fault, that is—"

"No." Sebastian shakes his head. "She was never mine. She was yours and now she is God's."

"But . . ." Etta shakes her head too, still sobbing. "But . . ."

"No," Sebastian says again. "Don't punish yourself. You have already borne suffering far too great for me to imagine. I have found and lost a daughter in the same hour. You loved her for a lifetime. I am the one who is sorry."

Sebastian holds Etta, his hands just resting on her shoulders, until at last she is silent again. Then she looks up at him, into his blue-gray eyes, with the slightest smile of hope.

"You have a granddaughter."

It took Judith and Cora two hours and thirty-seven minutes to find what they were looking for. Cora had been counting on the probability that once Judith started the search, unearthing old boxes and riffling through personal papers, the momentum of the mystery would pull her along until the end. Luckily for Cora, Judith's guacamole got forgotten in her curiosity.

What was left of her parents' papers fills a shoebox. After tipping up the entire contents of Judith's office (14 boxes, 29 files, 47 envelopes) that was all they found. But it was more than Cora had ever had of her parents before and she wept when Judith handed it over.

While Cora sat on the carpet holding the papers in her lap,

tears running down her cheeks, Judith made a quick exit to get on with preparing her long-overdue dip. When Cora finally wipes her eyes and descends the stairs, she stands in the doorway to the kitchen holding the burgeoning shoebox.

"I'm sorry about the . . . crying."

Judith waves avocado-smudged fingers in Cora's direction. "Take the box with you. And the one on the wall," she says. "It clearly means much more to you than it does to us."

"Really?" Cora asks, relieved since this means she won't now have to beg for or steal it. Either way, she hadn't been planning on leaving the house without it. Or the box. "That's very kind of you, thank you."

"You're welcome," Judith says. "But please, don't ever come back again."

"I won't." Cora nods. "I promise."

Gushing *thank yous*, Cora turns from the general mess of the chrome and marble kitchen and hurries back down the corridor to snatch the frame off the wall before the lady of the house changes her mind.

Dylan hasn't written another letter since his last one to Milly. Walt's unopened fan mail piles up in boxes and drawers, pricking Dylan with guilt every time he sees them. He'll get back to being an agony aunt to the lovelorn and lonely as soon as his own heart has healed just enough. But right now the idea of even picking up a pen makes him think of Milly. When he writes them this time, though, he won't sign Walt's name. He'll be himself, though exactly who that is, he isn't sure anymore.

For the last few weeks, writing to Milly has defined Dylan. He's uncovered elements about himself he never really knew, not consciously, or understood. He'd never talked much about his feelings before, certainly never told anyone he loved them (except his father, now and then, whispered in the dark as he tucks him into bed) and never really wondered what it was that made him tick.

Milly changed all that. She wanted to know all about him and, forgetting it was really Walt she was asking about, Dylan started to look and see what he could tell her. He'd never had anyone so interested before. Other women he dated asked questions, of course, but he never really felt it was *him* they were interested in. They had the image of an ideal man in their heads, along with the list of attributes he should and shouldn't have, and they only listened to see how closely he matched up to the man they wanted. But Milly seemed to want to know everything, regardless. And she opened her heart up to him in a way he'd never known before.

The last thing Milly wrote, before Dylan ended their correspondence, was of her overwhelming desire for a child. It was then that Dylan saw—so bright and startling he couldn't believe he hadn't seen it before—the line he had crossed. He'd always been aware that what he was doing wasn't remotely right, in any moral sense, but when he realized how much Milly loved Walt, how she wanted to start a family with him, Dylan knew it was time to let go and let them get on with their life together.

Now, as Dylan sits alone in his office surrounded by the letters of women he will never meet or miss, he only hopes that Walt will give Milly what she wants, that he will make her as happy as Dylan so dearly hopes she will be.

Cora can't wait two and a half hours for the next bus to Cambridge. She also can't wait the average of 3:39 hours it'll then take to get home. She doesn't know if a taxi would make the trip, so she calls Henry. 14 minutes and 27 seconds later he pulls up to the curb outside Jack & Jim's. Seeing his car through the window, Cora abandons her untouched coffee and, clutching her parents' papers to her chest, dashes out of the café and onto the street. Henry pops open the door and Cora slides into the passenger seat.

"Are you sure you don't mind?" Cora asks for the thirteenth time, purely out of politeness, praying Henry won't suddenly rescind the offer.

"Absolutely not," he says, pulling off the clutch and speeding off down the street. "Anyway, I'm not letting you meet a man who might be a murderer alone. If he did kill your parents to steal their research, he'll kill you to cover it up. Don't doubt it for a second."

"Do you really think he could have done that?" Cora asks. In her apocalyptic excitement at discovering her parents' research and the cataclysmic shock of realizing that Dr. Baxter, whom she's admired for so long, had stolen it, she had almost forgotten what else he might have done in the process. She certainly hadn't contemplated the possible danger to herself.

Henry shrugs. "Why else would he cover it up?"

"Yes," Cora says, still unable to imagine Dr. Baxter doing such a thing. Even if he was a despicable thief. Stealing was one thing, killing quite another. And Etta had never mentioned murder.

"I still can't quite believe any of it. I mean . . . I've been working with him for years. He was my supervisor for my Ph.D. He . . ." Cora sighs. "I just don't . . ."

"Well, perhaps there's another explanation," Henry says. "We'll have to confront him to find out. Tell me everything, all the facts, all the evidence you have before we challenge him with it."

Cora nods. "Okay, well, I suppose Dr. Baxter must have been at Oxford at the same time as my parents, probably working in the same field. These papers prove that they created the genetic formula to modify wheat seeds so that they could grow without water," Cora explains. "It's exactly replicated in the research paper he published before being awarded the Nobel Prize, so . . ."

Henry presses the accelerator and the car speeds along Woodstock Road toward the motorway. One hour, forty-three minutes, eighteen seconds later he pulls up outside the biology department in Cambridge and follows Cora as she jumps out of the car and runs into the building.

Chapter Twenty-Five

"Cora." Dr. Baxter smiles at seeing her. "I've been trying to find you. I might have a lead on securing us another grant—"

"That's not why we're here," Henry interrupts. "May we come in?"

Now that she's standing in front of him Cora cannot summon any words. She simply stares at him, quite unable to believe that he actually did what she thinks.

Dr. Baxter regards Henry with a frown. "Who are you?"

Henry shows his badge. "Detective Henry Dixon, Oxfordshire police."

Cora studies Colin as he receives this news and is certain she sees a flicker of fear in his face. But in the next moment, as he opens his door and invites them in, it's gone. As they step inside, Colin Baxter walks quickly across the room to stand behind his desk.

"Cora?" he asks. "Is everything okay?"

Henry glances at Cora, but she's staring at Colin.

"We're here," Henry begins, "to ask—"

But then, snatched up by some unseen force, Cora crosses the room toward Colin, until she's standing in front of him, separated only by his desk. Carefully, she places the box of papers in front of him.

"Did you do it?" she asks. "Did you really do it?"

"Do what?"

"Did you steal my parents' research?"

A flash of guilt passes over Dr. Baxter's face, so fast, but Cora sees it.

"Oh my God," Cora whispers, "I don't, I can't . . . How could you? How could you do that?"

Dr. Baxter stares at her, his eyes clouding with tears. "Cora, I . . ."

"Did you kill them?" she asks, her voice quivering. "Did you—?"

He stares at Cora, horrified.

"You're the one who profited from it," she continues. "You're the only—"

"Oh, God," he whispers. "Oh, God. Oh, God . . ."

Cora stares at him, wide-eyed. She steps back, away from Dr. Baxter, toward Henry. "You did? You . . . you killed my parents?"

Dr. Baxter starts to shiver, as if he's suddenly freezing cold. He drops down into the chair behind his desk and begins to sob. "I didn't mean to . . . that is, I did, at first, but as soon as the fire started I tried to stop it, I . . ."

"I don't, I can't believe," Cora stumbles. "But, how, why—

I've been working for you for four years and you've . . . you've always been so, so—I don't understand. I just don't . . ."

"It was an evil thing I set out to do." Dr. Baxter speaks so softly he's almost inaudible. "I knew your parents had made a great breakthrough. I overheard them in the lab one night. And I'd done nothing, nothing to help anyone, and I wanted it, I wanted to be a part of that."

"A 'part' of it?" Cora snaps. "You wanted to take it all, you took it all from them. Everything."

Colin Baxter nods. "But as soon as I'd done it, I knew, I did everything I could to stop it, to put out the fire and, when I couldn't, I ran upstairs to wake them. That's when you started to scream."

"What?"

Dr. Baxter walks around the desk until he's standing close to Cora.

"I've never forgiven myself," he says softly, "and I've tried to give you the life I knew they would have wanted for you. The postdoc position, to enable you to continue their work—I know that's nothing. I know I took your life from you and there is nothing I can begin to . . . But I've punished myself for it, every single day, you need to know that."

Slowly, Dr. Baxter rolls up the sleeves of his shirt. Every inch of his skin is scarred, the flesh burned away. "Every night," he says, "I pick a new piece of my body and I burn their memory into myself. This is my penance. And I know it's not enough, but it was the best I could do."

Cora glowers at him with absolute hatred but, quite in spite of herself, she feels the swell of her emotions start to soften. She may not have Henry's ability to detect liars but she can see the sincere regret and sorrow on Colin Baxter's face. Still, she won't forgive him. Not now, not ever.

In the silence Henry steps forward. There is something he needs to settle for himself. "Did you bribe Nick Fielding to corrupt those blood samples?"

Dr. Baxter nods. "I almost confessed that night, when they interviewed me. But then, I realized—if I went to jail it'd all be in vain, I couldn't do any good from there. My soul would burn and I could never . . . but if I carried on in this world, I could take their discovery and use it to help, to do so much good . . . I could make amends, I could try . . . to save as many lives as I could, to make up for the two lives I took."

Cora wants to say something but all she can think of is her parents, burning to death while the man she'd admired fled from the house, leaving with their lives and their legacy. She's so lost in these thoughts that it takes her a moment to realize that Dr. Baxter is speaking again.

"You screamed and screamed, so loud," he says, "I found you first and I took you and ran outside . . . But I couldn't save them. I couldn't get back inside the house. I tried, I tried, but I couldn't get down the corridor . . ."

"No, you didn't," Cora snaps. "You didn't save me."

"Then how did you escape," Dr. Baxter asks softly, "when they died?"

"I, I, they saved me, somehow they saved me." Cora grasps for answers, for memories, she doesn't have. "I don't know how, but they did."

Colin Baxter shakes his head. "It was me," he says softly, "I saved you."

In the corner of the room Henry gives a little cough. "He's telling the truth."

Cora glances over at him. Then she turns back to her former employer and shrugs. "It doesn't mean anything. You killed them. Nothing matters after that."

Dr. Baxter nods. "I've tried to turn myself in, a million times, and then I'd think that it would be better to live my sentence out here, instead of in jail, where I could do nothing—"

"You don't have that choice anymore," Cora says. "Now you're going to jail for the rest of your life."

"I know. And I'm sorry, not for that, but for what I did. To them, and to you. Every day of my life. I truly, truly am."

Cora glances at Henry, who nods.

"Well, I suppose I'm glad for that," she says. "But it doesn't change what you did. And I'm going to make sure you're punished for it."

Henry glances at the office walls, at the pictures of Colin Baxter in Africa surrounded by children, at the framed certificates and newspaper clippings. He coughs so Cora looks at him again.

"Are you sure?" he asks.

"Of what?"

"That you want a man, albeit one who has done something so dreadful, to be imprisoned when he could be out there, saving people's lives?"

Cora is silent for a moment. "He shouldn't be out there. He killed my parents. I don't care if he didn't mean to. It was his fault. And now he's saving people with stolen ideas and—"

"That doesn't alter the fact," Henry interrupts gently, "that he's doing it. Despicable as his actions were, it seems also that he's someone who does a lot of good."

"I don't care," Cora snaps. "It doesn't matter. He's going to pay for what he did. That's all I care about."

"Is it?"

"Yes." Cora spits the word at Henry's feet.

"No, it's not," Henry whispers, "you're lying."

"I'm not," Cora protests, her words drenched in sorrow. Tears fill her eyes and fall down her cheeks. "I'm not."

"Sorry," Dr. Baxter says, stepping toward her. "I'm so, so . . ."

Cora glowers at him. Then she raises her right hand and slaps him hard. Then again. Henry winces. Colin doesn't make a move to his red cheek but closes his eyes in surrender.

"Fuck you," Cora says. "Fuck you."

Colin Baxter just nods.

"You deserve to die for what you did," she says, and he nods again. "And, personally, I wish you would. But I won't be the one to take you away from what you're doing. If I did then I suppose I'd be doing something . . . Whatever, I won't, but I'll be watching you and you'd better save a bloody lot of people or . . ."

"I will, I, thank—"

"Don't thank me," Cora snaps. "You're the last person I'm doing this for. And you'll never make up for what you did, not if you save the whole world. But that's what my parents always wanted to do and, since you stole their work, now you'll keep doing it in their memory, every day for the rest of your life. And you'd better set the record straight—publically—you'd better give them the credit they deserve. You owe them that much, at the very least."

Dr. Colin Baxter says nothing, but nods.

Their office was downstairs, which was a stroke of luck. Although it shouldn't really be called luck, given what he was about to do. He didn't deserve a lucky break; that much was certain. Dr. Baxter fumbled with his torch, stumbling along the dark corridor. Warm, wet blood dripped slowly down the fingers of his right hand. Tiny shards of glass still pricked his skin from where he'd fumbled breaking the windowpane in the back door.

He found the safe almost immediately. Of course he couldn't crack it, he wasn't a thief, after all. But he kept looking, hoping they'd made copies, or left scribblings of calculations he could decipher. And then, less than half an hour later, he got lucky again. He found more than simply a copy. It was a folder—upon which were inscribed the words FINAL DRAFT FOR SCIENCE MAGAZINE—containing ten pages of type, pages covered with formulas and equations so close to the ones he'd been working on himself for the past decade, only—he could see straightaway—these worked. It was a major breakthrough in sustainable farming, a huge step toward a solution to world hunger that he'd been striving for every hour of every day of his twenty-year career. Now he held it, he had it, it belonged to him. When Dr. Baxter pulled the half bottle of sambuca out of his bag, he hesitated. Was he really about to do this? Was it possible?

He mustn't think about it, that was the answer. If he thought about it now, he certainly wouldn't do it. He'd turn around and run. Indeed, he was only here in the first place because the contents of the other half of the sambuca bottle were currently sloshing in his stomach and firing adrenaline through his blood. Dr. Baxter dropped the bottle to the floor. Clear liquid splashed the bookshelves and the hem of his trousers. He flinched, stepping back. It felt as if an hour passed until he flicked the lighter on, but it might have been less than a minute, even a few seconds.

The flare of the fire was so sharp and fast that he cried out. The heat was instant, flames lapping at the floor, engulfing papers and debris, swallowing the empty bottle. It was no longer an idea, it was happening. It was happening and he had done it. What had he done? *What the hell had he done?* Dr. Baxter looked wildly around the room, looking for something, anything that could be used to put out the fire. But everything was flammable, everything he could take hold of would only make it worse.

He sprinted out of the room—filling with fire and smoke—and turned into the hallway. Panic swept through his body, his heart beating so fast, his stomach lurching, his hands shaking. Dr. Baxter ran through the house, hoping desperately he was heading for the kitchen. As he passed the stairway he heard the screaming. He stopped, frozen. At first he thought it was Maggie and then—in the next moment—he realized it was a girl. A little girl.

Dr. Baxter nearly collapsed against the wall, paralyzed by the sudden urge to throw himself on the fire to put it out. He'd forgotten about the girl. How the hell could he have forgotten about the girl? She slept in the lab sometimes, while Maggie and Robert were working late; she ran up and down the corridors, giggling and calling out, inviting the biochemistry students to join in her games. Cora. Little Cora Carraway.

Dr. Baxter snatched the stair railing and pulled himself up two or three steps at a time—he almost slipped on a partially unwrapped present halfway up the stairs but caught himself in time. The air was filling with smoke and he ran as fast as his triple-beating heart would allow. He turned right at the top, with no clue where he was going, following the siren call of the scream. He started to shout himself, a sharp warning screech to alert the parents, needing to pierce their dreams and pull them out of their beds. When he reached her room, Dr. Baxter ran in and snatched up the screaming girl, holding her tight to his chest, pulling his coat over her head to keep her air clean. With every breath he took, the smoke was sweeping into his lungs, and—in a snap decision he's regretted every second of his life since—Colin Baxter didn't run farther down the corridor but turned down the stairs. As he clutched Cora (now silent) to his chest, he kept shouting for help as long as he could, reaching with his breath instead of his hands, until he was out of the door and onto the street, gasping, gulping up the sweet, fresh air, dragging it into his lungs. He didn't let go of the girl yet, but when he turned back to the door, planning to put her down and reenter the house, thick white smoke was billowing out in hungry clouds and the flames were gobbling up the doorway. Dr. Baxter stood rooted to the pavement, unable to let go of the little girl, thinking he'd never be able to let go of her again.

Chapter Twenty-Six

Walt is walking along the street in a daze. Now that he's away from Milly he can't quite understand what just happened. He'd been going to talk to her, to tell her that, while he cared for her deeply, he didn't think he could ever love her, not while there was a chance that Cora . . . But when he'd seen her, in that dress, those thoughts had been swept from his head and all he'd felt was passion and desire. It was very unlike him. The dress, he thinks as he walks, it was the dress that did it. He was enchanted. He was under a spell.

But now that he's alone again it's worn off, as if he's walked out of a smoky fog and only a faint scent of it still lingers on him. He must go back to her in the morning, while she's in the shop wearing sensible attire. He should speak to her before he speaks to Cora, it's only right.

Walt turns the corner of Trinity Street and into All Saints' Passage. He can see the door to the bookshop illuminated by the one streetlamp and he hurries toward it. When Walt reaches the door he stops to fumble for his keys in his coat pocket and that's when he sees them: Cora and another man standing outside the window of Etta's dress shop. They are standing close, heads dipped forward, talking. Walt cocks his head toward them, straining to hear. The name *Henry* floats toward him and he catches it just before it falls. A few other words drift over: *love* and *wife* and *hope*. Crouched down on the step, Walt listens, his spirits sinking with each minute that passes. When he sees them hug each other tightly, Walt closes his eyes.

"Thank you for coming with me," Cora says. She gives a nervous giggle. "I can't quite believe all that just happened. I'm still shaking."

"Me too." Henry smiles. "But you'll be okay."

"Will I?"

Henry looks at Cora, her eyes red and arms wrapped tight around her, and wants to give her a hug. In his professional capacity as a detective of course he really shouldn't, but since this hadn't been an official police investigation perhaps it doesn't matter. Instead he nods.

"You'll be better than okay. You've faced your demons. You've done what most people never do. After courage like that I doubt you'll be scared by anything else. And a life without fear, well, that's what everyone wants, isn't it? What could be better than that?"

Cora smiles. "Thank you."

"Anytime." Henry glances at his watch. "Are you okay if I go? I want to be back in Oxford in case my wife, well, you know . . ."

"Yep, of course, please," Cora says. "I've got my grandma. I'll be fine."

"And that chap you love."

Cora's smile widens, all the horrors of the day suddenly eclipsed by the thought of Walt. "Yes, well, I've not got him yet. But I hope . . ."

Henry reaches out and touches Cora's arm. She leans in toward him.

"No hope needed," Henry says. "I'm sure of it."

"Really?"

Henry nods. "Really."

Cora looks up to meet his gaze. "You know, you are, hands down, one of the loveliest people I've ever met."

When Henry laughs, his eyes suddenly wet, and Cora doesn't glance away, she realizes that what he said about courage and fear was absolutely true.

They are together, that much is clear to Walt. Why else would they be whispering to each other after midnight? Walt might have hoped it was a first date, but the words and the familiarity between them suggest otherwise. Could this man be proposing? Asking Cora to be his wife? Walt shudders at the thought. But when the man dips his head forward to rest it against Cora's shoulder, and when she pulls him into a hug, the shadows of Walt's fears solidify and his heart sinks. Unable to bear the sight of their kiss, Walt turns his key in the lock and pushes open the door. He almost made a horrible mistake, letting go of Milly just to tell Cora he loves her. He'd have broken Milly's heart and his, too. So, as he steps into his beloved bookshop, Walt vows once and for all to finally let Cora go and be with a woman who actually loves him back.

It is nearly dawn by the time Henry reaches Oxford. He wants to be back near Francesca in case he can help her, in case she needs his support. He's still in shock. Now he understands so much more about the last five years, why she hid from him, why they'd been to so many parties, why she hadn't fought for full custody. He's been replaying their last conversation over and over again since he last saw his ex-wife, but is still slightly unable to believe it's true.

"How long?" he'd asked her. "How long have you been an—?"

"Before I met you. A long time before."

"Is that why you're going back to Tuscany?"

Francesca nodded.

"Why?"

"I thought it would be easier out there, to be sober. I've tried so many times here and I've always failed. But there, with my family, without work."

"Is that why they gave you a sabbatical?"

Francesca sighed. "They gave me a sabbatical because one of my students reported me."

"What? Why?"

"I was drunk during a tutorial."

She waited after that, as if inviting Henry to chastise her, but he'd said nothing.

"Of course they wanted to fire me," she went on. "And God knows I deserve it, a million times over. But they can't. So instead they told me to take a year off and come back when I'm sober, God willing."

For a long time she didn't look at him and when she did she

saw the look of shock and sorrow on his face. He hadn't been able to hide it. A thousand memories had come flooding back to him: Francesca drunk at all those parties and Henry telling himself it must be an Italian thing, his wife drinking a carafe of red wine at dinner followed by a few nightcaps, the time he found two bottles of grappa behind a bookcase in her study, all those clues he'd never allowed himself to piece together for fear of the consequences. And he was a detective, for goodness' sake. It was shameful.

"I knew it," Francesca said. "I knew you couldn't keep loving me no matter what. That's why I sent you away. You always idealized me so much, you thought I was so perfect. You didn't know I drank while I was looking after Mattie, that I dropped him off the bed once when I'd had two bottles of wine. You thought I was always so effervescent and sparkling but that was only after three cocktails and then last night I—"

"Stop." Henry put a finger to her lips. "I'm not sad because of you, I'm sad because of me."

"I don't—"

"I should have seen it, I should have known," Henry said. "No wonder you felt unloved, you were suffering so much and your own husband didn't notice."

Francesca stifled a sob.

"What's wrong?"

"I think," she said, "I think you may just be the kindest man in the world."

It's six o'clock in the morning when she calls him. Henry isn't asleep and he picks up the phone before it even has a chance to ring twice. He's outside her house and standing on her doorstep twenty minutes later. She hasn't said outright that she's not going to Italy anymore, but he knows she won't, she doesn't need to now. She's confessed the dreadful thing to him and now he can help her. Whatever it takes, he will do it, they will do it together.

"Thanks for coming," Francesca says as she opens the door. "I couldn't sleep. I didn't want to be alone. I've got my first meeting this morning. And—"

Henry nods. "I'll make breakfast," he says, stepping inside. "What do you fancy?"

"Coffee." Francesca smiles. "And your company."

Upstairs Mateo wakes and calls for his mama. His calls drift down the staircase and into the hallway as they walk toward the kitchen. Francesca turns but Henry reaches for her arm.

"I'll get him," he says. "We'll meet you in the kitchen."

Francesca gives him a weak smile. "Thank you."

As he hurries up the flight of stairs, Henry allows himself—if only for a moment—to pretend that he still lives in this house with the two people he loves most in the world. And he hopes, with each step, that he's closer to that wish coming true.

"You made the right choice," Etta says.

"I knew you'd say that," Cora says, "saint that you are. Personally I'd prefer to see him dying of malaria or cholera or something similarly torturous. But I suppose I'll get over it."

At the word *saint,* Etta sits up. She still has to break the news of Sebastian and, in the echo of all that Cora has just told her, Etta isn't sure that her granddaughter will be able to take any more shocking news for at least another few years.

"He did save your life."

"There wouldn't have been a fire if he hadn't been there stealing my parents' research."

"But he's going to give up the Nobel Prize?" Etta asks. "And he's going to name Maggie and Robert as—"

Cora nods. "He gave me his word, he would. So, instead of prison, I suppose I'll have to settle for public humiliation instead."

Etta smiles.

"I've got something else to tell you," Cora says, finally ready to forget all the pain of the last twenty-four hours, at least for a while. Now she wants to wipe out death with love.

"Oh?" Etta asks, desperately hoping it's good news.

They are sitting in Etta's sewing room, a half-finished dress of moss green satin on the table between them. Cora absently runs her finger over a hem of 179 stitches, then bends down to pick up the bag at her feet and pull out Walt's notebook. She hands it to Etta.

"What is it?" Etta asks, staring at the symbols adorning the pages. "I don't understand."

"I found it in your dressing room a few days ago. It belongs to Walt, see." Cora points out his name on the cover. "It's in code. I deciphered it."

Etta closes the notebook. "Sweetheart, you shouldn't have done that. It's a private diary, not a mathematical puzzle."

"I know," Cora says, "I know, I just couldn't help it. But don't worry, I won't break any confidences by telling you what it says."

Etta smiles. "Tease."

Cora gazes down at the table, her fingers on the edge of the satin. For this confession she can't look her grandma in the eye.

"I love him," Cora whispers at last.

Etta leans forward. "Sorry? What did you say?"

Cora gives a little smile. "You heard me."

Etta grins. "Touché."

"And when I return his notebook, I'm going to tell him."

"Well, in that case, I think he'll forgive the fact that you read it."

"Do you think he loves me back?"

"Oh, my dear girl, of course he does." Etta laughs. "You know, for someone so exceedingly clever, sometimes you can be incredibly stupid."

"Shut up." Cora's smile reaches her fingertips. And, all of a sudden, Etta realizes that this is the perfect time to tell her granddaughter the great secret, while she's distracted by expectant happiness. Cora stands.

"Wait," Etta says. "Before you go, I've got something else to tell you."

Walt and Milly sit on a picnic blanket spread out on the floor of the Nineteenth-Century Literature section of Blue Water Books. They've finished the ham sandwiches Milly brought and are now slowly but steadily munching their way through the cherry tart Walt made an hour ago.

"Great pie," Milly says, though she'd meant to say something else.

"Thanks."

"Will you read something for me?" Milly asks, brushing away a crumb from her lip, though this isn't what she'd meant to say either. The confession is proving harder to admit than she'd thought.

"Sure." Walt nods, pushing the image of Cora and that man out of his mind as he stands. "What do you want?"

"Close your eyes and pick something."

Walt steps toward the shelf, closes his eyes, reaches up and wiggles a book into his hand. As he sits down again, he reads the spine. *"The Age of Innocence."*

"Wonderful," Milly says, grateful for the distraction. "One of my favorites."

Walt glances down at the book again. "Really? But it's not by Jane Austen."

Milly laughs. "I do read more than just Jane, you know. Anything with romance and sexy men, and I'm game. Though, as heroes go, Newland Archer isn't much of one, I'll grant you."

Walt sits down beside her. "Exactly how many times have you read this book?" he asks, giving her a sideways grin. He will learn to love these books, Walt tells himself, he will.

"I nearly know it all by heart," Milly admits.

"Why doesn't that surprise me?"

Milly raises an eyebrow. "Okay, test me. Open a page at random and read."

"All right, boss." Walt holds the book between his palms then slides a finger between the pages and lets them fall open. He looks down and inhales:

"'That is, if the doctors will let me go . . . but I'm afraid they won't. For you see, Newland, I've been sure since this morning of something I've been so longing and hoping for—'"

Walt breaks off. "Okay, what comes next?"

"Your voice when you read, I can't get over how beautiful it sounds," Milly says, though her own voice sounds strangely flat as she speaks. "You always make me feel so . . ."

"Enough of the flattery, you're stalling," Walt says. "What's the next line?"

"Her color burned deeper, but she held his gaze," Milly says,

soft and steady. "*'No; I wasn't sure then—but I told her I was. And you see I was right!' she exclaimed, her blue eyes wet with victory.*"

Walt looks down at the book, flicking the pages. He frowns. "No, that's not it. That's the last line of the chapter. Word perfect, I'll give you that, but not the right line, so I'll have to deduct points for . . ." He looks up at Milly, suddenly sensing how quiet she is, aware only now of the shift in the air between them.

"What's wrong, Mill?"

"She knows he's in love with another woman, so she traps him by—"

"By what?"

"The usual way they did in those days."

"Oh."

Can we have a baby? is what she means to say. But when she opens her mouth something else comes out.

"Walt?" Milly says softly. "Will you marry me?"

Utterly dumbfounded, Walt just stares at her, openmouthed. He had absolutely not seen this coming. He's not ready. He can't do it. He's in love with someone else. But such is the heartbreaking hope in her eyes and such is the conviction that Cora will never, ever love him that, before he quite realizes what he's doing, Walt begins nodding. And when Milly's face lights up as if she's just won the lottery, he's glad for this at least.

Cora runs the length of the alleyway separating Etta's dress shop from Walt's bookshop. She holds his notebook tight in her hands and its words in her mouth, sucking them like sweets—the facts to back up her feelings, scientific (sort of) proof to show she and Walt should be together. Etta's momentous revelation about her unknown grandfather, a priest no less, is still shaking through her head but, incredible and crazy though it is, even the fact of a new family member is submerged by the weight of thoughts of Walt and what she's about to do.

When Cora opens the door and steps into the bookshop she's out of breath. He's not standing at the counter. Cora glances around the shop, at the bookshelves she can see from the entrance. When she can't see him a wave of nerves floods her body and Cora focuses on the shelf closest to her, counting to calm herself. 278 books divided over 6 shelves, an average of 46.33 recurring on each shelf.

Thirty-three is Cora's favorite number and its appearance reassures her. It's an auspicious sign. She will find Walt, give him back his notebook, show him what it says, and they will be in each other's arms before another moment passes. At this thought, Cora realizes how long it's been since she's been in anyone's arms and the sad fact spurs her on. She hurries toward her favorite section: Scientific Biographies. If he's standing close to a biography of Gerty Cori then that will be it, their fate will be sealed. She'll run up and hug him without saying a single word.

As she passes the Nineteenth-Century Literature section Cora stops and doubles back. The first thing she sees is Walt, down on one knee, perhaps picking up a book fallen from the shelf. Cora's heart bangs against her chest. And then she sees the woman, the one she saw before eating cherry pie, on the floor next to Walt and smiling, her face radiant with shock and joy. The woman gets onto one knee and takes his hand in hers.

"You will?" she asks. "Really?"

"Yes," he says. "Yes, I will."

For a moment Cora is rooted to the spot watching. When the woman falls onto Walt, hugging him, laughing and exclaiming "yes" over and over again, Cora turns to sneak back across the floor without a sound, now no longer feeling her heart in her chest at all.

Chapter Twenty-Seven

"I'm not sure I want a white dress. I don't think it's appropriate for a second wedding," Milly says. "What do you think of cornflower blue?"

Etta nods, trying to hold her tongue and suppress her shock.

"I think a bride should have whatever she wants. But then perhaps you should give yourself time," Etta suggests. "There's no need to rush anything."

She wonders if she should be more direct, if she should tell Milly that she'd be making a horrible mistake marrying a man whose heart belongs to someone else. But Etta worries that, since she's far from impartial on the matter, saying something would be wrong. Etta has always regarded her role to her customers as rather like Sebastian's role to his parishioners. She is there to offer objective advice and emotional support. She's not afraid to say exactly what she thinks and, if this were any other woman, she would. She'd say that Milly shouldn't get married, that she should find someone else, a man with an undivided heart, a man who doesn't also love another woman. But since that other woman is Etta's granddaughter, it doesn't seem quite right to say anything. Not directly, at least, so instead Etta suggests and implies, as heavily as she can without compromising her integrity.

"How long have you known him?" she asks. "I think it's best to wait at least a year before jumping into anything. You want to be sure—"

"I am sure," Milly interrupts, "and we're not rushing. When I met Hugh I knew straightaway, before we'd even said a word to each other. And I fell in love with Walt the first time I heard him on the radio—actually, no, when I read his letters. That's when I *knew.* I would have married him then, if he'd asked." She giggles. "And then, somehow, I asked him instead."

"Okay," Etta says, "but I'm only saying, there's no need to do it so quickly—"

Milly's face lights up with a secret smile. Tonight is the night. This time, she's sure of it. "Well," she says, dropping her voice to a whisper, even though they are alone in the shop, "I'd like to fit into my wedding dress, so we can't wait forever."

Etta frowns. "You're . . . pregnant?"

Milly smiles. "No, not yet, but I'm hoping it won't take very long."

Just then the music shifts from the slightly melancholic tones of "Since I Don't Have You" to the sparkling notes of "All I Have to Do Is Dream." Etta glances up to see Cheryl walk through the door. Grateful for the chance to avoid the sorry situation of Walt's impending nuptials, Etta leaves Milly at the rack of dresses in every shade of blue—rustling and whispering to one another of shifting hearts and broken promises—and crosses the purple velvet floor.

"Hello," Etta says. "How are you?"

Seeing Milly, Cheryl blushes. "Oh, I'm sorry, Mill, I only nipped out of the shop for a moment."

"That's okay." Milly smiles at her assistant, still distracted by the dresses. "Take your time."

Cheryl beams, then turns back to Etta. "I've brought you a gift."

"You have? How lovely. I adore gifts."

Cheryl opens her linen shoulder bag, glancing up at the green-blue walls of raw silk that shimmer bright yellow toward the ceiling.

"Changing colors for changing seasons," Etta says, as if this explains everything.

"Ah, okay," Cheryl says. She pulls a parcel wrapped in brown paper and tied with string out of her bag. "Anyway, I made this for you. To say 'thank you.'"

"You made it? How perfectly lovely," Etta says, pulling off the string and ripping off the paper. She holds the picture poem: vines of violet wisteria wind around the words, leaves coiling through black letters. The dresses cease rustling and the music falls silent. Etta reads aloud:

When you speak
I will listen
You will be heard by me.

When you reach out your hand
I will take it in mine
You will be held by me.

While you live
I will be there
You will be seen by me.

Today, tomorrow, and
All the days of my life
You will be loved by me.

"I thought, perhaps . . ." Cheryl says, glancing down at her feet snug in the deep velvet carpet. "You could give it to the man you love."

Etta smiles. "How do you know I have one at all?"

Cheryl looks up, her eyes shimmering like the silk walls. "I don't, it's just a feeling I have."

"Well then, you're clearly a psychic poet," Etta says. "So, thank you. It's beautiful."

Cora ambles along the pavement behind her grandmother. Etta glances over her shoulder and urges her on. They are walking along Trumpington Street, on their way to the Catholic church. Cora slows to a stop outside the 14 grand white pillars and 4 stone lions of the Fitzwilliam Museum.

"I haven't been in there since I was at school," she says. "Why don't we go? I feel like lingering in the Egyptian Room, maybe slipping into a sarcophagus."

"Stop being so morbid and hurry up," Etta says, trying to sound flippant and light, as if her heart isn't aching for her granddaughter.

"I think we should postpone," Cora says. "I'm not in the mood to meet anyone, let alone a secret priestly grandfather I've only just found out about. Can't we wait for a time when my heart isn't cracked in half, when I'm in better spirits?"

"And when will that be?" Etta asks, knowing that the last few days have been the worst of her granddaughter's life but needing to push her on. "If we wait forever you'll just sink into a pit. I won't have it."

She reaches out and begins pulling Cora along with two hands, determined not to let her granddaughter spend any more time than she has to in mourning for lost love. If she made a mistake about Walt, if she got Cora's hopes up when she shouldn't have, then she's more sorry than she can say. But Etta will do everything in her power now to make sure that, before too long, Cora can put it all behind her and get on with her life. Etta desperately doesn't want her granddaughter to spend a lifetime pining away for a man she can never have. Etta lived that life and she won't have Cora living it, too.

"You sprung this new grandfather on me too quickly," Cora moans as she's dragged along. "I need to think about how I feel and what I'm going to say . . ."

"That's the last thing you need," Etta says, aware of how bullish she's being but believing that it's the best way to help her granddaughter right now. "If I leave you to stew in your own juices you'll shrivel up and die. You need to move on. Meeting Sebastian will help you do that."

Cora sighs loudly as they shuffle past the fancy French hotel on the corner. She glances in the restaurant window: 28 tables, 118 chairs, meaning 472 pieces of silverware . . .

"Speaking of which," Etta continues, "have you decided what you're going to do with yourself workwise yet?"

"No," Cora snaps. "I'm taking a bit of a break, okay? Perhaps I'll have a holiday, go traveling in Asia or some such thing."

Etta laughs as she pulls Cora into Lensfield Road. "That actually sounds like a great idea, but you'll never do it, not in a million years."

"Why not?" Cora glares at her grandmother. She's about to say something witty and withering in return but when she glances up at the sky for sudden inspiration she sees the spires of the church and instead holds her breath.

"I was thinking of a summer wedding," Milly calls out from the kitchen, "the first of August. What do you think?"

"Sure," Walt says from the sofa, "whatever you want is fine with me."

The television is on and the opening credits for *Howards End* play. Milly walks into the living room carrying a china bowl brimming over with popcorn. Little kernels drop to the floor as she crosses the carpet.

"If we're really lucky we'll get one of those beautiful, breezy days," she says, "and a confetti of flower petals. It'll be lovely."

She sighs happily as she snuggles in next to Walt, balancing the bowl on his lap then taking a handful.

"Oops, I forgot the salt." Milly stands again and hurries back to the kitchen. "Pause the film for me, will you?"

"Yep." Walt leans over to the tiny desk upon which the remote controls are balanced, picks up the bigger one and points it at the television. "It's not working."

"What?" Milly calls. "I can't hear you."

"It's okay." He reaches for the smaller remote and notices that the desk drawer is open. Glancing inside, Walt sees it's stuffed full of letters addressed to Milly, the postmark on the top dated only a few weeks ago. Frowning, Walt reaches in and removes a letter. He slides three pages out of the envelope and begins to read.

A moment later Milly steps back into the living room holding a salt shaker. "Oh!" She smiles. "You found them."

Walt looks up, his face a confusion of shock and pain. "This is a love letter," he says. "These are love letters."

"Yes," Milly says, "so beautiful they should probably be published."

"What?"

"Don't you think so? Of course I wouldn't, they're private. I only meant—"

"What the hell are you talking about? You're not even trying to deny it?"

Milly frowns. "Deny what? Why would I deny it?"

"You're having an affair and—"

Milly's eyes fill with tears. "What? I know we said we'd keep it a secret; that we wouldn't talk about it. But it's not funny now . . ."

"I know it's not funny, it's a bloody shock is what it is." Walt pulls the drawer open so far that it falls out of the desk and clatters to the floor, scattering letters across the carpet. He jumps up and starts to stamp on them. Milly drops to her knees, grabbing the letters from beneath his feet.

"What are you doing?" she shouts. "I adore these letters, I reread one every day. I fell in love with you through these letters. I—"

Walt stops stamping. "What are you talking about? Me? How could you fall in love with me? I didn't write them."

Tears roll down Milly's cheeks as she clutches an armful of letters to her chest. "Stop! Stop!" she sobs. "I don't want to play this game anymore. It was silly and romantic before, now it's just horrible. Please, please stop."

With great force of will, Walt steadies his voice. "What game? What are you talking about?"

Milly gazes up at him through her tears. "We were writing to each other. We agreed to keep it secret, not to talk about it, just to write—"

"But I didn't," Walt says, "I've never written you a letter in my life."

"No, no, no." Milly shakes her head. She sets the letters she's holding carefully down on the floor, then picks one up, opens it, pulls out the last page and holds it out to Walt. "You did. You wrote them all. See."

He takes it from her and reads his name. *With all my love, Walt xxx*

"This isn't my writing," he says. "I didn't write this."

"What do you mean?" Tears run down Milly's cheeks. "You didn't mean any of the beautiful, wonderful things you said?"

"How would I know?" Walt asks. "I haven't read them."

As the shock of this slowly sinks in—the revelation that not only does Walt not love her in the way she thought, but that she doesn't love him in the way she thought either—Milly suddenly realizes something else.

"If you didn't write them," she says slowly, "then who did?"

"He's not here," Cora hisses, as soon as they step inside the church. "Let's go back."

"Don't be silly," Etta says. "Of course he's here, he's expecting us."

Cora waits just inside the ancient oak door counting 14 pews on each side of the aisle, 168 Bibles, 7 statues of the Virgin Mary, 23 flickering prayer candles in the far corner by the lectern . . .

"Stop stalling," Etta says. "Come on." If it were any other time, Etta would be much gentler on Cora. But Etta firmly believes in the art of distraction, of distracting the mind in order to help the heart forget. In this instance, a found grandfather is perfect to shift the focus from a lost love, especially a grandfather as special as Sebastian.

After lingering awhile at the statue of St. Francis, Etta glances at her watch and beckons Cora to follow her along the aisle. Reaching the lectern, they hear the hum of voices a few feet away.

"Confession," Etta whispers. "Let's wait here."

She slips onto a pew a respectful distance from the confessional and Cora sits next to her.

"How long will we have to wait?"

Etta gives her granddaughter a sideways smile, ignoring her sullen disposition. Just then, a sudden sharp sob makes Etta and Cora turn toward the confessional, then back to each other with raised eyebrows. A moment later a man hurries out of the booth, past the pew and down the aisle. It's only when he's nearly at the door that Cora realizes she's staring at the rapidly disappearing head of Dr. Baxter. For a moment she's about to tell Etta, then decides against it, keeping the imprint of his shadow to herself.

Etta nudges her granddaughter. Cora looks up to see a man with thick gray hair and a brilliant smile walking toward them.

"Hello," Sebastian says.

Etta grins. "Hello."

As Sebastian briefly clasps her grandmother's hand, Cora watches them curiously. Etta hasn't exactly been forthcoming about her history with this man who happens to be Cora's biological grandfather. Etta only said she loved him once and neglected to mention whether or not she still does. But, looking at them now, Cora would estimate with a probability of 98.7 percent that Etta is head over heels. She feels a pang of sorrow and regret for her grandmother, since being in love with a priest is about as bad as being in love with a man who is about to marry someone else.

"And this is Cora, my granddaughter," Etta says. *Your. Our.* She wants to say but now it feels too strange, too sudden.

Hearing her name, Cora looks up to see Sebastian reaching out his hand to her. She stands and takes it.

"It is an honor and delight to meet you," he says, grinning. "I must say I can't quite believe it, even as you stand here."

"Thank you," Cora says, glancing at her grandmother. "It's lovely to meet you, too."

The three of them stand in silence for a few moments. Cora looks at Sebastian again and takes a deep breath. "I, um . . ."

"Yes?"

"The man who just confessed to you," she says, "do you know him?"

Etta frowns. "Cora, you can't ask that sort of thing."

"I know, I know, but I'm not asking what he said, I'm just wondering if he's one of your regulars," Cora says, "that's all."

Sebastian looks at his new granddaughter, then at his old lover. When he opens his mouth he means to explain that he can't say anything, given the confidentialities of the confessional. He wishes, more fervently than he's ever wished before, that he wasn't a priest anymore.

"He's been coming to see me every week for nearly twenty years," Sebastian says. "But, strangely enough, until today he never spoke. And he confirmed . . ." All of a sudden Sebastian seems to realize he's not saying what he'd meant to say. He frowns, not entirely sure what's going on. Secrets just seem to slip out when he's around Etta. "I'm sorry, I can't—"

"It's okay, I don't need . . ." Cora says. "I just want to know—was he sorry?"

Almost against his will, Sebastian finds himself nodding. "Yes, yes, he was."

Cora smiles, feeling her heart lift. "Good," she says. "That's good."

Henry sits on a park bench with Francesca next to him and Mateo playing with a stick in the grass a few feet away.

"You didn't have to come with us," he says. "You could have taken some time for yourself. Read a book, gone to the cinema, had your nails done."

Francesca laughs, a hearty, dirty laugh that sends shivers of pleasure through Henry. It's been a long, long time since he's heard that laugh.

"I'd rather be here."

"I'm glad." Henry gives her a sideways glance. "Does it get easier?"

Francesca gives a little smile. "It's hell. It's the hardest thing I've ever done. But it's okay." She reaches for his hand. "Because I'm not . . . I'm not doing it alone anymore."

Henry takes her hand and holds it in his.

"Daddy! Daddy! Look at me!"

Henry looks up at his son, who's holding an enormous stick above his head.

"You're so strong, Mattie," Henry calls out. "You're even stronger than me."

Mateo giggles and starts running in circles, the stick aloft, a thick black line against the light blue sky. Henry and Francesca clap and cheer. A gust of wind blows through them and Francesca pulls her coat tighter. She holds her son's woolen scarf up and calls to him.

"It's getting cold, Mattie. Come and put your scarf on."

Mateo gallops over to his parents, snatches the scarf up and dashes off again.

"He'd freeze to death if we let him," Henry says.

Francesca nods, then mumbles something he can't hear.

"Sorry?"

Francesca looks down at her gloved hands and presses her fingers together. "I said . . ." She takes a deep breath. "I said that I never stopped loving you."

Her words are dripping with honey and sugar again and, as he swallows them, the sweetness rushes through his blood. He feels light-headed and wonders if he might faint. He grips the bench and opens his mouth to breathe. Then he nods. "I know," Henry says, "I knew you didn't."

Francesca turns to him. "What do you mean, you knew?"

Henry gives a shrug and tries to sound nonchalant. "It's part of being a policeman, I suppose. I just know when people are telling the truth or not."

"So when I told you I didn't love you anymore, you knew I was lying?"

Henry nods.

"Why didn't you say anything?"

"Because what difference did it make? You wanted to leave me. And you wouldn't tell me why. So what could I do?"

"Why didn't you fight for me?"

"I asked you," Henry says. "I asked you again and again. What more could I do?"

"In Italy we fight for love," Francesca says. "An Italian man would have knocked my door down until I took him back, if he knew I still loved him."

"So you left me because I didn't fight hard enough for you when you left me?" Henry frowns. "That makes no sense."

"No. Sorry. I'm being silly, of course that's not what I mean."

"Well, what do you mean?"

Francesca shrugs.

"Why didn't you tell me? Why couldn't you let me help you then? Why did you hide yourself from me?"

Francesca is silent. "I was scared of you."

"Scared?" Henry is incredulous. He's one of the gentlest men he knows, he's never once lost his temper with his wife or his son. "Why?"

"You didn't *do* anything," she says. "But you can see everything, you just proved it. I always felt like you can see inside my soul with a single glance."

Henry frowns again. He glances back at the grass to check his son is okay, then turns back to his ex-wife. "What's wrong with that?"

"Not all of us have souls as clean as yours," Francesca says quietly. "I had so much I was ashamed for you to see."

Henry lifts his hand to her cheek and gently brings her face toward him until she meets his gaze. "You thought there was anything you could tell me that would stop me loving you?"

Tears fill Francesca's eyes.

"There is nothing," Henry says, "absolutely nothing. You could have told me Mattie wasn't mine, I'd still love you. You could have told me you'd killed a man. I wouldn't have cared. Alcoholism is nothing."

A tiny smile slips onto Francesca's lips.

"Hell, you could tell me you *are* a man," Henry continues. "Say whatever you want, it won't matter to me."

Francesca giggles. "Now you're being silly."

Henry shrugs. "I'm a man in love, that's all."

"Then not many men love like you do." Francesca leans toward Henry, rests her head on his shoulder and looks up at him. From his spot on the grass Mateo stops playing and watches them as they move closer together.

"Mama and Papa in a tree," Mateo sings, "k-i-s-s-i-n-g."

Then he claps and cheers, throwing his stick high into the air.

Walt's mind races and finally slows as he alights on the answer. Of all the people who might possibly have impersonated him in a letter there is really only one. Though he still has absolutely no idea why on earth he would do it.

"Dylan."

Milly frowns. "Who's Dylan?"

"My boss."

"Your boss?" Milly's frown deepens. "But why would he?"

Walt shrugs. "I have no idea."

Then Milly remembers. "I started it," she says.

"What?"

"I wrote to you, when we were first together. I sent it to you at the radio station. I thought it would be romantic and I wrote things I was too shy to say to your face. You wrote back to me the next day." Milly swallows. "At least, I thought you did."

"But it was Dylan."

Milly shrugs and nods all at once. With every second that passes she is being slowly torn in half, ripped down the middle by feelings that fight inside her: sorrow that Walt isn't who she thought he was, regret at being fooled, confusion about whom she really loves, hope that perhaps Dylan . . .

Walt watches Milly's face changing and suddenly, with a great flood of relief, realizes what she's feeling.

"It was the letters you loved, that was the man you fell in love with."

Milly nods. "I'm sorry—"

Walt smiles. "Don't be."

Milly reaches for his hand. "I didn't mean to hurt you."

Walt kisses her fingers. "You didn't. It's fine. It's perfect. You're in love with someone else and so am I."

Chapter Twenty-Eight

Henry stands in his kitchen in his pajamas, pouring Francesca's coffee with one hand and stirring Mateo's porridge with the other. His son plays on the stone floor with his Legos, building an enormous and elaborate kingdom. BBC Radio Four plays in the background, the comforting hum of eloquent voices drifting through the air, bringing Henry home again. He'd only ever listened to the radio for music—local rock stations while driving around in the patrol car—before meeting Francesca. She introduced him to the joys of *The Archers* at seven o'clock every evening and *Woman's Hour* at ten o'clock every morning.

"Daddy, look, I've added a castle," Mateo says. "What do you think?"

Henry lifts the pot of porridge off the stove, sets the French press on the counter and crouches down on the floor to inspect the newest development in Legos.

"Here it is," Mateo says, pointing to a tower of red and green bricks.

"It's very cool," Henry says and, when his son frowns, adds, "really quite magnificent."

Mateo grins. "Papa?"

"Yes?"

"Now that you are back home again, can I have a baby brother?"

Henry regards his son with a smile. "Whatever gave you that idea?"

Mateo shrugs. "Tommy has one, he's okay. I thought I might get one, too."

Henry smiles and tousles his son's hair. "I don't know, Mattie, we'll have to see. But don't ask your mama about it, okay?"

"Why not?"

Henry considers, wondering how best to explain. "She's just feeling a bit—" He glances up, hearing the radio presenter say a name he recognizes.

". . . has, in an unprecedented move, relinquished his Nobel Prize and named two deceased scientists, Drs. Robert and Margaret Carraway, as the original authors of . . ."

"Papa?"

"Just a second, Matt-Matt." Henry stands, reaches for the radio and turns the volume up.

". . . Dr. Colin Baxter said in a statement that he deeply regretted his actions in taking credit for their research and would be setting up the Carraway Foundation to fund aid work, specifically the planting and distribution of sustainable foods in third world countries. In other news . . ."

Henry leans against the counter, thinking of Cora and smiling.

"Papa, can I have my breakfast now?"

Henry turns back to his son. "Of course, Matt-Matt, of course you can."

Milly knocks on the office door, thinking again what a strange situation she has got herself into: thinking she was in love with a man with an enchanting voice and then discovering she was actually in love with a man she'd never met. Now that she's about to meet him Milly is oddly calm. Even though she's never seen his face, and has no idea of the color of his hair, if indeed he has any hair, or the color of his eyes or how tall he is. Not that she cares, not at all. She only hopes that he's as uninterested in physical beauty and not too young or too handsome to be interested in her.

Fifteen seconds later, when Dylan opens the door, she can only gawp at him. He is, without a doubt, one of the handsomest men she's ever seen. Suddenly Milly feels shorter, fatter, uglier and older than she's ever felt in her life. But, when his face lights up with delight at the sight of her, all of a sudden Milly doesn't feel so frumpy anymore.

They stand in the doorway and stare at each other for what feels like both a single second and an eternity. Then Dylan steps back.

"Come in."

Milly steps inside and stands in the middle of the room, before Dylan nods at the small sofa in the corner.

"Please, sit down. Would you like tea? Coffee? Anything?"

"No thanks." Milly shakes her head and perches on the edge of the sofa. Smoothing her skirt over her knees, she glances around the room: books on the shelves, open boxes overflowing with letters scattered across the floor, pictures of exotic places on the walls, then back at Dylan.

"I don't know what to say."

"I know." He grins. "Me neither."

As the shock of it all slowly begins to subside, Milly thinks of something, the thought she has been thinking, mulling over in her mind for nearly every minute of the last forty-eight hours.

"Why did you do it?" she asks.

"I've been trying to think of an answer to that, a good, sane answer that doesn't make me sound like a crazy person, ever since Walt called." Dylan starts pacing up and down the room. He gestures at the boxes around him. "I started answering his fan mail. All these women were writing to Walt with their problems and broken hearts and it seemed so sad just to leave their letters flapping in the wind . . . Not that I'm the sort of man who'd usually do that sort of thing, not before I started listening to him read. It changed me, I don't know how but—"

Milly nods. "I know what you mean."

"Exactly, right? He's so strangely . . . enchanting. When he started reading *Sense and Sensibility* I turned from the tough, rugged specimen of a man I've always been"—Dylan gives a self-deprecating smile—"and became some sort of gooey little girl. When your letter arrived, I started reading it before I knew I shouldn't. And by the time I finished it, well, I couldn't help myself. I had to know you, I had to keep knowing you. So I sat down and wrote back."

Milly closes her eyes and sighs.

"I'm sorry," Dylan says. "I'm so sorry I ruined everything for you. Do you hate me for it?"

Milly opens her eyes and smiles. "How could I possibly hate someone who says something like that? And anyway, you didn't ruin anything."

Dylan stops pacing, overcome with relief. "Really?"

Milly nods. "Everything you wrote, your letters, I loved every word. I must have read them a million times over. I could quote them all to you, line for line, right now. Oh God," Milly says, suddenly blushing, "I shouldn't have just admitted that."

"It's okay." Dylan smiles. He walks over to the sofa, then crosses his legs and sits on the floor in front of her. "I could do the same with yours. But I'd just be mortified with embarrassment if you reminded me what I wrote."

He dips his head toward his lap and picks at the rug on the floor between his legs.

"Yes, of course," Milly says, studying the thick dark curls of which she now has an unsullied view, "me too."

"So, I was wondering . . ." Dylan looks up, the vanished curls replaced by his beautiful face and the gaze of his deep blue eyes.

Milly swallows.

"I was wondering if . . ." Dylan laughs. "Bloody hell, I never realized how much easier writing is than speaking—you don't have to look at someone while you do it. It's hard to find the words for—"

"Would you like to go for a walk," Milly offers, "and see if, after all those letters, we still have anything to say to each other?"

"Those are the perfect words." Dylan smiles. "Yes, I'd like that very much."

I'd like you to meet my father. I'd like us to get married and have a million babies. These are the things Dylan wants to say next. But so as not to scare Milly off, he decides to save such sentiments for a while. At least until tomorrow.

Cora steps into the cemetery ahead of her grandparents. Reaching the pebbled path running alongside the medieval stone church, she turns back to see Etta and Sebastian walk through the wrought-iron gate. She watches her grandmother ambling across the grass and all of a sudden realizes that Etta is being slow on purpose, to give them more time alone.

Cora hurries along the path and ducks around the corner into a graveyard surrounded by ancient walls obscured by heavy ivy hanging to the ground. Cora steps carefully around the graves, 47 in total, most of them hundreds of years old, one from 1423: WALTER COOPER, DEAREST HUSBAND, REMEMBERED AND LOVED ALWAYS. Cora thinks of Walt, then shakes her head to dislodge the thought.

When Cora arrives at the two headstones at the farthest corner of the garden of graves she stops at the edge where the grass is scattered with wildflowers: 58 daisies, 23 cornflowers, 17 violets, 9 foxgloves . . .

"Hi, parents," Cora says, slipping a small packet out of her coat pocket. "I've brought you something." She opens her palm and tips out a handful of seeds. "Your legacy," Cora explains, as she scatters them over the grass among the flowers.

She takes a step back, smiling, though tears fill her eyes. "This is a sample of that rather special wheat that will grow anywhere, though of course you already know that." Cora hears her grandparents approaching through the grass. Etta gives a self-conscious cough from a few feet away.

"Everyone is talking about you," Cora whispers. "Daddy, do you remember when you said to me: *I couldn't be more proud if you went out and saved the world.* Well, I suppose, you and Mum sort of did that. And I couldn't be more proud of you both, too."

Etta's hand rests lightly on Cora's back and she turns to her grandmother with a smile, quickly wiping her eyes. Sebastian tentatively touches the edge of Cora's arm and the three of them stand in a line, with Cora in the middle, each tucked inside their own thoughts.

"Hello, Maggie," Sebastian says softly.

"Mags," Etta says, "my darling girl."

"Don't forget Dad," Cora adds.

"Yes, of course," Etta says. "Your father was a good man, a great man. He and your mother were as happy as two people could possibly be. They met at university, they had ten years together," Etta tells Sebastian. "It's not an eternity, but it is more happiness than many get in a lifetime."

"More than we got," Sebastian says softly.

"We had, what?"

"Two months."

As her grandparents talk Cora stands between them, feeling the sizzle in the air, wondering if she should sneak away and leave them alone, but feeling rooted to the spot.

"Speaking of lifetimes," Sebastian begins. "I've been thinking . . ."

After a moment or two of silence Etta gives a little cough. "Yes?"

"Well, the thing is," he says, "I've given most of my life to God. And I've been thinking I'd like to give the rest of it to you, if you'll have me."

After postponing the inevitable for as long as possible, Cora pushes open the door to Walt's bookshop with his notebook in hand. Praying that she'll find him alone this time, unencumbered by a cherry-pie-eating fiancée, Cora ambles along the entrance aisle of books, counting the totals on each shelf at eye-level as she walks: 33, 45, 28, 37, 41 . . .

Walt is standing at the counter alone with stacks of books laid out in front of him. One by one he lifts them off the piles and sticks bright white price labels on their back covers.

Cora creeps forward, half thinking she might just sneak the notebook onto the counter edge then dash off without him noticing her. But when she is within twenty feet of him, Walt looks up. A shadow of a frown sweeps over his face and he says nothing. Cora's chest tightens as she walks slowly up to the counter, squeezing out her breath and all the words she'd prepared to say, leaving her mind blank so all she can say is "Hello."

Walt nods.

Wanting to get out of there as soon as possible and bang her head hard against a wall, Cora holds out the notebook to him.

"I found this, it's yours."

"Bloody hell!" Walt's stony face suddenly illuminates with joy. "Where on earth did you find it?"

"At Etta's shop, in the changing room."

"But I went there, I looked . . . Anyway, it doesn't matter. Thank you. Thank you so much," Walt says, though he doesn't look at Cora as he speaks, just at the notebook, flipping the pages, tracing his fingers over the symbols, letters and numbers.

It's the perfect moment for Cora to turn and leave. She can walk away now, she can crawl across the carpet, and Walt won't notice. But something stops her. She isn't sure what it is, or why, but Cora waits. She holds on to the counter to steady herself before speaking.

"That's a pretty incredible code your mother wrote," Cora says, thinking of the things she has read in its pages: prophecies and predictions made by a mother for her son. She frowns, wondering at the unscientific strangeness of it all.

"Yes," Walt says, "and I've spent my whole life trying to decode it. I'm so happy to have it back, you have no idea."

"You don't know what it says?" Cora asks.

"No, it's bloody impossible. I haven't got the brain for it. I'm not sure I ever will, but of course I'll never stop trying. I just don't understand why she wrote it like this. What was the point? I don't know."

Cora just stares at him.

"What?"

"I've read it, I mean, I—"

Walt drops the notebook. It falls with a clatter to the counter. "Are you joking?"

"No."

"So what does it say?"

A spark of hope flickers to life in Cora's chest. "Shall I read it to you?"

"Yes, yes." Walt nods. "Yes, please."

"Okay," Cora says and, with her blood pumping in her ears and her heart pounding in her chest, she reads him the first line. As the words float through the air between them Walt's mouth drops open.

"Really?" he asks at last. "Is that really what it says?"

"Yes." Cora smiles. "Yes, it is."

"Bloody hell."

"Indeed."

"Do you think . . . ? Could it . . . ?" Walt ventures. "But it can't be true."

"Why not?"

"Because you've got a boyfriend."

"What?" Cora asks, incredulous. "No, I haven't. I've never—anyway, you're engaged."

"I'm not," Walt says. "I was, for about a day."

"Really?" Cora exclaims, trying to tone down her delight. "Really?"

Walt nods. And, without another word, he takes three steps around the counter to stand in front of the woman he has loved all his life.

"Really," he says softly, inclining his face toward hers.

"Really," she repeats, tipping her head up to him.

When their lips are only an inch apart Walt speaks again, in a whisper, postponing the moment he's waited twenty years for, just a little longer. The little piece of velvet Etta gave him, the one he's never taken out of his pocket, tugs at its tiny red threads. And then he kisses her for the first time, light and quick, a promise and prelude of what is to come.

"My goodness," Cora says softly, "that's amazing."

"Why, thank you," Walt says, with a little bow of his head.

Cora laughs. "Well, yes, the kiss too, but that wasn't what I meant."

"It wasn't?" Walt feigns crestfallen features. "I'm crushed."

"Hush," Cora says. "I meant, it's amazing how I never knew."

"What?"

"That I loved you all my life."

Walt grins. "How you could be so clever yet so dumb at the same time?"

"Hey!" Cora gives him a gentle slap.

Walt takes the hand that hit him and kisses her palm, holding it between both of his.

"Please," he says, "read it to me again."

Cora points to the first line, sliding her fingers across the symbols as she translates them. Walt watches her lips as she speaks.

"The woman who deciphers this notebook will be the love of your life."

The Dress Shop *of* Dreams

A Novel

Menna van Praag

A Reader's Guide

A Conversation with Menna van Praag

Random House Reader's Circle: How did you become a published writer?

Menna van Praag: Just before I turned thirty, I wrote a little book called *Men, Money, and Chocolate*. I'd written numerous (unpublished) novels before that, but I had a special feeling about this one. It wasn't a great work of literature, just a little fable, but it was *true*. I believed in it. I still didn't fully believe in myself as a writer, but I believed in this book. So, full of confidence and excitement, I submitted it for publication . . . but it was rejected. So I self-published. I went all over London, Oxford and Cambridge, bribing independent bookstores with my homemade flapjacks and begging them to sell my book. Eventually people started reading it and loving it. About a year later, when I'd sold nearly a thousand copies, I submitted it again and this time it was picked up. It was subsequently translated into twenty-six languages. That was just the beginning. . . .

RHRC: Do you have a writing routine?

MVP: I don't have a particular routine but write whenever I can. Before my son was born (three years ago), I'd often write for ten hours a day. Nowadays, if I get two hours in a row I consider myself lucky! I can write anywhere, but my favorite place is at my desk on a sunny day. I have a window that looks out onto my garden. Whenever I'm stuck for words, I go for a walk, and the next sentence will come to me soon enough. I adore notebooks and often scribble ideas, sentences and paragraphs down in them, but when it comes to writing the story, I always go to the computer.

RHRC: Where did the idea for *The Dress Shop of Dreams* come from?

MVP: I saw a TV spot about Cuban cigar rollers who pay a percentage of their wages to a reader who will read them stories while they work. They then name some of the cigars after their favorite tales. I thought how it would be if the reader had a magical voice, and I fell instantly in love with the character of the Night Reader.

RHRC: What do you love most about writing?

MVP: While I fall absolutely in love with my characters, losing myself in their stories (these are often as much a surprise to me as to anyone), most of all I love the words: the way a beautiful sentence feels on your tongue, the delightful surprise of a startling and lovely simile or metaphor. I simply love words.

RHRC: What are some of your favorite books and authors?

MVP: Magical realism has always been my favourite genre. I like to think there's more to reality than our five senses show us. My favorite author, above all others, is probably Alice Hoffman. I love the magic in her tales, along with the acute realism of the worlds she creates. Other favorite magical-realism authors include: Isabel Allende, Laura Esquivel, Sarah Addison Allen and Barbara O'Neal. Other favorite authors, who don't write specifically in that genre, include: Erica Bauermeister, Maggie O'Farrell, Ann Patchett, Tracy Chevalier, Carey Wallace, Anita Shreve, Kate Morton, Anne Lamott, Anne Tyler, Neil Gaiman and Sue Monk Kidd. I've just finished *The Age of Desire* by Jennie Fields, which I found to be a beautiful book. I'm always on the look out for new authors, so if we share similar tastes and you have any recommendations, please get in touch!

RHRC: Did reading a particular book inspire you to want to be a writer?

MVP: As a child I was a typical bookworm, reading everything I could get my hands on—aren't all writers? The first book that had a significant impact on me was *The Water Babies* by Charles Kingsley. It opened up the idea of magic hiding within the mundane. The book that made me want to be a writer was *The House of the Spirits* by Isabel Allende. I read it as a young teenager, and it was so startling, so magnificent that it ignited within me a desire to write something like that. I didn't believe I could (that came much, much later), but I desperately wanted to and was determined to try.

RHRC: What advice would you offer an aspiring writer?

MVP: Write all the time—as often as you can—read nearly as much as you write. And, if you want to get published, simply never, ever, ever, give up. It's simply a matter of deciding how much you want it (it can take years, decades even—it took me just over a decade), so determination is the most valuable trait you can employ. Oh, and if you're just starting out and need a little help with inspiration, self-belief and all that, read *The Artist's Way* by Julia Cameron. I read that book at age nineteen—I longed to be a writer, but I couldn't write—when I started reading it, suddenly, there was light and possibility and hope.

RHRC: Do you ever feel stuck?

MVP: I used to feel stuck all the time. In my twenties I was full of self-doubt and could barely finish a first chapter. But, following years of attending inspirational seminars and writing workshops, I'm no longer a perfectionist, which, of course, makes finishing a book a lot easier! I now simply write because I love to express myself. I no longer care that it's not Shakespeare. I don't suffer from stuckness anymore, but if things aren't flowing as they should be, then I stop for a while and go for a walk, read a book or watch a film instead. I take an inspirational break, and when I return to my desk, the words are usually there waiting for me.

RHRC: What do you hope to accomplish with your writing?

MVP: I once got an email that actually made me cry. It was from a woman who worked in an office job that she hated. She went to a bookshop over lunch, bought *Men, Money, and Chocolate* and read it under her desk that afternoon. Then she replicated the main character, Maya, and booked a fortnight off work. She wanted to be a singer, so she arranged time in a recording studio, made an album, and now she gigs all over the country. It's incredible that something that I wrote actually helped someone transform her life. It's a glorious thing to feel that you're somehow being a little piece of goodness in the world; it's a gift.

RHRC: What next?

MVP: I've just started running writing workshops in person and online. Teaching was a dream I had a long time ago, but it's taken me until now to have the courage to do it! It's a process I find extremely inspiring, both professionally and personally. I love witnessing my students becoming better writers while we're working together, and I'm certainly becoming a better writer myself in the process, which is a lovely, unexpected bonus.

My next book, *The Witches of Cambridge*, is about a secret society of women (and one man) who are all professors at the university and all witches. It's the most fantastical book I've written so far, and I'm absolutely loving it. I'm also musing on an idea I had (about ten years ago) for a children's book. I might be nearly ready to start writing that now. . . .

Questions and Topics for Discussion

1. Etta's dresses give their wearers a magic push to go after their dreams. Have you ever had an item of clothing that especially inspired you to take action that you might not have otherwise? Or perhaps someone or something gave you a push to do something that you might not have initiated on your own?

2. Why do you think Etta's magic doesn't work on her?

3. Cora's father tells her the chemical formula for love is "One proton of faith, three electrons of humility, a neutron of compassion and a bond of honesty." Do you agree? Would you add anything to this equation?

4. Dylan's letters bring comfort to many lonely fans of the Night Reader. Do you think that justifies his duplicity?

5. Another possible title for this book was *The Night Reader*, after Walt and his special secret. Does it change the story for you if you think of Walt as the main character? Which of the characters do you most identify with?

6. On page 142, Cora tells her grandmother that "all the great leaps are made when a scientist thinks of something she can't yet prove, then dedicates her life to trying." All of the characters in this book have to make leaps of faith to get something they want. What are some examples?

7. Do you think Etta made a mistake when she decided not to tell Sebastian about their daughter? Would you have made the same decision? Are secrets inherently wrong or sometimes justifiable?

8. Should Henry have fought for Francesca even when she told him she didn't love him anymore? Do you think she was right to send him away?

9. At the start of the novel, Cora protects herself from pain by focusing on numbers and lab work. But all of the novel's characters have ways of hiding from their feelings. What do you think these characters are afraid of? Do you ever notice yourself or others around you strategically avoiding difficult truths?

10. As he reads, Walt notices similarities between himself and the characters in his books: he identifies with Emma in *Madame Bovary*, Marianne from *Sense and Sensibility*, and Cyrano de Bergerac. Are there other great literary figures you would compare him to? What about Etta? Cora?

11. On page 37, Etta thinks: "It's a great shame . . . that the heart cannot feel joy without also feeling pain, that it cannot know love without also knowing loss." Do you agree that it's true that we cannot love without also suffering?

Read on for a sneak peek at

The Witches of Cambridge

A Novel

by Menna van Praag

Chapter One

Amandine closes her eyes as the clock ticks past midnight. She tries to ignore the tug of the full moon and the flutter in her chest as its gravity squeezes her heart. Instead Amandine focuses on her husband's soft snores and wonders, as she has every night for the last few months, why she feels so numb.

When they met thirteen years ago, she thought him the most beautiful man she'd ever seen, and he's still a handsome man, strong and lean and dark. Amandine Bisset was so passionate for Eliot Walker that tiny silver sparks flew from her fingertips when she touched him. When they made love, her whole body filled with white light so bright Amandine believed she might explode. Now she wonders when the last time sex was like that. Before the babies were born?

Now they have two rambunctious, full-blooded, glorious boys

and hardly enough energy left at the end of the day for a goodnight kiss, let alone anything else, like wet kisses scattered across warm skin. At least, that's what they tell themselves. Thirteen years ago, when they were both undergraduates at Magdalene College, Amandine's skin had shimmered at the sight of him. The first time Eliot Walker entered her world she was standing in the foyer of the Fitzwilliam Museum gazing at *The Kiss* by Gustav Klimt and wondering if, among all the glistening gold, she'd ever be blessed enough to feel the passionate desire depicted in that painting.

A moment later, the thought still lingering in her head, Amandine had heard laughter as bright and brilliant as moonshine. She turned to see Eliot standing alone in front of a van Gogh, his laughter flooding the painting and filling the room. Seized by a sudden urge she couldn't explain, Amandine found herself walking toward him. When she reached him, she didn't reach out her hand and introduce herself.

"Why are you laughing?"

Eliot turned his smile on her. "What?"

She asked again and he shrugged.

"I don't know. There's a quirky joy about it, the sky rolling like waves, the moon and stars like little suns. I think the artist wanted to make us smile."

"I don't think so," Amandine said. "Van Gogh was a depressive. This painting was the view from his sanatorium window. I doubt he was smiling at the time."

Eliot's own smile deepened, tinged with cheeky triumph. "But he didn't paint it there, did he? It was done from memory, years later. He might have been laughing then."

Amandine frowned, not because he was wrong—indeed she knew for a fact that he wasn't—but because he was so sure of himself, so arrogant and argumentative. It brought out her own fire.

"Before or after he cut off his ear?" she declared.

Eliot laughed again. "You don't like to be wrong, do you?"

Amandine's frown thickened. "Does anyone?"

"Not me," he agreed. "But that doesn't matter, because I never am."

Now Amandine laughed. "Everyone's wrong sometimes."

"Something you know more than most, I imagine." Eliot's eyes glittered.

For a moment Amandine felt the fire rise up in her throat, but just before she retorted with words that would singe Eliot's eyebrows, she realized he was flirting. She suppressed a smile and feigned a nonchalant shrug.

"I'm as wrong about life as anyone, but I'm rarely wrong about art," she said. "Are you a student here? You're not art history. I haven't seen you around Scroope."

"Law. Finalist. Trinity." He gave a little bow with a flourish of his hand. "Eliot Ellis Walker-Jones, at your service."

"Ah, so you're one of them." Amandine raised a teasing eyebrow, her glance resting for a moment on his thick dark hair. "I should have known."

"One of whom?"

"A lawyer. A snob."

"The first charge I already confessed to," Eliot said, "but how can you claim the second?"

"Your accent, your name, your knowledge of art even though it's not your subject." Amandine smiled, feeling a sparkle on her skin as it began to tingle. "You probably play the piano disgustingly well and row for Trinity, too. I'd bet a hundred quid you went to Eton—"

"Winchester."

"Same difference."

"Well, not unless twenty thousand pounds a year means nothing to you."

Amandine rolled her eyes, finding it harder and harder not to stare into his: vivid green with flecks of yellow, bright against his pale skin and dark hair.

"So, you're an art historian then?" Eliot asked, shifting the tone.

Amandine gave a little curtsy, still wanting to keep it light, slightly scared at the rapidly growing intensity of her feelings for him.

"Amandine Francoise Héloïse Bisset."

"Pretty name."

"Merci."

Eliot met her eyes. "You don't have an accent."

A rush of warmth rose in her throat. "My parents are French, but I grew up here. I had a brother, but he . . . he died when he was a little boy."

"Oh, I'm sorry."

And he was. Amandine felt gentle waves of sadness wash over her as Eliot spoke. She could feel what he felt just as she could feel what van Gogh had felt when he painted *The Starry Night* in 1889. Every artist—painter, writer, musician—put their spirit and soul into their work, along with their emotions, and Amandine had always been able to feel exactly what the artist had been feeling when she looked at a painting or read a book. Music was trickier because the emotions of the musician always mixed with those of the composer, and she felt confused and cloudy when confronted with conflicting or unclear emotions.

Amazingly, though he clearly wasn't a witch, Eliot was right about van Gogh, though Amandine would rather die than admit it. Besides, she couldn't say so without also telling him her deepest secret. And she had absolutely no intention of doing that. Even her father hadn't known about her mother. Héloïse Bisset had kept her true nature from her husband, and although she'd never explicitly told her daughter to do the same, Amandine had always assumed that it wasn't safe to share such things with people who were purely human. It was likely, if nothing else, to shock them so much that they'd never see you in the same way again.

"I don't suppose . . . ?" Eliot began, tentative for the first time.

"What?" Amandine asked, though she already knew the answer.

"I don't suppose you fancy taking a cup of tea with a snobby lawyer? My treat."

"Well," Amandine pretended to consider, "since you're not a lawyer yet, I suppose I could make an exception. And if you like van Gogh, you can't be so terrible."

"Ah, high praise indeed. I should ask you to write my references," Eliot said. "And when I am a lawyer, what will you do about fraternizing with me then?"

They began to walk, past the paintings and toward the door.

"We'll still know each other then, will we?" Amandine swallowed a smile.

Eliot paused for a moment in front of *The Kiss*.

"Oh, yes," he said. "In ten years or so I'll be a London lawyer and we'll be married with two kids. Boys."

Amandine raised both eyebrows. "Oh, really?"

They began walking again.

"But I don't want children," Amandine said, "so I'm afraid that might put a little crimp in your plans."

"You might not now," Eliot said, "but you will."

"Now you're taking arrogance to a whole new level." Amandine laughed. "But I'm afraid you are wrong this time. I admit I might change my mind in many ways in the next ten or twenty years but not about that."

"Ah, but I told you," Eliot said, still smiling,. "I'm never wrong."

And then, with one bold move following another, he reached out and took her hand in his. Amandine almost flinched, thinking perhaps she ought to be shocked, affronted at his arrogance again. But the thing was, she wasn't. So she let her hand soften in his, and as they walked together, Amandine wished that her mother had given her psychic powers, along with extraordinary empathy, so she could know whether or not this man she suddenly loved might be right.

Now Amandine lies in bed next to her husband who has changed so much, and so suddenly, from being the light at the center of her life to someone currently trying to hide at the edges. Lately there's something else Amandine has begun feeling from Eliot, emotions coming off him in swells so strong she could swear she can almost smell them. Wafts of guilt and fear float about the house in great ribbons, trailing through corridors and lingering in the air so Amandine could track his every movement if she so chose. Her first assumption, of course, was that he was having an affair. It wouldn't be difficult. He commutes to London every day and often works late and on weekends, no doubt spending time with a wide variety of ambitious young lawyers who might set their sights on a successful and handsome barrister.

However, if Eliot's having an affair then he's as careful and cunning as an MI5 agent. No emails, no texts, no phantom phone calls. Amandine's few routine investigations have failed to unearth anything remotely suspicious, and she's sure he's neither discreet nor deceptive enough to pull off such an obvious secret right under her nose. Eliot Walker is clever, certainly, and as a lawyer he has probably pulled off a few tricks in his time, but as a husband and father he's always been transparent and true. At least as far as Amandine knows. It's just a shame that her gift for feeling what other people feel isn't accompanied by the ability to know their thoughts. Empathy balanced with telepathy would make sense. It would provide the whole picture. Without it Amandine is left knowing how people feel but not knowing why.

Noa Sparrow has never been much liked by people, and she doesn't much care. That isn't strictly true, of course. She tries not to care, she pretends not to care, but she doesn't do a very good job. The problem is that most people don't like to be told the truth. They prefer to hide things from themselves, to act as if everything is okay, that stuff doesn't bother them when it does. They think, rather foolishly, that what they ignore will simply disappear.

Noa can't help it that she's always been able to see the truth. What's worse though, is that she's unable to keep silent about what she sees. The words escape her lips, no matter how hard she tries to clamp them tight shut. How often she longs for the ability to feign and fake, to be two-faced, to be a bold and brilliant little liar. Most people seem to manage it easily enough, but sadly it's never been one of Noa's gifts.

She was twelve years old when her need to tell the truth ruined her life. It was two weeks before Christmas and Noa was sitting at the dinner table with her parents, wondering about what she'd get in her stocking that year, while they talked about fixing the dripping tap in the sink, when she saw something—a dark truth snaking underneath benign sentences about faucets and the price of plumbers—that she couldn't keep secret. Every day since, Noa has cursed her awful truth-telling Tourette's syndrome, wishing she'd been able to keep quiet on that dreadful December night. But, since she can't undo the past, she's spent every day instead hating herself for doing what she did.

Diana Sparrow didn't speak to her daughter for three months after Noa, reaching for more potatoes, suddenly burst out with the fact of her mother's affair with her tango teacher. The shocking secret had just slipped out. Noa clamped her hand over her mouth as the words tumbled into the air, but it was too late. Both her parents had turned to look at her in shock, and the stunned guilt on her mother's face was unmistakable.

In the months of ear-splitting, heart-shattering pain that followed, Noa prayed every night that she'd be struck down and her "gift" for seeing and telling the truth would be stripped from her. She cut off her long blond hair in penance and denied herself any treats. She took a vow of silence, not opening her mouth to say anything at all, so no hideous, undesirable truths could sneak out. Noa watched, helpless, while her mother relocated to the sofa, then moved out altogether. She listened to her father sob behind his bedroom door in the early hours of the morning. And all the while she said nothing. Not a single word.

Noa had hoped she would somehow be able to go through

the rest of her life like that, silent and unseen, never upsetting anyone again. But when she returned to school at the end of the summer, Noa found that her teachers weren't willing to let her tiptoe through her education undetected, especially when they noticed the quality of her written work. Seeing they had someone rather special in their school, they encouraged her to participate in class, to join in with everyone else. So, in spite of her desperate efforts to remain anonymous, Noa was frequently forced into class discussions, team projects and group assignments. And, although she tried very hard to monitor words very carefully in her mind—planning them once and checking them twice—before she let them out of her mouth, every now and then someone's secret would break free. Perhaps unsurprisingly then, Noa's childhood passed without the comfort of friends.

By the time she reached university, to study the history of art at Magdalene College, Cambridge, Noa had almost convinced herself that she didn't need anybody else, she was perfectly fine going through life alone. She could quite happily spend entire days in the Fitzwilliam Museum on Trumpington Street, passing the morning with Renoir, Matisse and Monet, sharing her lunchtime sandwiches with van Gogh and Vermeer, having a quick supper snack in the presence of Picasso and Kandinsky. But at night, as she lies alone in her bed, all the unspoken thoughts of the day pinballing around her head, Noa's loneliness is bitter and sharp.

Noa sleeps with the curtains open, allowing as much moonlight as possible to flood her bedroom, allowing her to see each and every picture on the walls, if only a rather pale glimmer. It took Noa weeks to perfect the art display. Reproductions of Monet's gardens at Giverny blanket one wall: thousands of violets—smudges of purples and mauves—and azaleas, poppies and peonies, tulips and roses, water lilies in pastel pinks floating on serene lakes reflecting weeping willows and shimmers of sunshine. Turner's sunsets adorn another: bright eyes of gold at the center of skies and seas of searing magenta or soft blue. The third wall is splashed with Jackson Pollocks: a hundred different colors streaked and splattered above Noa's bed. The fourth wall is decorated by Rothko: blocks of blue and red and yellow blending and bleeding together. The ceiling is papered with the abstract shapes of Kandinsky: triangles, circles and lines tumbling over one another in energetic acrobatics.

Noa adores abstract art. It quiets her mind; it throws up, for her, fewer questions than figurative art. She doesn't wonder—though perhaps she ought—what intention lay behind the placing of a square or the choice of yellow or blue. Noa can simply gaze at the colors and shapes and enjoy the emptiness inside her, the rare absence of thought, together with a feeling of connection—the shadow of something she misses and longs for.

With the exception of a few cursory words exchanged with librarians and museum curators, virtually (with the exception of her beloved aunt, Heather) the only people Noa speaks with are her professors. So far, to her great fortune, her only two teachers have been so boring and lifeless that they harbour no hidden truths for Noa to blurt out and offend them with. Today, though, she's meeting a new professor, Amandine Bisset, and Noa can already sense that she won't be so lucky this time. This new teacher's name alone suggests sensuality and secrets, veiled lives and lovers, concealed longings and desires. Noa imagines her: tall and willowy with long black curls, enormous brown eyes and lips that have kissed a hundred men and brought them to their knees with whispered French words coated in black coffee and chocolate. Noa is absolutely certain that this woman will be her undoing. After years of carefully clipped silence, she will be unable to contain herself anymore.

It's a surprise then, when Noa opens the door to Professor Bisset's office and steps inside. The room is large and the walls are bare—a strange quirk for a professor of art—except for a big, bright poster of Gustav Klimt's *The Kiss* hanging opposite a large oak desk, behind which sits Amandine Bisset, head down, scribbling into a notebook.

"Give me a sec," she says, without a French accent and without looking up.

Noa stands at the edge of the room, not sitting down in her allotted chair, antique and upholstered in dark red leather, wanting to give her new teacher at least the semblance of privacy. While Amandine writes, Noa watches her. She's been right about the beauty and the black hair but it's very short, her eyes aren't brown but green, and Amandine isn't tall and willowy but average height and verging on voluptuous. More important, however, Noa instantly sees that she's absolutely accurate about one thing, the worst thing of all: Amandine Bisset is full of secrets.

"It's strange that your walls are empty," Noa says, before she can help it. "Why do you have only one painting? Don't you get bored?"

Professor Bisset looks up from her writing, eyes green (not brown as Noa predicted), almond shaped and pinched in a frown.

"I have a good imagination," she says, her voice a little sharp and a little shocked. "And you have a rather impolite way of introducing yourself."

"I'm sorry," Noa says as she sits. "I can't help it. I . . ."

"Oh?" Amandine's frown deepens, though she sounds more curious than annoyed. She studies Noa, then, about to say something, seems to change her mind. "I'd get bored looking at the same paintings every day, no matter how much I loved them."

"Except for the Klimt."

"Yes."

Amandine glances back at her notebook.

Noa bites her lip, but she can't stop herself. She sees what her teacher isn't saying as if it were written on a teleprompter that someone is insisting she read aloud.

"Your husband. That's why you keep that painting. It reminds you of when you were happy."

Amandine's eyes snap up again.

"How did you know that?" she says, her mouth still open as if she wishes she could swallow the words back down now that they're out. But she can't, of course, and the truth once spoken is undeniable.

Noa gives a little shrug and starts fishing around in her canvas book bag for her essay. "I've been looking forward to the French impressionists," she mumbles, hoping her teacher will appreciate the swift change of subject and let her off the hook. If Noa's really lucky she'll be able to get through the next hour without saying something really off-limits, something that will have Amandine refuse to keep her on as a student. It's happened before.

"Fuck the French impressionists."

Having just pulled her essay out of her bag, Noa drops it. Five pages flutter to the floor, but Noa just stares at her teacher, wide-eyed, her fingertips already sticky with fear. Mercifully, the shock empties her mind and silences her mouth.

"Sorry," Amandine says softly. "I didn't . . . of course, that was very rude. But you can't say something like that and then expect to start talking about Monet. You have to explain yourself first."

Noa nods. Her mouth is dry. She swallows. "I didn't mean to upset you. It's just . . ." Noa has no idea how to explain herself so that she doesn't sound crazy or scary or both.

Amandine takes a deep breath and sits up. She pulls her long fingers through her short hair. "You don't have to give me a rational explanation," she says. "I'm not a rational person myself. I'm . . ."

It's then that Noa sees what Amandine is. And she smiles, just a flicker at the edge of her lips, but a sense of relief that floods her whole body from fingertips to toes. Now she knows that it's safe, for the very first time in her life, to reveal herself. Noa has only just met this woman, but she knows that Amandine won't judge, reject or punish her. She knows that it's finally okay to tell her own secret, to be honest about who she is.

"I see things I shouldn't," Noa begins, her voice soft. "I see all the things most people don't want other people to see. I don't want to say anything, I want to keep their secrets, but I can't seem to help saying what I see. I don't have any control over it, I don't know why not."

Amandine sits forward. "How do you see what you see?"

Noa shrugs, twisting a piece of her hair around her finger then smoothing it against her cheek. "I don't know. I've always just known things. That's okay, I guess, but not being able to shut up about it, that's a shame."

Amandine nods. "It doesn't make you many friends, I suppose."

"No," Noa says, "not many."

Amandine sits back in her chair. "You mentioned my husband." Her eyes flicker to the one painting on the wall. "And how we used to be happy. So, so happy."

"But something changed, quite recently. It's like . . . a wall between you." While Noa speaks she looks at her teacher, who's still gazing at the painting. "You don't know what's happened. You wonder if he's having an affair. You wonder if he loves you anymore."

Still staring at the painting, Amandine nods, very slowly, as tears pool in her eyes and drop down her cheeks.

"Do you want me to leave?" Noa asks, her voice so soft she almost can't hear her own words.

"No." Amandine pauses, taking a long moment before she brushes her cheeks with the back of her hand and looks up at her student again. "No, I don't want you to leave. I want you to meet my husband. I want you to tell me the truth about him."

ABOUT THE AUTHOR

MENNA VAN PRAAG is a writer and creative writing consultant. She graduated from Oxford and lives in Cambridge, with her husband and young son. She's also the author of *Men, Money & Chocolate*, *Happier Than She's Ever Been*, and *The House at the End of Hope Street*. Her next book, *The Witches of Cambridge*, will be out next year.

www.mennavanpraag.com